STEVEN M. ROTH

A SOCRATES CHENG MYSTERY

THE MOURNING WOMAN

Published by Blackstone Press, A Crime Novel Imprint

Cover Design and eBook & POD Formatting: Streetlight Graphics

SECOND EDITION

ISBN 978-1-938701-03-0 (ePub)
ISBN 978-1-938701-04-7 (Paperback)

Visit the author's website: www.stevenmroth.com

ALSO BY STEVEN M. ROTH

The Socrates Cheng Mystery Series:
Mandarin Yellow

For Dominica

"The past is a foreign country."

Epicurus

PART ONE

CHAPTER 1

As I stood in the hallway and waited for the old woman to answer my knock and open the door, I thought about the rumors I'd heard that she was a descendant of the ancient Greek Oracle at Delphi, and that she could accurately foretell the future.

I looked at my watch and knocked again.

The door opened and revealed the partly exposed face of the woman, who stood behind the door and peered around its edge, looking at me. She stared at me briefly, then opened the door all the way.

She said nothing to acknowledge my presence, but held up her hand and slightly moved her crooked index finger to beckon me into her apartment.

As I stepped across the threshold into the foyer, the woman turned away and started walking, leading me along a windowless hallway, the walls of which were covered with Greek Orthodox religious ikons. She tapped a wooden cane on the floor ahead of us as she walked.

I followed her into a room — she later referred to it as her parlor — over to a chair with frayed, overstuffed cushions. She pointed at the chair and said her first word to me: "Sit."

I lowered myself onto the seat, then watched as the

woman crossed the room over to a chair similar to mine. She turned back and started walking toward me, dragging the chair behind her, tapping her cane on the worn carpet as she struggled forward.

I stood up, intending to help her, but she waved me off with a brusque shake of her head. I sank back down onto my chair, and watched and waited.

When she reached me, the old woman placed the chair in front of me, then carefully lowered herself onto its seat. We sat so close to one another our knees almost touched. I could smell the sour odor of advanced old age and bad teeth that leached from her.

When she finished settling herself among the cushions of her chair, the woman looked into my eyes and nodded. I took that as permission to speak. I decided I'd tackle the rumors first, then get to the real reason I'd come here.

"They say you can predict the future," I said. "Can you?"

She didn't answer me. Instead, she looked down at her lap and, with slow, deliberate gestures, ran the palms of her hands across the top of her thighs, over her ankle-length black dress, smoothing away invisible wrinkles. When she finished, she looked up and said, "Some people think so, some don't."

"What should I think?" I said.

She looked into my eyes and held my gaze, then said in a voice that had the measured cadence of someone who had said the same thing so many times, her answer took on the power of truth, "You would be wise, Mr. Cheng, to respect my powers."

I didn't know what to say to that, so I nodded once and said nothing.

"Your mother says you're a detective, Mr. Cheng. Are you?" she asked.

I nodded. "Private, not a cop. Please call me Socrates."

She dragged the tip of her tongue across her upper lip, then back again, leaving tiny droplets of glistering moisture on her dark mustache. When she again spoke, she changed the subject.

"My ancestor was the Greek Pythia, the Homeric $\Pi v\theta\omega$," she said, "the one the ancient Hellenes called the Oracle at Delphi."

I assumed from this statement that she thought because I'm half Greek I'd get her cryptic allusion to Apollo's ancient spokeswoman. She was right. I did get it.

"How long have you been a detective?" she asked.

"Almost three years," I said. "So, going back to before, can you?"

The woman wrinkled her forehead as if puzzled by my question. "Can I what?"

"Predict the future."

She shrugged slightly. "Sometimes yes, sometimes no," she said. "It depends."

I sighed silently. The woman's equivocal reply certainly imparted credibility to the rumor she was descended from the Hellenic Pythia. The ancient Oracle was renowned for her power of obfuscation when responding to an inquiry from a supplicant.

I was tiring of our verbal jousting and sorry I'd ever brought up her purported powers, so I said no more about it.

I briefly looked the woman over to get her physical details set in my mind.

She definitely was old, probably in her late 80s or early

90s, and petite, perhaps 4'10" at the most. She was pencil thin, maybe no more than ninety-five pounds, if even that. Her arms were match sticks covered with translucent, wrinkled skin that draped over her bones in loose folds. Dark spots the size of dimes and occasional warts sprouting wiry gray hair speckled her arms and neck. She was balding, too, having only wispy white hair that forced me to see more of her scaly, yellowed scalp than I cared to see.

Time to get to my reason for being there.

"My mother said you have a problem you'd like my help with. Why don't you tell me about it."

I waited while she closed her eyes. I assumed she was composing her thoughts. After a few seconds she gripped the arms of her chair and leveraged herself up and out of her seat into a standing position.

She thrust out her right arm and opened her hand, offering to shake mine.

"I'm Eugenia Stamos," she said, "you mother's friend." She smiled, giving me a fleeting glance of dark teeth. "I need your help, Mr. Cheng, because someone is going to murder me."

CHAPTER 2

Panos Makeresos, hoping to settle his chronically dyspeptic stomach, poured himself a second glass of licorice-flavored Mastika, closed the thickly bound green-page accounting ledger he used to record his clients' financial accounts, and settled back into his reading chair. He picked at a plate of olives and fried octopus he'd precariously balanced on the arm of his chair.

Seventy-two year old Panos lived an idiosyncratic and moderately solitary life that suited him just fine. He lived alone in his three bedroom condominium apartment in the Mount Parnassus Condominium, just two doors down the hall from Eugenia Stamos. He was a licensed financial planner and certified public accountant, and used his condo both as his home and business office, employing the smallest bedroom as his office, the middle-size room as his bedroom, and the largest bedroom as his secret, secure Treasure Room.

Panos dressed every day in a dark blue double-breasted suit and solid blue tie. He wore shoes with elevated heels that offered him greater imagined stature than his natural 5' 6" frame tendered him. He had thick, wavy black hair with fingers of silver running through it, ruddy skin, and a deceptively soft face. He was youthful, but not young, having been blessed with the good fortune some Greek men have of remaining much younger looking than do their women.

Panos' eyes were dark brown and masked something lurking there that gave pause to anyone who stared too long at them. His smile, while readily offered and often accepted as a signal of a tender personality, was wanting in warmth and full of hunger. Yet people liked Panos because he habitually offered the world his guileful smile and a kind word or inquiry. His neighbors and clients thought of him as old-world charming. Panos thought of himself as the Ice Man.

Panos had lived at the Mount Parnassus — a pre-World War II Washington, DC mid-rise structure located on Kalorama Street near the former site of the Embassy of the People's Republic of China — since 1968 when the building still operated as a rent-controlled luxury rental building.

He had come to Washington from his home in Piraeus as a twenty-eight year old mainframe computer and COBOL programming language prodigy who had lost his position in King Alexander's Ministry of Communications when the junta of Colonels overthrew the King in 1967, and established an authoritarian military government in Greece. Panos, never one to put himself at risk, fled the new despotic state and resettled in America.

Panos savored everything about the Mount Parnassus: its baronial stone façade; its small staff of obsequious, pretentious doormen and porters; its mahogany-paneled elevator operated by a middle-aged Greek immigrant with one blue eye and one brown eye; and, its eighty-eight living units, each with spacious rooms, 12-foot high ceilings, walls of thick plaster, and oak floors.

In his role as financial planner and advisor, Panos offered

his clients — some of whom were his neighbors; some of whom were his fellow parishioners at Saint Sophia Greek Orthodox Cathedral — sound, conservative financial advice calculated to produce investment returns which, although modest by Wall Street's standards, suited his clientele because their investments always generated returns to them within the parameters of Panos' forecasts.

Many, if not most, of Panos' clients considered him to be not only their financial adviser, but also their friend and personal confidant. He was their neighbor, a fellow Saint Sophia congregant, and, above all, like them, a refugee from Greece. It was this blended perception that enabled Panos to stealthily worm his way into his clients' personal lives so that he also tended to their daily and routine financial affairs, paying their bills for them from their checking or money market accounts against checks he drew and signed on their behalf, with their consent.

All in all, Panos' neighbors and clients were happy with him, but that was because they didn't know that Panos was a committed and cunning embezzler who scrupulously stole from his neighbors, clients, and fellow parishioners, all of whom he deemed to be his rightful treasure trove.

CHAPTER 3

EUGENIA'S ASSERTION THAT SOMEONE WANTED to kill her certainly grabbed my attention, but I had mixed feelings about helping her.

Although she was my mother's friend, my impression so far of Eugenia wasn't favorable. Actually, I didn't like her very much at first, especially not her imperious attitude. Yet I knew enough about me that I knew this might change, that my habit of compassion for old people was strong enough to paste over my immediate distaste for her and eventually convince me that what I really felt about Eugenia was pity.

I leaned in close to her and placed Eugenia's hand between both mine in order to comfort and reassure her I was taking her statement seriously. Her hand felt like a paper mâché theater prop.

"What makes you think someone wants to kill you?" I asked, wondering if this would be the divination that would test her purported powers.

Eugenia pulled her hand away and resettled herself deep in the back of her chair.

"I take walks every afternoon if the weather is good," she said. "For the past three weeks when I came home, some of my things were moved while I was out. Someone had been in my home."

"You mean like some person moved a table or chair?" I said.

She shook her head. "No. Small things, things only I would notice living here alone for so many years."

She turned her face away from me and canted her head toward the book shelves across the room.

"One time it was a small *krater* turned so its design was not facing exactly the way I keep it. Another time, a porcelain figure was no longer on its same spot on the shelf. Once, an ikon on the wall in the hallway was hanging crooked when I came back." She paused, then said, "That's what I mean."

I glanced around the room. I saw nearly thirty Greek Orthodox ikons hanging on the walls of the parlor, none crooked. I turned my attention back to Eugenia.

She was deep in thought, her head tilted toward the ceiling as if I wasn't here.

"I am talking about changes I would never cause myself," she said, not opening her eyes or leveling her chin, "would never leave that way if I had accidentally caused them."

She opened her eyes and looked at me. She shivered and shook her head.

"*Ti yinete* — What's happening?" she said. "I don't know who it is coming in my home when I'm out," she said, "but I'm frightened by it."

I thought about this. I had to be careful how I responded. I didn't want to seem either to be patronizing Eugenia or summarily rebuffing her. In fact, I wanted to help her, if for no other reason than to please my mother. I also wanted to alleviate Eugenia's fear, whether or not she actually needed my assistance.

I couldn't help wondering, however, if Eugenia's fear was rooted in her aging imagination, the byproduct of a mind afflicted with some level of dementia. My mother and I had lived through that affliction with my father a few years ago before he died, and had watched helplessly as his illness and its attendant paranoia slowly took control of him. It wouldn't surprise me to find out that Eugenia had herself moved her things and then forgotten she'd done so, and then attributed it all to some nefarious intruder into her life.

I considered this, but dismissed the thought for now. Although Eugenia was very old, there was an intelligence in her eyes that belied dementia.

Eugenia must have read my mind or perhaps guessed my thoughts from my facial expression and body language because she said, "I told your mother you wouldn't believe me. I was right."

She twisted her hands together on her lap and stared briefly at them, then looked up and locked her gaze on my eyes. I saw resolve in the expression that overspread her face.

"I'm not just a doddering old woman," she said. "Although I'm almost ninety-four, I'm not yet forgetful or confused." She slowly wagged her head. "You young people always think us old ones aren't right in the head. Well, in this instance, Mr. Cheng, you're wrong."

I blushed, but said nothing. What could I say? She had nailed me.

"Besides," Eugenia said, as she slowly shook her head and kneaded her hands together, "there's something I haven't told you yet." She paused, then said, "When I go out walking, someone follows me."

She punctuated this statement with a sharp bird-like peck of her chin. "And that, Mr. Cheng, in spite of what you might think, is not the product of an old lady's imagination."

CHAPTER 4

P ANOS WAS NOT AN INDISCRIMINATE thief. He didn't loot his clients' bank accounts and investment and retirement funds merely because he was greedy, although greed played an indirect role in his thefts. Panos' motivation was far more pragmatic. When all the possible reasons and motivations were examined, given their due weight, and the false or trivial ones stripped away, two reasons remained: Panos stole from his clients because he was able to and he stole to feed his voracious appetite to build a collection of Greek antiquities.

Although it might be expected that Panos' felt sense of entitlement and his desire to build an antiquities collection would drive him to embezzle as much money as he could, just as fast as he could, this was not the case. Panos' ease of theft and his wolfish desires to acquire antiquities never propelled him into acting precipitously to satisfy his cynicism or collecting cravings. In fact, for someone who innately believed that his so-called friends were not his friends as far as he was concerned, that he was superior to his neighbors, fellow church congregants, and clients, and that it was their God-given purpose on Earth to satisfy his desires and self-perceived needs, Panos acted with anomalous restraint and measured patience until that time came, as it inevitably did, when he finally set his sights on a specific quarry to add to his growing collection of pots, vases, sculpture and jewelry. When that occurred, all bets were off.

Panos used a remarkably simple technique to embezzle. It was one he hadn't invented, but he applied it religiously. It was the conjuring trick of the stage magician in which Panos symbolically induced his clients to look at his left hand while he deftly picked their pockets with his right hand.

Panos' technique required that he never steal a large sum of money from any one client at any one time. Instead, he stole in small increments, setting loose a small sum each month from each client so that his thefts went unnoticed, at worst appearing to be rounding errors, and providing Panos with a unfaltering pipeline of flowing funds from many sources. The FBI called this technique the Salami Technique because its perpetrator took a thin slice of the whole sausage many times.

This worked well for Panos because he accepted the long-term nature of his undertaking. He understood it would require time to build a significant acquisition fund using his method of theft. In this regard, Panos was like a sophisticated stock market investor who, having a long-term goal, never loses sight of that strategy, never worries about the daily, weekly or monthly fluctuations of the stock market, but instead maintains his long-term view and quest.

So much for theory. In practice, Panos' steadfastness always weakened once he identified an antiquity as one he wanted to acquire. When that occurred, he couldn't just walk away and hope no other collector would learn of his target while he built his acquisition fund to a sum sufficient to purchase his quarry. When this occurred, Panos had to have his prey, and would not willingly suffer the possibility of losing it to some other occupant of the savannah.

CHAPTER 5

WASN'T READY YET TO TELL Eugenia if I would help her. I needed more information, specific information.

"Start at the beginning," I said. "How long has this been going on?"

Eugenia closed her eyes as if trying to recall the first time she'd noticed. Then she opened her eyes and reached into her dress pocket. She pulled out a pack of *Marathon* brand cigarettes, shook the deck once, and lipped a cigarette that had jumped up, taking it into her mouth. She struck a long wooden match on the arm of her chair and fired up.

She inhaled deeply, tilted her face toward the ceiling, and streamed smoke up from her nostrils. She seemed to be a million miles away. After a few seconds she looked back at me and flicked an ash into the palm of her other hand.

She again reached into the pocket of her dress. This time she pulled out a set of worry beads. She wrapped one finger around the leather string and swung the beads into her palm. She worked the *koumboloi* — the beads — with the fingers of the hand that held them, first smacking her palm with a sharp crack and then slapping the back of her hand with a reverse motion, while she looked sternly at me.

She began to talk, and digressed, but I decided to let her

go without interruption. It would be my best shot at hearing not only her version of the facts, as she thought she knew them, but hearing her feelings about the events, too.

"The first time would have been three weeks ago, maybe longer. I was gone an hour. When I came back, my late husband's photograph wasn't how I keep it on the piano."

"Was anything taken?" I asked.

Eugenia shook her head and slapped her worry beads. "Just moved."

I reflexively cocked one eyebrow, a habit my mother tells me I've had since childhood and have unknowingly invoked whenever I mistrusted what I was being told. Eugenia must have noticed this because she said, "I have lived alone here since my husband was murdered in Greece, almost thirty years now. That was when I came to America." She snapped her wrist, vigorously flicking her *koumboloi*.

Eugenia raised her arm and gestured with a backhand sweep, corralling the whole room with her gesture. "When you live in a small apartment like this as long as I have, you know it well. Besides," she said, "I am extremely tidy. You young people would say I'm crazy because I have a place and a position for everything. I know when things are not as I left them."

I nodded. I was that way myself so I took her point.

"Do you have visitors sometimes?" I said. "Is it possible they moved things without you noticing?"

She shook her head. "No, I would have known as soon as they left and I saw the changes."

"All right," I said. "I understand." I wasn't sure where to go with this next. Eugenia bailed me out.

"Your mother comes here for tea sometimes, but she

wouldn't be so rude as to pick up my things without asking first."

She looked across the room, seemingly lost in thought. Then she turned back and said, "Other than Sophia, some of our neighbors come for scheduled readings. I would have noticed when they left if they had moved anything. Besides, I never leave my clients alone here."

I decided to run through my mental checklist with her. "What about pets? A cat or dog?" I hadn't noticed any signs of an animal, but you never knew unless you asked. "Or visitors like children, grandchildren, perhaps, or nephews or nieces?"

She wagged her head resolutely. "No pets and no children."

This was going nowhere fast and I was running out of ideas.

"Do you have any valuables someone might be after, something they haven't found yet, something important enough or valuable enough to keep drawing them back until they find it?"

She looked over the shelves across the room, then gazed briefly at one of the groups of ikons on the opposite wall, then looked back at me. "Nothing like that," she said. "I have very little money and nothing valuable. I live on my husband's small pension from the Greek government. I don't live in a way to suggest I am wealthy. No one would have any reason to think I am hoarding large amounts of money here."

I looked over at the ikons hanging on the walls, then looked back at Eugenia who seemed to be blushing.

"They are copies, those ikons," she said. "I couldn't afford to own even one real one. I have nothing of any value except sentimental value to me. No one would come in here to get what I have or, if they did, they wouldn't bother coming back another time once they saw how little I have."

I thought about Eugenia's answers. She was right, of course, in principle. If all she had was what she described, what I could see from where I sat, an intruder wouldn't return after the first time. Yet, if Eugenia was to be believed, the intruder did come back, time and time again. There had to be something here he wanted, either something Eugenia knew about but wasn't disclosing to me or something the intruder wanted that drew him back, although Eugenia wasn't aware of what it was.

"Does anyone have a key besides you?" I said.

She nodded. "Your mother, for emergencies. And the condominium management company. No one else. I keep my two keys for the regular and security locks on a key ring in my pocket." She reached into her dress pocket and pulled out a key ring the size of a silver dollar. "It's always in my pocket, even when I'm home."

After thinking about what I'd heard from Eugenia, I had serious doubts about my ability to help her, assuming she really needed my help. I needed to come up with some gracious way to extricate myself, perhaps by saying, truthfully, that I didn't know how I could help her based on what she'd told me, then add that she should call me if she ever had more concrete evidence of a break-in or of being followed.

This, of course, was wishful thinking on my part.

I knew better than to think I could pull off such a smooth, but totally disingenuous exit from Eugenia. After all, Eugenia, in this scenario, was almost a bit player, the prop on which to hang the plot. The real player in this little drama was my mother, the catalyst who had caused me to meet with Eugenia as a favor to her. That meant that disentangling myself from Eugenia's situation, whatever that situation actually was, was not in the cards for me. I would have to see this through no matter where it might lead or how much time I might waste.

I could feel my face and neck grow warm as I considered the subtext of my next statement, a statement that had to be said to make sure Eugenia and I were on the same page.

"In other words," I said, "if I understand you right, beginning about three weeks ago you came home from your walks and you believe someone entered your home while you were out, moved some of your things, but removed nothing from your apartment. Is that right?" As I finished saying this, I watched Eugenia's eyebrows knit together and her body stiffen.

Eugenia's tone shivered with ice; her eyes narrowed and fixed on mine. Her voice was infused with contempt. "Except for the part about *I believe*. It's not just what I believe, Mr. Cheng. It was exactly as I described for you. You can trust me or not, but I know what happened."

The edge in her tone stung me. *Time for damage control*, I decided.

I blushed again. "Sorry," I said. "I didn't mean that to sound the way it came out. I have to be skeptical in my business. Sometimes I have to ask probing, unfriendly, even painful questions that might give the impression I don't believe you. That's the nature of my work. It's nothing personal."

Eugenia said nothing, not revealing whether she accepted my explanation or not. I decided to move on and make my interpersonal repairs as we moved along, hopefully in the context of gathering more information.

"I take it you never walked in and caught someone here,"

I said. "Not a handyman or some other building or condo person?"

She shook her head.

"Any idea who the intruder might be?" I said.

"No." She pulled hard on her cigarette, then softened her voice. "Will you please help me? I have told you everything I can. I'm old and vulnerable, and although I have a special gift, I need your help."

This was the moment I'd been avoiding by asking questions that evoked responses I'd already expected based on her previous answers. It seemed I'd bought all the time I was going to buy for now. I decided I'd try one more approach, see how she responded.

"Just one more thing," I said, "then we're done for now. Did you report this to the police?"

"*Ach!* — Of course, for all the good it did me."

I could hear her impatience. "Sorry, but I had to ask," I said, "to have the whole picture. What'd they say?"

"Unless I could convince them someone had entered my home or I actually caught someone, or could prove it to them some other way, there was nothing they could do."

"Did they say anything about you being followed?" I asked.

She nodded, but frowned at the same time. "The same. Unless I was stalked and could convince them it was not my imagination, there was no crime, nothing for them to act on. *Dhén katalavéno* — I just don't understand."

I again took her hand in mine and held it, trying to join with Eugenia in her frustration. "That's always the official position," I said, "in cases like this. Sorry."

"Will you help me or do you still doubt me?" she said.

I wasn't ready to give her my answer. I wanted to talk this over with my mother, see what her expectations were. Eugenia's story had started out as tenuous, at best, and hadn't improved with my questioning of her. Had she been a walk-in client at my Dupont Circle office, I would have politely shown her the door.

"Eugenia — Mrs. Stamos, I mean — I believe you, but I want to think about your situation overnight. I want to help you, but need to consider whether I'll be able to help you."

"Speak to your mother then," Eugenia said. "Sophia will set you straight."

I blushed at being so easily seen through by the woman her neighbors called the Oracle. Was I really that transparent or were her neighbors right about Eugenia's gift?

My recovery from this question was half-hearted, but practical. "In the meantime," I said, "call a locksmith and have him rekey both locks on your door. If nothing else, that should stop the intruder."

I hoped I was right.

CHAPTER 6

E IGHTY-ONE YEAR OLD ARÊTE XANDEREAS shuffled across the darkened front room, her lips silently moving as she repeatedly sucked them. She held a cigarette in her left hand and a feather duster in her right as she made her way through the parlor performing her morning ritual — dusting the three saints' stations, several framed photographs, and many mementoes she had set up to honor her deceased husband, Petreus. She paused at an end table and stabbed out her cigarette, taking a long time doing this, moving the dead stump around and around in the heavy ceramic ashtray.

Arête was part of a group of women living in and around Washington who comprised the three basic political factions present in Greece in the twentieth century: those women and their families who had supported King Alexander; those who had supported the Colonels when they overthrew the king in 1967; and those women who had championed democracy and the Colonels' overthrow in 1974. All three groups consisted, in part, of women who continued to mourn their dead or missing husbands, sons and other relatives who had died or gone missing, first, after the Colonels took power from the king, and next, when the Colonels fell. The women were known in the Greek-American community, facetiously, at best, and sarcastically, at worst, as the mourning women.

Arête had one daughter, Toula, who lived with her, and one son, Ari, who she had left behind in Greece when she and Toula immigrated to America because he suffered from a lung contagion.

During the years when Toula was a child, and continuing to this day, Arête frequently told Toula that Petreus had been misjudged by the members of the democracy movement, and had died in prison of a broken heart after having been falsely accused of being a war criminal.

Arête carefully lifted and dusted the 8"x10" framed black and white photographic portrait of her husband, the framed letter of appreciation he had received from King Alexander when Petreus was only twenty-seven years old, the photograph of Petreus standing with Prince Mekos, and the two medals given to him one year before the king's overthrow. Each photograph was draped in sepulchral bunting.

Arête finished dusting her husband's shrine and lit another cigarette. She inhaled deeply, held the smoke in her lungs for almost one minute, then grudgingly let it stream out her nostrils. She moved over to dust the saints' stations honoring the images of Saint Michael, Saint Gabriel and Saint Pareskavi, the latter being the saint who heals eye problems. Arête bowed her head, crossed herself, and proceeded to attend to the stations. When she completed this task, Arête fired up an incense stick and yet another cigarette.

CHAPTER 7

LEFT EUGENIA'S APARTMENT, BYPASSING THE elevator and its taciturn operator, Nikos, and headed for the interior stairwell. I jogged up two flights, taking two steps at a time, heading to my mother's condo apartment on the sixth floor.

I rapped twice on the door to alert my mother I was coming in using the key she'd given me. The two quick knocks were my mother's idea so I wouldn't frighten her by suddenly appearing without warning.

As I stepped through the doorway into the foyer, I immediately succumbed to the felt warmth and aromas I've always associated with every home my mother has ever kept. I smelled the basil, the sage, and the oregano plants that were scattered throughout the apartment. I inhaled the pervasive fumes of the balsamic vinegar she uses in salads. And because she'd been cooking recently — perhaps today — I could taste the fragrances of lamb rub and Locanico sausage in the air. I could even identify the cheeses she'd served today or yesterday — Dodoni feta from the region of Epirus and aged Kasseri from central Parnassus. Above all, of course, this being my mother's home, I could taste the aroma of her Papagalos Loumidil coffee that overlaid all the other scents.

Yet all these sensory comfort triggers were not sufficient to fully tamp down the disquiet I also felt when I entered and became painfully aware that my mother was gradually expunging from her home most evidence of my father's Taoist existence, replacing it with indicia of her fervent return to the Greek Orthodox Church and to her Greek heritage.

Gone now from one foyer wall above the sideboard, for example, were the three small calligraphy scrolls my father and grandfather had cherished, and my mother had placed in her new home when she moved to the Mount Parnassus from Long Island. Gone, too, was the small seventh century BCE life size limestone Bodhisattva head that had been the pride and joy of my father's modest collection of China's historic artifacts. In their stead, my mother had substituted two sweet basil plants, and a small ikon station she'd erected honoring Saint Stephanos, the patron saint of martyrdom.

To some extent this was understandable. Even though my mother grew up in Shanghai after age eight because her father's work took her family there, she was raised by her Hellenistic parents in the Greek Orthodox Church which permeated all aspects of their life. For her parents and for my mother's formative years, being Greek Orthodox was tantamount to being Greek.

While I understood this intellectually, I wasn't comfortable with the effect this had upon the receding memory of my deceased Chinese father.

I walked into the kitchen and startled an elderly woman who was sitting at the table facing my mother, who stood at the counter with her back to the woman. My mother had hold of a large rolling pin and seemed about to flatten out a fist size ball of what I assumed was filo dough.

The woman at the table picked up a cigarette from the ashtray in front of her, flicked off an ash, and inhaled a long drag. She stared at me with bulging eyes.

"Hello," I said, smiling at her. She quickly looked over at my mother, then turned her head to look back at me again. I watched her tighten up.

"I'm Socrates," I said. "Sophia's son." I smiled and tilted my head toward my mother as I said this. The woman noticeably relaxed. "Sorry if I frightened you."

The woman nodded, and said, "I am Selena Kostas, your mother's neighbor."

She turned back toward my mother, who now faced us and boasted a large, maternal grin.

"I'll go, Sophia," Selena Kostas said. "*Evcharist* — I thank you. The coffee was good." She looked at me again, said nothing, then stood up and walked stiffly out of the kitchen, heading toward the front door.

"*Adio* — Goodbye," I said to the back of her fleeing ankle-length black dress. "Nice meeting you." Then I added, *sotto voce*, "I'll try not to scare any other old ladies today."

Selena's reaction to my presence stirred up memories for me of many of my mother's Greek relatives who had refused to accept my father as one of their own even after he and my mother had been married for more than forty years. If you could believe my father, my mother's cousins, aunts and uncles had a deep and ancient inbred distrust of all outsiders, meaning everyone, even other Greeks, who were not members of their immediate family or members of their own village. My father described it as a prison mentality. So I understood

Selena's reticence to stay and converse with me present, and regretted my flippant remark made to her fleeing back.

"There's no reason to be sassy with my friend, Socrates," my mother said. "Selena's very Old World and not comfortable sitting in a room with a strange man. She's been a good companion to me since I moved here. In fact, she's the one who introduced me to Eugenia. The three of us have become *parea* — close friends."

I acknowledged Selena's role in my mother's new life with a nod, but thought, *Definitely a prison mentality.*

"Did you meet with Eugenia?" my mother said. "How will you help her?"

"I just left her," I said. "I spent almost an hour with her."

As I stared at my mother, I realized that she'd put on weight in the two years since my father died. She was now built for labor, for house work, now having heavy hands, a thick waist, and broad shoulders. She wore her braided gray hair pinned up behind her neck.

I walked over and kissed her on the cheek. "You look nice, Ma. Real pretty."

"*Ach!*" she said, dismissing my comment with the flip of her hand as if ridding herself of a irritating insect. "You always say that, ever since you were a little kid. Don't change the subject. How will you help Eugenia?"

"I don't know yet. I have some questions. Maybe you can clear up some things."

My mother frowned and looked impatient. This was not the answer or level of enthusiasm she expected from me. She pointed with the rolling pin to the chair Selena Kostas had just vacated.

"Sit," she said. Her tone made it clear this was not a request.

My mother took the chair across the table from me, set down two small empty coffee mugs and two glasses of water, and poured coffee. She placed the *briki* — the long-handled brass pot she used to make the coffee — in the middle of the table, next to a small potted basil plant she probably planned to take to Easter week services at Saint Sophia so it could be blessed. I preferred my coffee *sketos*, without sugar; my mother took hers *gliko*, sweet.

"Explain yourself," she said. She reached out and pulled the basil plant over to her and began snapping off leafs, stacking them on a paper towel in front of her. She never stopped looking at me even as her hands mechanically defoliated the plant.

"Well—" I started to say.

"What's your problem helping my friend?" she interrupted. "I don't understand. Eugenia's my friend and she's in trouble. I want you to help her. What more do you need to know than that?"

If we had been playing chess, my mother could have said 'check' at this point and skipped the preliminaries of giving me an illusory opportunity to wriggle out of her trap.

"I know that, Ma, and I'd like to help her. But at her age you have to wonder if Eugenia's fears are real or imagined."

I considered drawing an express analogy to my father, but decided not to.

"The fears are real to Eugenia, Socrates, real enough, anyway. That should be good enough for you," she said, "because she's elderly, and she's my friend."

Checkmate. I mentally knocked over my king and surrendered the game.

I hadn't seen my mother this worked up since my father was first diagnosed with dementia. Seeing her this way stirred my atavistic and unyielding desire to protect her from further anxiety and bad memories, to keep her safe from all that and more.

"Eugenia does not exaggerate or give in to hysteria," my mother said, "not in the two years I've known her. You can ask Selena, she'll tell you." She shook her head as if to say, 'I just don't understand you sometimes, Socrates.'

"If Eugenia says someone entered her apartment when she was out, then someone entered her apartment. That's all there is to it. End of discussion."

She picked up my tepid, untouched cup of coffee and dumped its contents into the sink. Then she poured a fresh cup for me, and said, "I want you to help her. Understand?"

I did understand. The bare truth was that it really didn't matter if Eugenia's worries were real or imagined. My mother's concern for Eugenia was real, and that was all that mattered.

"I'll do what I can for her," I said.

My mother smiled and reached across the table and patted my hand. "Thank you, Socrates. I knew we could count on you. I told Eugenia and Selena you would come through for us."

I got up to leave, leaned over, and again kissed my mother's cheek. She wrapped her meaty hands around my waist and squeezed.

"*Náse kalá* — Be well!" she said.

"And you, Ma. I love you."

I figured I could wrap up Eugenia's problem, one way or

another, in a week or so, then get back to my real job and earn some much needed money.

I left my mother and walked over to my office near Dupont Circle to arrange my affairs so I could be away for the week or so I expected it would take me to resolve Eugenia's problem. With the benefit of hindsight, I must admit, I was being very optimistic or very naïve. Probably both.

CHAPTER 8

LATER THAT SAME AFTERNOON WHEN I'd finished up at my office, I returned to my mother's apartment.

"I have some questions," I said. "I need a fuller picture of Eugenia."

My mother shrugged. "Whatever I know, you will know," my mother said, as she patted my forearm. "Just ask."

"Tell me everything. Facts, gossip, whatever. I need it all if I'm going to figure out why someone would repeatedly enter Eugenia's apartment, but not steal anything."

My mother, as usual, was standing at the counter near the stove with her back to me. She held a long-handled wooden spoon she was using to stir a pot of soup simmering on the front burner.

She was dressed in her post-husband uniform: an unadorned black dress, black stockings, and black shoes that would have been referred to years ago as orthopedic shoes.

She put down the spoon and grabbed a pile of basil leafs that were sitting on the countertop by the sink and started rinsing them. She spoke with her back to me.

"Eugenia is one of the most interesting and complex women I have ever known. You'll love her, Socrates, although not everyone at the condo feels that way about her."

That last statement sparked my interest.

My mother finished rinsing the basil and spread the leafs out on a paper towel to dry. Then she walked over to another counter and retrieved a serrated bread knife and a large section of *Spanakopita*. When I realized what she was doing, I smiled and said, "Yesssssss," stretching out the word for all it was worth. My mother was about to serve one of my favorite baked treats.

"I made this yesterday," she said. "Enjoy." She cut a large slice and placed a fork, paper napkin and the plate containing the treat in front of me.

As I slowly ate, relishing every bite and savoring the blended flavors of feta cheese, spinach, and baked filo, my mother described how she'd first met Eugenia through Selena Kostas, and how, over time, she'd become one of the few people in the building (other than Selena) who liked Eugenia, and did not gossip about her.

"Why would people gossip?" I asked.

"It's her gift," my mother said, "or, maybe, her curse, depending how you see it. Most people don't understand it. Some people fear it; others resent her for having it. And some people think she's faking when she goes into one of her states. So people talk behind her back."

"What do you think?" I asked.

"I believe her," my mother said, but a little too quickly to comfort me.

I'd heard this sort of response from my mother on other occasions in her life when her voice would become truculent and take on an edge because she was defending a belief rather than stating a fact. I let it pass.

"Does she abuse her gift?" I asked.

"Not really," my mother said. She paused. "Oh, a little, I suppose."

She looked away briefly, then faced me again and said, "Yes, I suppose she does abuse it. Eugenia has a tendency to offer a prophecy even when she isn't asked to. Some people resent that, especially when it isn't good news."

"Not a good idea," I offered. "I think it's called meddling," I said, trying to be facetious. My feeble attempt at humor sailed right over my mother's head.

"Some of our condo neighbors think she's crazy, but harmless, an old fool. Others think she's crazy and dangerous, a meddler who stirs up trouble by poking her nose where it isn't wanted."

"What's your take?" I said.

"She's a bit of all that. I also think, as I learned from dealing with your father as he approached his end, that certain privileges come with old age and illness.

"Eugenia is not malicious, as far as I can tell," my mother said, "but she certainly doesn't know about boundaries or tact in dealing with other peoples' lives."

I handed my empty plate across the table and silently begged for another slice by raising my eyebrows, canting my head in the direction of the *Spanakopita*, and miming a hangdog face.

My mother smiled and made a *tsk, tsk, tsk* noise as she spooned another piece onto my plate. "That's my boy," she said. Then she slipped back into her chair across the table from me.

She waited until I'd swallowed my first bite, nodded her approval, then said, "If I had to sum her up, I would say Eugenia gives the impression she thinks she's special because of her gift and is, therefore, absolved from the usual rules of community life. It's not a popular attitude."

"Is she delusional?" I asked.

"Depends on what you mean, Socrates. Some people would say the fact she thinks she has the gift means she's delusional."

"What about her thinking someone entered her apartment and moved things," I said, "or that she's been followed?"

My mother wagged her head and made another *tsk, tsk, tsk* noise. A big smile gradually overspread her face.

"Now, Socrates," she said, "isn't that why I brought you in on this, to find out the answers to those questions? You're the detective, not me."

"Touché," I said. I could feel my neck and face grow warm with embarrassment. "I'll take another piece of *Spanakopita*," I said, changing the focus of conversation away from me and back to my mother's favorite topic, her cooking, "if that's okay. A small piece this time." I loosened my belt buckle one notch.

"Eat, Socrates, eat. It's all for you. Who else is going to eat this if you don't?" My mother acted for all the world as if this was a new and insightful question. "I made it just for you," she said.

I slowly chewed this third piece, considered where I wanted to go next with the information my mother had just given me, and then said, "How'd you meet Eugenia?"

"The way most neighbors meet. First we saw each other at the Hellenic immigrant support group that meets here biweekly. Selena introduced us. Then we saw each other a few days later at the book discussion group I organized when

I moved here. We briefly talked before the group's fireworks began."

"What do you mean, 'fireworks'?" I said.

"You don't know? *Ach*! Of course you don't," my mother said. "Eugenia was one of the few people who supported the group's decision to read Kazantzakis' novel, *The Last Temptation of Christ*. The book has been very controversial here and has caused angry discussions in our meetings." She smiled innocently and shrugged.

I knew better than to think my mother innocent if there was controversy afoot.

I could tell she enjoyed recounting this. The black cast iron pot usually sitting on her stove was not the only pot my mother enjoyed stirring. That was part of her charm. At least that's how I saw it.

I remembered Kazantzakis' book from my third year at Penn State. My professor had described how Kazantzakis had created Judas as the hero of the book and had explicitly shown Jesus' humanity, making him free from sin, but challenged by many human temptations. The professor, who made it plain he was no devotee of the author, said that Kazantzakis should have titled his novel, *The Re-Crucifixion of Christ*, because of the negative, fictive and defamatory aspects of Jesus' human-side personality shown in the book.

"I'm surprised your group selected that book to discuss," I said. "It's pretty controversial for religious people in an informal book group. Weren't you worried how people would react?"

"Worried? Me? Are you kidding? Of course not," my mother said. "I wanted to get some blood boiling and flowing in my neighbors' clogged arteries, ignite those idle grey cells up in their thick skulls. The book has done just that, Socrates. Perhaps more than I bargained for though." She chuckled.

"Getting back to Eugenia," she said, "after those two times when we met, we occasionally ran into each other in the mail room, said 'hello', and talked briefly. One day, she invited me to tea in her apartment. I accepted. Now, we try to have tea two or three times a week."

"Okay," I said, "tell me, what do *you* think about her so-called gift?"

"I don't know. I want to believe her, but I don't know. There are times she seems so rational and other times she's completely out of it, like she is in a trance or some strange state." She paused, looked across the room, then back at me, and slowly fanned out her upright palms. "I just don't know."

"Do you know if she's always had the gift?" I said. I lifted the coffee pot from the table and asked, "More?"

My mother shook her head. I poured the remainder of the coffee into my mug.

"Eugenia told me she's had the gift since she was a child in her village near Sparta. When she was nine years old she was taken from her family and moved to Delphi at Mount Parnassus. There, she and other young girls from other villages were trained in geography, history, religion, politics, mathematics, philosophy and the arts, with the intention that one of them would be selected to join the Cult of Apollo and eventually replace the current Pythia. Eugenia was the one chosen. The other girls returned to their villages. Eugenia became the official Oracle at Delphi on her nineteenth birthday."

I picked up my cup and blew a stream of air across the surface of the steaming coffee. "What made her come to the

United States?" I said. "Why didn't she stay in Greece and continue as the Oracle?"

"That's a little unclear to me," my mother said, "although I have put together some of it from gossip and the little Eugenia told me."

She stood and walked her empty cup over to the sink and rinsed it out. I could tell from her body language she was giving my question thought.

She returned to the table and sat down.

"It seems Eugenia met her husband, Christos Stamos, when he visited Delphi from Athens. Eugenia was about forty years old at the time. They soon married and lived at Delphi, while Eugenia continued to utter prophecies in the manner of the ancient tradition. That ended, however, when the Colonels overthrew the king."

"Why?" I said. "She still was in Delphi, far away from Athens and the Colonels' center of power."

My mother gave a slight shrug. "For reasons she hasn't told me, Eugenia quit her role as the Pythia and moved with Christos to Athens. He became a minor official in the new government because he was related to one of the Colonels. Seven years later, when the Colonels were overthrown, Christos was executed as a war criminal by the new democratic regime, and Eugenia immigrated to America."

She looked over at the counter, stood, and said, "I'm going to put on a fresh pot of coffee. You want?"

I nodded.

I waited until she finished with the coffee pot, returned to the table, and settled back on her chair.

"You said you met Eugenia at the immigrant support group. What's that?"

"Many of us in DC meet and talk about being immigrants in this country. We're mostly Greek in our chapter. I don't know about the other chapters around the country because we're a lodge, a secret society, part of *Philiki Eteria*, and don't share information with other chapters."

"What do you do when you meet?" I said.

My mother smiled. "Oh, you know, Socrates. We complain a lot, argue about the past, especially about politics in Greece, and fight battles that once might have mattered, but no longer should. But we do support one another, too.

"We're all different in our politics," she said. "Some members supported the king, some the Colonels, and some the current government. Others, like me, curse them all," she said.

"We usually talk about the problems of moving to a new land and a different culture. Since we are predominately Greek and mostly elderly, we more often than not argue about having fled Greece, whether we should have stayed and ridden it out or if it was okay to leave. You know, things no longer relevant, things like that."

I smiled. I'd heard this all my life at the dinner table, this familiar debate between my father and mother. The only difference in their positions, although neither would have understood it or acknowledged it if I had raised the point, was in their degree of cultural paranoia.

"What about you, Ma?" I asked. "Where do you fit in? None of what you described seems to apply to you. You and pop lived in the U.S. long before the time of the Colonels. And growing up you barely even lived in Greece. What's the attraction of the support group for you?"

My mother picked up her cup and sipped her coffee. I

could sense the wheels turning in her head. She replaced the cup on the table and stared at it, seemingly thinking about her answer.

After a few more seconds, she looked up at me and said, "Attending the meetings and listening to my neighbors has reawakened my interest in my heritage. I like that. It has put me back in touch with my Church, too. I'm observant again after all these years away. I regularly attend Saint Sophia now. I never realized how much it meant to me, all those years when your father was alive and I didn't go to Mass," she said.

That bothered me, the backhanded reference to my father, as if he had held her back from attending her Church, the slam on all the years they were married and she chose not to attend. I'd never heard my father discourage her from going and I never heard my mother express any interest in attending, not before today. It just hadn't been an issue as far as I knew.

I thought about saying something, but decided to let it sit. I would raise this some other time and deal with my feelings then, when we could talk in a more relaxed context than we found ourselves in now.

"Anything else I should know about Eugenia?" I said.

"Just this. I don't know if Eugenia has the power of prophecy or not. I don't know if I even know all the reasons she came to America. But I do know she is a very old lady who thinks she has a gift and who believes someone is going to harm her. I also know, Socrates," my mother said, locking her eyes on mine, "she's my friend."

And that, I knew, was the bottom line concerning this matter.

I had one more question. "Do you think Eugenia's powers

have anything to do with the break-ins or why she's been followed, assuming it's true?"

My mother shrugged. "I don't know." She paused, looked me in my eyes again, then said, "Have I helped you?

I nodded and reached over and squeezed her hand. "You've helped me, Ma, and I'll help Eugenia for you." I stood up to leave.

My mother smiled and clasped her hands together. "*Adāo*," she said.

"*Yasou, re*, I answered, and kissed her cheek.

CHAPTER 9

P
ANOS' SYSTEMATIC LOOTING OF HIS clients' accounts
provided him with the means to build a moderate size
collection of Greek antiquities, but not with sufficient
funds to acquire first rate, museum quality artifacts as he
would have liked. His limited legitimate income, together
with his limited embezzled income, enabled Panos only to
purchase objects that, at first sight, appeared to be high
quality, but which upon inspection would be found to be
seconds. In every case, with Panos' acquiescence, all of his
acquisitions had discernible defects such as small cracks,
repairs, or tiny chips.

This collecting strategy - actually, collecting necessity
although Panos thought of it as his strategy - reflected Panos'
concession to reality and enabled him over twelve years to
acquire antiquities he otherwise could never have dreamed of
owning. But this strategy came at a high psychological cost,
and carried within it its internal death wound.

One of Panos' few pleasures in life was to enter his Treasure
Room — his secret room, the vault no one knew about except
the five workers Panos had temporarily imported from Piraeus

to build the room for him, workers who then returned to Greece pledged to secrecy.

Once inside the Treasure Room, Panos typically settled into the cushioned, motorized chair in the center of the room, and faced one of the twelve pedestals that ringed the room's perimeter, in anticipation of soon gazing upon the first of the eleven antiquities on display. He never knew which treasure he would begin his day's admiration with because he started the process by closing his eyes, then pressing the chair's Rotate button while he counted to that day's arbitrary number. When he finished his count and stopped the chair, he would open his eyes and begin his visual examination of whichever object was directly across from him.

The twelfth pedestal, like the others, also held Panos' collected artifacts, but artifacts in a very different condition. The twelfth pedestal displayed a small pile of shards created when Panos decided that one of his treasures might be a fake, and he then crushed the offending artifact using a heavy rubber mallet he kept in the Treasure Room for this purpose. The debris on the twelfth pedestal was intended to remind Panos to be vigilant in his acquisitions, and always was the last pedestal he looked at when he visited his Treasure Room.

Panos stopped the chair's rotation and opened his eyes. He was directly across from the fifth century BCE limestone *Head of Athena*, one of his most prized possessions. He smiled. This, and the other ten artifacts spread around the Treasure Room, made life worthwhile for him.

He pushed the button on the armrest once. The chair rotated 10o counter-clockwise. He now faced the pedestal supporting the 14" draped female sandstone figure, *circa* sixth century BCE, dedicated to *Nikandre on Delos*. This was another prized purchase, one of his first from the Theodoros brothers. This acquisition had taken Panos seventeen months to pay off, but it was worth it. The figurine's serene beauty was Panos' daily palliative.

Slowly, deliberately, Panos rotated the chair and faced the remaining pedestals. He paused before the Black Figure *amphora* and lingered for five minutes, drinking in the power of the cup which had the painted interior showing Ajax carrying the body of Achilles.

He paid short shrift to the sixth century BCE vase decorated with the figures of Dionysus and the two Maenads — a recent acquisition he hadn't yet resolved his doubts about concerning its authenticity — and then spent contemplative time staring at his Red Figured *amphora* showing Herakles attempting to steal Apollo's tripod. Last, he gazed at the bronze charioteer statuette from Delos. He ignored the others for now.

Panos' last act before he left the Treasure Room was to rotate his chair until he faced the pile of rubble displayed on the twelfth pedestal, rubble that once had been an Attic Black Figure vase.

Panos smiled as he thought about the shards. The object they represented had been his only purchase from a dealer other than the Theodoros brothers, and he'd learned his lesson when he showed the artifact to Milos Theodoros who had quickly identified it as a fake.

Panos had intended to return that purchase to the dealer, but he was nowhere to be found so, instead, Panos acquired the mallet and used it on the fake. Panos chuckled thinking about it. If he'd had his way, he would have kept the fake intact as an object lesson and turned his mallet against the dealer. *But,* as he often thought in other circumstances, *you make do with what you have.*

Although Panos loved his time in the Treasure Room, it came with a steep price. Once Panos entered the Treasure Room, and continuing for hours after he left, his emotions ran the gamut from exaltation to despair and anger. The pattern was this: Initially after acquiring an object, Panos saw only its beauty and only his contorted visual sense of the object that had originally fueled his desire to possess it. His joy at owning the object during this stage of his mood swing constantly ascended until it reached a crescendo of pleasure almost unbearable for him. Then, inevitably, as the climactic moment occurred, it was followed by the headlong downward rush of his emotions and his attachment to the object as he recalled what he'd known all along, that the object was damaged goods — cracked, chipped, or repaired - not the high quality artifact his emotions had originally blinded him to delight in.

Eventually, Panos grew to loath his collection. Its very existence ate away at him like a slow growing intestinal parasite.

CHAPTER 10

I'S TIME I INTRODUCE MYSELF. You already know my
name — Socrates Cheng.

I am a licensed private investigator working mostly
in Washington, DC, although my cases sometimes take me
from the city to suburban Maryland or northern Virginia.

When I acquired my PI's license, I went to work
conducting investigations for my former law partners. As a
result, my PI practice has almost always involved white collar
matters.

I don't have to do much fieldwork in my business. I don't
carry a weapon, although I'm licensed to do so, and I don't
engage in car chases. I haven't been in a fist fight since before
I was in junior high school.

Much of my investigatory work is done from my office
using my computer to search various databases I subscribe to.
I don't peek through keyholes; I don't sift through anyone's
dirty laundry or trash or garbage — not literally — and I
don't snap clandestine photos of wayward spouses.

What I do in my practice are forensic investigations to
help defend my clients when they've been charged by the
government with various types of white collar crimes —
embezzlement, tax fraud, Medicare fraud, and sundry other

alleged dubious or illegal practices. I also investigate employee thefts, trade secret thefts and creative accounting methods generally referred to as *cooking the books*. I've promised myself that if I ever am reduced to keyhole peeping or the like, I'll make another career change.

Why, then, would I agree to help Eugenia find out who had been illicitly entering her apartment (a misdemeanor trespass, at best, or a felony attempted burglary, at worst) and try to learn who had been following her when she took her walks (assuming, of course, all this wasn't a figment of her imagination)? The answer is simple: to appease and, if necessary, protect my mother.

I'll do almost anything my mother asks me to do for her. That's my felt obligation since my father died two years ago. I perform this responsibility without any reluctance or resentment on my part, although not always without trepidation.

CHAPTER 11

I CALLED EUGENIA FROM MY MOTHER'S apartment and told her I would help her. I asked if she'd mind if I stopped by in a few minutes so we could talk some more.

I knocked on Eugenia's door and was surprised when Selena Kostas opened it.

"Hello again," I said, trying not to seem surprised. "I'm here to see Eugenia. She's expecting me."

Selena raised her hand to her mouth and rolled back her eyes in a movement that seemed so melodramatic and contrived it had to be natural.

"I'm leaving," Selena said. "We have finished my reading."

"I hope it went well" I said, trying to make some innocuous small talk.

"It did not," Selena said, "and it's not your business."

Eugenia appeared at the door and rescued me before I put my other foot in my mouth. I said *Adio* to Selena, and, feeling duly chastened by her, followed Eugenia back to the parlor.

Eugenia seemed different to me. Her eyes were glassy, her pupils large and unfocused. She walked from the front door to her chair in the parlor with exaggerated deliberation, like someone inebriated who took each step with overstated care, hoping to project a portrait of imagined sobriety.

We settled into the same two chairs, facing one another again. I said, "I was surprised to see Selena here. Sorry if I spoke out of turn. I was just making small talk with her."

"It doesn't matter. Your curiosity about her reading won't change anything for her. We were completing her session when you called. Your timing was good. I did not feel comfortable continuing with her today."

Tempted though I was to ask why, to latch onto Eugenia's throwaway remarks, I minded my manners and didn't follow-up. Instead, I said, "Does she come for readings often?"

Eugenia interlaced her fingers, put her hands on her lap, and frowned. "Often enough," she said.

I had the impression I was marching through forbidden territory and that Eugenia wanted to change the subject. To my surprise, she continued. "We've known each other for several years. You interfered with our reading."

Now I was the one who wanted to change the subject.

"I'm sorry, but I didn't know she was here when I called. Given our conversation earlier this morning, I assumed you'd want me to—"

"That is not what I meant," Eugenia said. "Your telephone call was not the problem, not the interference I referred to."

"Then what?"

"I saw a vision of you while I performed Selena's reading," she said.

My breath caught and I realized I was holding it in. "What do you mean?" I asked, although I wasn't sure I wanted to know.

Eugenia looked into my eyes and studied them, but I

had the feeling she didn't see me. She still seemed to be in a trance-like state.

"In my vision, you were under threat by someone from your past who intends to harm you."

This wasn't what I expected or wanted to hear, not why I'd come back here to see Eugenia. "Who?" I stammered. I felt my gut tighten.

"This is all I know. I cannot say anything more about this."

I didn't want to drop the subject. "Why would someone want to harm me?" I said.

Eugenia shook her head. "I have told you all I can for now," she said.

I nodded, signaling my wiliness to drop the subject. *At least for now*, I thought.

As it stood, as we left it standing, I would have been better off if Eugenia hadn't said anything at all to me, validating the old bromide that ignorance is bliss.

Eugenia stood up from her chair. As I started to follow suit, she signaled me with the palm of her hand and a shake of her head to stay put. I settled back into my chair and watched as she left the room.

CHAPTER 12

Toula Xandereas adjusted her black eye patch and checked herself in the mirror.

She was happy with what she saw. She was attractive for her forty-six years, and often thought of by strangers as someone a decade younger. She had raven black hair, Chiclet-white teeth, and radiant olive skin. In this regard, she was indistinguishable from many other comely Greek immigrant women raised in America. But in one regard, she was different. Toula invariably wore the expression of someone intent on being disappointed.

Toula had been well educated and was an honors graduate in Greek Classical Studies from American University in Washington. When it came to religion, however, including the religion of her heritage — Greek Orthodoxy — Toula practiced a healthy skepticism and worshipped at no God's alter save that of the home-bound shrine she and her mother maintained for Toula's mythic father.

CHAPTER 13

EUGENIA KEPT ME WAITING IN the parlor for twenty minutes before she returned. She carried a watering can with her.

As I waited, I looked around the room. The parlor's windows were covered with heavy burlap curtains. The only light source was a table lamp sitting behind me. The room's air was redolent of stale cigarettes, sweet basil, camphor balls, certain odors characteristic of old people that came from clothing and skin that had gone too long without washing, and some underlying sweet fragrance I couldn't identify.

As Eugenia walked past me, she said, "We will talk while I water my plants. This is the time each week I nourish them."

"That's fine," I said.

Eugenia had dozens of basil plants scattered throughout the parlor.

"How will you help me?" she asked.

I studied Eugenia's face for a few seconds before I answered. She was holding a watering can with its long spout swallowed up by the leaves of a succulent basil plant. I looked hard at her, trying to uncover some clue whether she believed I sincerely wanted to help her or cynically thought I was agreeing to appease my mother. Had she asked me, I couldn't have told her which it was or if it was both.

"How I'd like to approach this," I said, "is I'll go with you on your walks. The walks will be our *volta* — our stroll. But each time, first I'll look around your home to get a picture how things appear before we leave. When we get back, I'll do another walk-through to see if anything's been changed, been moved, I mean. Let's try that for a week or so, see how it goes, then we can take it from there."

"What about the person following me?" Eugenia said.

"I hope my presence will put an end to that," I said. "If not, I'll deal with that, too."

Eugenia and I kicked-off my plan the next morning at 10:30. I started by walking around Eugenia's apartment, taking care to examine and mentally inventory her framed ikons hanging along several walls in different rooms, her knickknacks and curios, and her framed, free-standing photographs, all of which were in great abundance. I was surprised how dusty the standing objects were.

The rest of Eugenia's apartment — at least the parts I had access to — seemed to be an homage to a cleaning obsession. I recognized, of course, that if Eugenia wanted to keep all her objects and the surfaces under them dust free, she'd have to spend hours each week carefully moving each object while she dusted, *ad infinitum*. She'd be like those window washers you see working on a skyscraper who start at the top floor windows, wash their way down to the ground floor, then start right over again at the top floor in an endless loop.

This operated to our advantage. Because Eugenia could

not just engage in a broad, rapid, once over dusting, she necessarily allowed dust to accumulate on the bookshelves and piano top, even as she studiously dusted the hanging ikons. This meant that any object that might be moved by an intruder would disturb the dust layer so that all I would have to do when we returned from our walk each day would be to complete another walk-around, but this time looking only for disturbed dust. It was an anal retentive archeologist's dream scenario.

It didn't take me long to discover the obvious: Taking walks with a ninety-four year old woman was not, as they say, a stroll in the park. Eugenia moved along so slowly and so unsteadily that I constantly had to adjust my pace to accommodate hers. I didn't want Eugenia to think she had to hurry to keep up with me or that she was being a drag on me, although, if truth be told, she was.

Beyond this, Eugenia's steadiness — her balance — was shaky. She probably should have been using an aluminum walker. Several times she seemed to teeter on the brink of falling so I had to stabilize her by looping her arm in mine. The first time I did this she looked up at me, smiled, and said, 'Thank you. Mr. Cheng'. After two more times doing this, I automatically kept my light grip on her.

As we walked, I not only paid attention to Eugenia's physical stability, I also tried to maintain an inconspicuous lookout for anyone following us. I never saw anyone.

After each of our walks, when Eugenia and I returned to

her apartment, I unlocked the door and entered alone while Eugenia waited in the hallway. I wanted to assure myself that no one was inside before she entered.

To clear the apartment, I first looked carefully at every shelf and the piano's top, eyeballing all the knickknacks and curios, and examining the framed photographs cluttered across the top of her grand piano. I then made a quick mental inventory in several rooms of the hanging, framed ikons.

Having satisfied myself each time that nothing in the apartment had been disturbed, I then invited Eugenia to enter and asked her if anything seemed out of place. She invariably gazed over at the walls, the shelves and the piano, sighed, and shook her head. She almost seemed disappointed when she said each time, "No, Mr. Cheng, nothing appears moved. Not today."

After the first few days walking together, I reflexively adjusted to Eugenia's pace so I no longer had to consciously restrain my stride. Beginning on the fourth or fifth day, we automatically fell into the routine of interlacing our arms like a young couple out for a stroll. This offered stability to Eugenia, which in turn enabled her to walk more quickly and with confidence she would not lose her balance. It also made our time out together much easier for me because I could stop thinking about Eugenia's uncertain gait and instead concentrate on spotting anyone who might have been following us.

On the ninth day, after we returned to Eugenia's apartment, and I finished my walk-around to check for signs of an intruder, Eugenia said, "You must think I'm demented, don't you."

I was tempted to answer honestly, but didn't. For reasons I didn't understand, or perhaps were too tangled for me to sort out, I had come to like this old woman and did not want to say anything that might offend her.

"What I think is, you believe you had an intruder, and maybe you did have one, but not over the past week and a half. At least I didn't see any sign of one." I paused, then said, "Maybe my presence scared him away."

Eugenia frowned.

"Why don't we walk again tomorrow," I said, "make it an even ten days in a row. Then, if things haven't changed, I'll back off and we'll see what happens. Maybe that will flush out the intruder."

I kept a close eye on Eugenia's face as I said this. She seemed bothered by my suggestion, probably because she understood the implication of my words — that no matter what I said, I didn't believe there had been an intruder or that someone had followed her. I felt bad about this, but what could I do? I had to get back to earning a living. I was a one man PI shop with a few clients and a few ongoing cases to attend to. I had to work the cases I had and get out there and find more business.

At any rate, I thought, *if I was scaring away an intruder, I couldn't keep this up forever. I'd have to call a halt to the walks at some point, after which, if there had been an intruder, he'd return when I left.*

Eugenia agreed, reluctantly, it seemed to me, so the next day we took our last walk together. I still didn't see anyone following us although I noticed that this time Eugenia seemed to be relying less on my powers of observation and more on her own. On this day's walk, she frequently slowed her pace, gripped my arm more tightly, and turned and looked behind us, something she hadn't done the other days. *Maybe, I thought, she was hoping to see someone I'd missed so she could keep our time together going along.*

CHAPTER 14

P ANOS STEPPED UP TO THE steel door that sealed
the Treasure Room and placed his eyeball up to the
biometric reader. When the LCD screen flashed red,
then yellow, then green, and finally spelled-out the word,
Valid, he punched his nine digit password into the key pad
and entered the vault. Then he bullied the heavy door closed
behind him, again punched in his code — this time to lock
the door — and glanced around the room. The recessed
lights, constructed to respond to motion, winked on one by
one around the ceiling's perimeter, bathing the room in a
warm, amber glow.

Panos settled into his chair and slowly rotated from left to
right, brushing his gaze over several displayed artifacts.

When he set up the Treasure Room, he had placed each
object far enough away from his chair so he could not see its
defects under the friendly, camouflaging amber light, but not
so far away he could shield their flaws from memory.

His eye fell upon an Attic Black-Figured column *krater*,
circa 540-525 BCE, which depicted a youthful horseman in
pursuit of two armed warriors. Panos had purchased this vase
seven years before from Aristides and Milos Theodoros.

The *krater*'s beauty still took away Panos' breath when

he viewed it from the distance of his seat, bathed as it was in soft, diffused amber light. But when he thought about the *krater*, as he often did, all Panos could see were the two cracks and the one inch chip that marred its side facing the wall, the side deliberately away from Panos' conscious view.

He turned away from the *krater*.

Panos stood up and walked across the room to a waist-high pedestal on which he displayed a 6" tall bronze mask of Herakles, attributed to the late Classical Period, *circa* 4th Century BCE. He loved this mask, and sometimes, but not always, regretted he was not able to dismiss his knowledge of its missing rear quarter.

Panos turned away from the mask and shifted his gaze to a clay-fired vessel, an Attic white-ground *lekythos, circa* 470-450 BCE. He had acquired this 6-7/8" high vase four years ago from the Georgetown-based Theodoros brothers. It depicted a seated woman, with a column behind her, holding an oval mirror in her right hand. Her hair was bound by a fillet and pulled back in a chignon. This ceramic object was one of his favorites.

Panos picked up the *lekythos* and stared intimately at it. Its beauty never failed to bring tears to his eyes. He held the vessel in his left palm and gently ran the fingers of his other hand over the figure of the seated woman. He could almost feel her suck in her breathe as he touched her. His fingers walked around the object until they came to the missing wedge located on its blind side. His fingertips dug into the depression, traced its jagged edges, and rubbed its rough underglaze. His brief action sent ugly remembrances racing to his consciousness.

Panos sighed a long, plaintive moan, shook his head, and

looked briefly at the ceramic lady in his palm. He shook his head again, then abruptly fast-balled the lady to the floor, smashing her into hundreds of shards.

He paced the room. He eventually knew what he must do. He'd made up his mind. His decision was a long time coming, had evolved slowly and painfully, but in a rare show of self-awareness, Panos was satisfied it was the correct decision for him.

He would go to the Theodoros brothers and insist they repurchase his surviving collection at the same price he'd paid them for it. His days as the brothers' willing customer were over. He would no longer collect seconds. And, since he could not afford to collect what he wanted, he would not collect antiquities at all. Not any more.

CHAPTER 15

EUGENIA AND I RETURNED TO her apartment almost seventy-five minutes after beginning our tenth and, presumably, our last walk. This last time together had been our most time consuming, as if we both were reluctant to return to her apartment and once again find disappointment awaiting us.

We stood in the hallway outside her door. Neither of us said anything. What, after all, could we say that wasn't implied by the circumstances? As she usually did, Eugenia handed me her key ring. I checked the apartment and found no evidence of an intruder. Eugenia agreed to call me again if she felt someone was again entering her apartment or following her.

I turned away to leave, when Eugenia said, "I need your help with another problem, even if you are not willing to help me with this one."

That stopped me cold. *Not willing to help her? This was not a nice lady. I could see why her neighbors didn't like her.*

I turned to face her. *Now what? Is she just trying to prolong this, hoping I'll change my mind? Trying to make me feel guilty because no intruder or stalker showed on my watch?*

"What's that?" I said, speaking softly, trying not to betray with my voice either my anger or my misgivings about her motive.

"My neighbors downstairs," she said, "they make too much noise. All hours of the day and night."

"What's the problem with them?" I asked.

"Noise. I just told you," she said. "You need to listen when I speak to you."

I held my tongue and reminded myself that this cranky old woman was both old and my mother's friend.

"Would you like me to talk to them for you?" I said. "I'll do that if you want."

Eugenia nodded, but didn't smile. "Make sure they understand they are disturbing me."

"I'll talk to them and see what I can do."

———————•◦•———————

I rode the elevator down one floor.

"Hello, Nikos," I said to the elevator operator as he dragged open the steel mesh gate, pulling it slowly across the elevator's entrance to admit me. He nodded and moved over to his corner to work the controls.

"I'll get out one down," I said. I looked at Nikos as we road down. He had a crooked thumb that intrigued me. It looked as if it had been broken and not reset. If I had to describe it, I'd say it looked like a hitchhiker's thumb.

Nikos frowned as if to say, "Why are you bothering me to go down one floor? We have stairs for that." I felt no need to explain myself, and let it ride.

I walked up the hall to the apartment below Eugenia's and paused in front of the door. I wanted to compose my thoughts before I knocked so I wouldn't inadvertently make matters worse. After all, I didn't really know how bad the situation was. I only knew what Eugenia had said. I was about to accuse someone of disturbing an old lady, but without being armed with the facts when I did so.

I decided to be deferential and to try to form a bond with the apartment's dwellers as if we had to endure together the burden of humoring a grouchy old woman. That wasn't so far from the truth.

I knocked lightly on the door.

My knock was answered by someone examining me through the door's security peephole. I stared back. After a few seconds, the door opened.

A man in his middle or late 20s, who looked as if he'd been cast for the movie *Night of the Living Dead,* stood facing me, partially concealed by the door. I could see enough of him to know he was not a lawyer or an accountant dressed for work. *Meth-head,* I thought. His left hand was curled inward to the palm concealing a smoke. I could smell the unmistakable, delicious scent of smoldering pot.

"Fuck you want, Dude?" he said, eyeballing me up and down.

So much for bonding.

"The old woman who lives above you asked me to stop by. Do you have a minute?" I said. I smiled.

"What's the old bitch complaining about now?" he said. He stepped out from behind the door and squarely faced me. He curled the fingers of his right hand into a fist, but kept it by his side.

"Useless old hag," he said, eyeballing me up and down as he spoke. He raised his left hand and hit the blunt he held in his nicotine stained fingers.

I felt my stomach tighten and my face grow hot. I might not be crazy about Eugenia, but he had no right to talk to me about her like that. I hadn't done anything to offend him.

"There's no need to call names," I said, struggling to keep my tone level. "I'm here to talk about a problem, to resolve it." I intentionally spoke softly.

"So talk, Dude," he said. "Clock's running. I don't got all day." He blinked hard several times, using his eyelashes as exclamation points.

I tried to look beyond him into his apartment. He noticed this and stepped toward the left side of the doorway, blocking my view. He pulled the door partially closed, effectively keeping me from seeing into his condo.

I looked him over, slowly, up and down. He was a mess. He had several swollen red bumps on his face, and dark, bad teeth. His hair, which he wore down to his shoulders, looked like a rat's nest, with the burnt straw texture common to malnutrition. I noticed a few bald patches on his head. His shirt, a faded and stained wife-beater, was torn in several places and stained with food. His jeans had the authentic look of long-term wear and misuse that modern vendors try to simulate by deliberately tearing the knee areas of new jeans and then stone-washing them to death. Even standing a few feet away from him, I could tell he sorely needed time in the shower.

"There's no reason to get nasty," I said, deliberately modulating my voice to sound warm and conspiratorial. "Mrs. Stamos upstairs thinks you're making too much noise at all hours. Even if she's imagining it, couldn't you make some effort to accommodate her?"

"Fuckin' bitch," he said. "Why she wanna mess wit' me

for? I'm trouble, bad trouble." He started to close the door, but I pressed the sole of my shoe against the door's bottom, stopping him.

"Look," I said, "just quiet down so I don't have to come back here again, understand? We'll let it go at that for now. Believe me, you don't want me coming back." I tried to stare hard into his eyes, but his rapid blinking won out, and I looked away.

"Woman's messin' with the wrong dude," he said.

He slammed the door again, but again I blocked it with my foot. He looked in my eyes with venom in his own; his mouth curled as if to growl. He took a step toward me.

I quickly moved forward without a word, cutting him off, and planted my right knee swiftly and firmly in his groin. I lifted his emaciated body several inches off the floor with my follow through, then pulled back and let him drop to the wood like a lead shot. His face now was sheet white; his eyes wide open as if he'd seen a ghost. He curled into a fetal position, with his hands tucked between his closed legs, and groaned. It hurt me to watch him.

"Let's see if we can avoid bad language and calling names in the future," I said. "Let's see, too, if you can behave yourself and not disturb your neighbor so I don't have to come back here and get serious with you. Understand?"

He didn't say anything. His wide-open eyes locked on mine.

I kneeled on one knee alongside him and put my face near his. I had to hold my breath as I spoke.

"*Katalavenis*?" — Understand?" I said, softly. "Pretend *I'm* the wrong dude to mess with."

I had no reason to think he spoke Greek other than the

fact he lived among a Greek population, but I thought he'd get my meaning from my tone and my head nod. He remained silent. I wanted to leave on a high note, so as I stood up, I smiled, and said "*Adio*."

As I neared the elevator, I heard him say just before his door slammed, "*Poosti*."

I couldn't help smiling. He had a big set, all right. I had to give him that much.

CHAPTER 16

T O SAY MY MOTHER WASN'T happy with me would strain the boundaries of sarcasm or understatement. She was furious I'd stopped accompanying Eugenia on her walks. And, although she did not come right out and say so, I also had the feeling she was disappointed in me, perhaps even embarrassed I had walked away from her friend's perceived problems.

For the next week, I immersed myself in my PI practice, and pretty much forgot about Eugenia, her putative intruder, and her purported stalker.

But not for long.

I was sitting at home, sipping a McCallum single malt Scotch and listening to John Coltrane's *Blue Trane* on my iPod, when my cellphone rang.

"Hello, this is Socrates," I said. I didn't recognize the caller's number, and the CallerID screen said, Caller Unknown.

"Socrates, it's me, Mom. I'm with Eugenia at her apartment. We have a problem. I need you here right now."

My stomach tensed. I realized I was holding my breath. "What's wrong?"

"It's Eugenia," my mother said. "I told you she was telling the truth, but you wouldn't believe us. Now you'll have to."

"What happened?" My insides roiled.

"She found someone in her apartment when she came home from her walk — her walk alone, I might add."

"Is she all right?" I said. I felt an undulating wave of guilt.

"If you mean did the trespasser hurt her, no, but she's not all right. She's very upset."

"Did she recognize the intruder?" I asked.

"It was our neighbor, Selena Kostas."

I never expected that. Why would Selena Kostas enter Eugenia's apartment without permission?

"There's more," my mother said. "Selena's dead."

CHAPTER 17

M Y MOTHER'S PHONE CALL SERVED as my wakeup call. She said that she and Eugenia hadn't called the police yet, so I told her to hold off for now. I also told her to lock Eugenia's apartment door from the hallway, and to wait for me with Eugenia in her own apartment.

It took me ten minutes to arrive there. I went directly over to my mother, hugged her, and said hello to Eugenia. I thought, *Thank you both for not saying, I told you so.*

We decided we'd all go to Eugenia's apartment so I could look around, then I would call the police. I wanted to experience what Eugenia and my mother had seen before the police arrived and sealed off the crime scene, barring civilians like me from entering the apartment. I knew I risked being charged with tampering with a crime scene — I assumed this was a crime scene since Selena had entered Eugenia's home without permission — but I wanted to make up my perceived indifference to Eugenia's fears by now being proactive. *The things we do to please our mothers*, I thought.

As we stepped onto the elevator to go to her apartment, Eugenia said to me, "I told you somebody was coming into my apartment."

I nodded, thought, *touché*, and said nothing in response.

When we arrived at Eugenia's place, she and my mother waited in the hallway while I went inside and looked around. Although I didn't intend to touch anything, I put on latex gloves I'd brought with me.

I opened the door slowly and looked in. Then, seeing no one, I cautiously entered the apartment.

Selena lay on her back staring at the living room ceiling with her eyes opened wide. Her face was contorted into a scowl as if she had suffered some trauma. Her open eyes screamed pain.

I've seen a few dead bodies at crime scenes in the last four years, but I still hadn't gotten used to it. Now, at the sight of Selena's body, I felt a familiar shudder in my legs, a weakness I only experienced when I was in the company of dead crime victims. I knew this response wasn't professional, but this was the way I responded. I doubted I'd ever become used to viewing DOAs.

I checked her for a pulse to see if I needed to call for an EMS bus. As I expected, I did not have to.

I didn't see any signs of trauma, wound or assault, so I had to consider the possibility that Selena hadn't been the victim of a crime, but had succumbed to some illness or natural tragedy. Maybe a painful heart attack. But if that was the cause of her death, this still begged the essential question: what was she doing in Eugenia's apartment without Eugenia's permission?

I looked back at Eugenia, who stood in the hallway by the door looking in, and shook my head. Then I quickly checked the other rooms and closets to be sure no one was hiding in the apartment. When I was satisfied no one was there, I retraced my steps back to the entrance and stepped out into the hallway.

I explained to Eugenia that until we knew the cause of death, since Selena was not supposed to be in the apartment, we had to treat Eugenia's home as a crime scene. Eugenia seemed to understand this and seemed content to wait in the hall with me and my mother.

I called the Second District Precinct — the 2D — and reported the body. Then I tried to comfort Eugenia while she and my mother waited for the authorities to arrive. I could see the physical change that had come over Eugenia as she withdrew into herself. She remained silent except to say, once, to no one in particular, "I warned her to be careful, that she was in danger. Now she knows." My mother and I slipped each other quizzical glances.

The District of Columbia's EMS vehicle arrived about twenty minutes after I called the 2D. It was soon followed by two uniformed police officers.

The EMS personnel indicated Selena was dead, but, as expected when I asked, did not offer a preliminary, off-the-record, opinion on the cause of her death. A few minutes later someone from the Medical Examiner's office arrived and began constructing a crime scene perimeter using yellow crime scene tape. Then the 2D homicide detectives arrived because, as I already knew, any unexplained death in the District was treated as a possible homicide until that cause was ruled out.

I was standing in the hall looking through the doorway into the apartment, watching the ME's representative dictate notes into a handheld recorder, when I heard someone say, "Well, well, well. If it ain't Socrates Cheng, my favorite Chinese amateur detective. Carrying on your tradition from four years ago, I see."

I groaned inwardly because I knew whose voice that was. I turned to face the detective as he made his way from the elevator to Eugenia's apartment.

Just my luck he caught this call, I thought.

I looked the detective in his eyes as he approached me, offering him fictive bravado, not willing to disclose to him my apprehension that he was going to conduct another investigation in which I was involved. As he drew near, I saw the same feral smile I remembered from the last time I'd crossed his path.

Not willing to concede anything to him, I said, "No longer amateur, Detective Thigpen. I'm licensed now and make my living as a PI. And, as you know, I'm not just Chinese," I said, emphasizing with my imperious tone my distain for his familiar dredged-up bigotry, although I knew my blowback would escape his notice. Nonetheless, it felt good to dish it out to him.

As if I didn't know what he'd been referring to, I said, "What tradition are you talking about, Detective?"

"I'll tell you, Cheng." He gave me an unfriendly *got-you-now-sucker* smile. "Your old habit of gathering dead bodies around you," he said. "It's still risky to associate with you and not wind-up a DOA." He paused and plugged a toothpick into the corner of his mouth.

Physically, Thigpen hadn't changed much in the four years since I last saw him. He still looked like a street thug badly dressed up to play at being a cop. He wore a suit jacket he'd obviously cannibalized from a worn-out suit, but now used as a sports coat he paired with slacks that had, themselves, originated with yet another suit. He'd also put on about fifteen pounds, showing a pot belly that draped over his wide belt buckle.

Yet I knew from experience that Thigpen was a good cop. He would ask no-nonsense questions, never crack a joke except occasionally at my expense, and never smile at me unless it had a predatory foundation. I expected him to continue to act out his unrelenting bigotry and contempt for me because of my two disparate heritages.

Thigpen turned away from me as if I wasn't worthy of any more explanation. He nodded once at his partner, as if with the few words he had directed at me, he'd told her everything she could possibly need to know about me. Then he looked back at me, and said, "Don't go anywhere, Cheng. I want to talk to you when I'm done inside."

Thigpen brushed past me and ducked under the yellow tape that had been stretched across the apartment's entrance. The young woman plainclothes officer, who had been silently watching us joust, looked at me and rolled her eyes as she leaned under the tape and followed Thigpen into Eugenia's apartment.

I wondered where Detective Harte was, Thigpen's partner four years ago. Harte, at least, had usually acted evenhandedly toward me and had actually seemed pleased when I solved the theft of Chinese cultural treasures from a Georgetown art gallery, and had exposed the murderers. Thigpen, on the other hand, had treated me as a suspect from the get go, or, at best, as an unwelcomed interloper into his official investigation.

———— •••• ————

One of the EMS women checked Eugenia as we stood in the hall. She pronounced Eugenia fit to stand by and wait for the detectives to take her statement.

After thirty minutes, Thigpen and his partner emerged from Eugenia's apartment. They pulled Eugenia aside and told me to wait my turn. Then they encircled Eugenia.

While I waited, I looked through the doorway into the apartment. A second crime scene unit had arrived and begun processing the scene — taking photographs of the body and the room, dusting for fingerprints, taking measurements, and so forth — the standard bouillabaisse of modern forensic procedures generated by the now antediluvian OJ Simpson trial, and by CSI-NY and its brethren forensic television shows.

I debated whether I would mention to Thigpen why I was with Eugenia today, and whether or not I would tell him that Eugenia believed her apartment had been entered on other occasions while she was out walking. I decided to wait and see how his interview with me played out before I made a decision. Besides, I thought, Eugenia would probably tell them before Thigpen ever got to me.

I watched as Thigpen nodded at Eugenia and then waved his arm at me to join him. He again cast his menacing grin at me.

I walked up the hall toward Thigpen and his partner. I felt more apprehension at the prospect of being interviewed by him than I would have expected.

"Move it, Asshole," Thigpen said, from twenty feet away.

I smiled at Eugenia as we passed one another, and said softly, "Call me if you need me." I handed her my business card with my cellphone number on it. My mother stepped over to me, and said she and Eugenia would be upstairs in her apartment waiting for me when I finished with the police.

"Step on it, Cheng," Thigpen said. "Let's get started." He paused until I reached him and his partner, then said, locking eyes with me, "And no bullshit from you this time around. Not like four years ago. Harte's not here to protect your ass." A wolf-like grin slowly spread across his face.

CHAPTER 18

T HIGPEN, HIS NEW PARTNER, AND I stood in the hallway
near Eugenia's apartment.

"There won't be any bullshit, Detective," I said in
response to Thigpen's snide remark.

"What were you doing here, Cheng?" Thigpen said.
"How'd you know the DOA?" Thigpen's eyes scanned me up
and down as if he was looking for something.

Given our prior history, and Thigpen's continuing
hostility toward me, I changed my mind from a few minutes
ago and decided to tell him everything, including my previous
skepticism about the break-ins at Eugenia's apartment.

I told him about my entire experience, so far, with
Eugenia. Then I added, "The dead woman's name was Selena
Kostas," I said. "She lives — lived, I mean — in the building.
We'd been introduced once or twice. Other than that, I didn't
know her and had nothing to do with her."

"Why was she in the Stamos woman's apartment?"
Thigpen said. "Did she have a key?" Before I could answer,
he pointed his chin at Eugenia, and added, "And why'd that
Stamos woman call you instead of us?"

I said that no one, as far as I knew from Eugenia, had a

key to the apartment except my mother and the building's management company."

Thigpen immediately dispatched his partner to talk to my mother.

I also told Thigpen that based on what I'd learned about Eugenia, I doubted she would give anyone, including Selena Kostas, permission to be in her apartment when she was out. I described Eugenia's surprise and distress, as told to me by my mother, when they discovered Selena's body in the apartment.

"I don't know if she was more upset because the woman was in the apartment in the first place," I said, "or because the woman was dead."

Thigpen frowned and said, "What else?"

"Nothing I can think of except I never saw anything to confirm Eugenia's suspicions."

Thigpen squinted at me and wiped his lips with the back of his hand.

"You're not holding out on me again, are you, Cheng," he said, "not like last time? Because if you are, I'll come down on your throat with both feet."

My stomach ached as I listened to his threat because I knew he not only meant it, he'd enjoy doing it to me.

"Where's Detective Harte?" I asked, pretending his remarks hadn't upset me. "Isn't he your partner anymore?"

Thigpen ignored my attempted deflection. "Keep your distance from my investigation," he said, "You get in my way this time, you won't walk, not like before." He paused, then said, "Keep yourself available."

After I finished with Thigpen, or, to be accurate, after he finished with me, I stopped by my mother's apartment and spoke with her and Eugenia. An hour later, I headed home to my condo on 22nd Street.

During my walk home, my thoughts focused on the events at the Mount Parnassus Condominium and their possible implication for my mother's safety. That was my prime concern. Until I knew more, I couldn't dismiss the events — including Eugenia's fears which now seemed more rational to me than before — as no concern to me and my mother. I would have to start my own investigation, independent of Thigpen's investigation, and try to get to the bottom of Eugenia's and Selena's roles in all this. I'd have to be careful, however, to keep clear of Thigpen, and not interfere with the official investigation. My butt was on the line.

I thought about the questions I had no answers to: Why was Eugenia's apartment repeatedly entered, if it had been? Why was Eugenia followed, if she had been? How did Selena Kostas enter Eugenia's apartment without a key, or did she secretly have a key? Had Eugenia given her a key, but mislead me about it? Was Selena Kostas the one who had entered Eugenia's apartment on other occasions? If so, why? And, finally, why did Selena die in Eugenia's apartment?

CHAPTER 19

Panos walked into the Theodoros brothers' gallery on 30th Street, just off M Street in Georgetown, and paused inside the doorway to look around for Aristides, the older brother, or Milos, the younger brother. He brought with him a large manila envelope stuffed with photographs of the objects in his collection and with pages from the computer database printout he'd made showing the name of each object, its description, its date and cost of purchase, and its known defects.

The Theodoros brothers operated a small exhibit gallery and retail store from which they sold ancient Greek, Roman and Byzantine artifacts that were not quite museum quality, as the brothers euphemistically described their faulty wares. Their clients, for the most part, were wealthy private collectors, small colleges, and private museums, all of whom avidly acquired the brothers' wares because, like Panos, they could not afford to purchase museum quality objects. The gallery's walk-in trade was negligible.

Milos and Aristides were not just soft-spoken, well-mannered and well-dressed hucksters preying on their clients' vulnerabilities. They also were students of their trade and occasionally published respected, peer-reviewed articles in scholarly journals — articles that often strategically anticipated their acquisition of an object or group of objects, and thereby made a market for such items.

The brothers' gallery/store combination was located in the two story, red-brick building that for many years had been occupied by novelist Larry McMurtrey's rare book store, called Booked Up, until he closed the business and moved back to Texas. The premises now housed antiquities from all parts of the world, but with an emphasis on artifacts from ancient Greece and its Hellenistic neighbors.

Aristides and Milos had cultivated Panos as a customer for approximately twelve years, and in that time had turned him from a curious, occasional purchaser of Greek objects into a serious collector who ravenously acquired Greek antiquity seconds.

"Ah, Panos, my good friend," Milos said, as he emerged from behind a curtained doorway in the far corner of the store and entered the retail area. "To what do we owe the honor of your visit?" He smiled big. "Come in, my friend, come in." He gestured with his arm, propelling Panos deep into the gallery.

Panos reached into his envelope and retrieved a two inch thick stack of paper and photographs. "I'm giving up collecting," he said. "Take this." He handed the computer printout and photos to Milos.

"I'm selling most of my collection," he said. "Keeping some items, but not adding any. Not anymore. It's all there and described in the database printout." Panos inclined his head toward the printout and photographs clenched in Milos' hand.

Milos frowned. "That's a serious decision, my friend. I thought you loved collecting." He paused, squinted, then said, "Come. Come with me. We'll talk." He gestured Panos over to a table and began to spread the photos across its surface.

"I'm not happy about my decision," Panos said. "It was a difficult one, but I've made up my mind. Since I'm not able to collect as I would like to collect, I will not collect at all."

Milos had occasionally encountered this buyer's remorse syndrome with other collectors who also had compromised their collecting standards for financial reasons. They inevitably became ambivalent about their collections, then frustrated, then disenchanted, and eventually lost the collecting bug. That was not good for business, and therefore not acceptable. Milos would have to change Panos' decision. Fortunately, he had just the remedy.

"Ah, Panos, my friend, yes, how sad, but of course I understand and commiserate with you. It is, unfortunately, a common problem. I've seen it before with other serious collectors and scholars such as yourself."

"Some comfort," Panos said. "Well, be that as it may, my collecting days now are over." He sighed and raked his fingers through his hair.

"Fortunately, my friend, it does not have to be that way," Milos said, "not at all." He paused. "Sit," he said, flicking his hand toward an overstuffed chair. "I might have just the solution for you." Milos paused to stare at Panos' face, to appraise Panos' response to his assertion. "Do you mind if I ask, specifically, why you are giving up collecting, forsaking your passion?"

Panos shook his head. His face cried anguish. "I can't bear

to look at my collection, not the way I used to. All I see now are the flaws."

Milos nodded knowingly several times, tented his fingers, and rested his hands on his chest as if he were in prayer, suggesting by his beatific gesture that he understood and fully commiserated with Panos.

"If I cannot collect what I want to collect," Panos said, "then I won't collect at all. That's my final decision."

"Ah," Milos said, "that is exactly as I thought. Fortunately, my good friend, I have just the solution for you."

CHAPTER 20

T HE DAY AFTER I HAD my run-in with Thigpen in the
hallway outside Eugenia's apartment, I was sitting in my
kitchen drinking orange juice and reading the *Washington
Post* when my cellphone rang.

I looked at the read-out on the cell's screen. The caller's
DC telephone number was vaguely familiar, but CallerID
didn't identify it, and I couldn't place it. I answered the call.
"Socrates here."

"Cheng?" the caller said.

I immediately recognized the caller's voice. *This cannot be
a coincidence.*

"Cheng, it's Ralph Harte," the caller said.

"Hello, Detective. What a surprise."

"Still a wise ass, I see," Harte said.

Harte, a senior Metropolitan Police Department detective,
had detected the sarcasm in my statement. I wondered if he
could also detect the wariness in my voice.

"I saw your partner yesterday," I said. I waited for Harte
to say something about this, but he didn't respond, so I
continued. "You calling me today can't be a coincidence," I
said. "It's Thigpen, right?"

"I'm at the Dupont Circle Starbucks," Harte said.

"Outside on the 19th Street-side patio. We need to talk." He paused, then added, "And, by the way, Cheng, it's ex-detective these days." He ended the call before I could respond.

Harte's words, "We need to talk," tripped an alarm bell for me. I didn't like the feel of this. My gut told me something was wrong. Why else would Harte call me after almost four years of silence, the day after I'd had a minor brush with his former partner?

I walked the five blocks from my condo to Starbucks. When I arrived, Harte was at a table with a cup of coffee in front of him.

I stepped over, said, "Nice to see you again", and sat. I was in no mood to spend time in line buying a cup of coffee. I wanted to know what had prompted Harte's call to me. I had my suspicions, and I was a little worried I might be right.

Harte looked pretty much as he had the last time I saw him except his hairline had receded a bit, his red hair now had streaks of grey in it, and he'd put on a few pounds. He still dressed himself as before, favoring a style I thought of as High School Physics Teacher couture.

"You look good," I said. "Haven't changed a bit in four years."

"Right." He paused and smiled. "And you still don't lie good."

We stared at each other for a few seconds, then I shook my head, blushed, and said, "How about we agree that's the last time we bullshit each other."

"Sounds good to me," he said, nodding, "but it won't be easy with you. I'll have to practice."

I leaned across the table and shook his hand. "What's up, Detective?" I said, as I lowered myself onto a chair across from him.

"Call me Harte," he said. "Everybody does now I'm not on the Job."

I was curious to learn what was so urgent we had to meet on short notice, but I bided my time and went along with Harte's meandering pace.

"You're young to retire, aren't you?" I said.

"But it wasn't my call. Got shot in the knee on my day off busting up a liquor store holdup. The brass upstairs forced me to take an early out."

"Sorry," I said. Then, wanting badly to stop digging the hole I'd started working on, I changed the subject. "You wanted to talk to me about something. Is there a problem?"

He smiled. "Oh, yeah," he said, "there's definitely a problem." He stared briefly at me, then said, "Thigpen's after your ass."

I gave him my *so-what-else-is-new* smile and raised my eyebrows. "No surprise there," I said. "I could've predicted it after yesterday."

"No, no," Harte said, "you don't get it. I mean, he really, really wants your ass, with a vengeance."

Time to be serious, I decided. "Okay, tell me about it."

"Sometimes I consult for private clients, now I'm off the Job," Harte said, "so I drop by the 2D a few times a week to shoot the shit and press the flesh. My daughter tells me it's networking, important for business." He slipped his finger between his shirt collar and neck, and tugged at his collar.

"Usually Thigpen nods at me from across the bullpen and keeps doing whatever he's doing. Never leaves his desk and comes over to talk. Never, that is, until today. This morning he made a point of crossing the room and pulling me aside to tell me he ran into you yesterday." Harte picked up his coffee, sipped it, then immediately put it down, spilling some over the lip onto the table. He wiped up the splash with two fingers, and wiped his fingers on his sports jacket.

"I did run into Thigpen yesterday," I said, "at my mother's condo. The Mount Parnassus. One of her neighbors died in someone else's apartment. I called it in for the old lady who lives in the apartment. As far as we know, the DOA wasn't supposed to be in there. Thigpen and his new partner caught the call."

Harte stared at his stained cardboard coffee cup, ran his index finger once around the rim, and licked the coffee off his finger. He then slowly rotated the cup counter-clockwise. He paused for a few seconds, seemingly lost in thought, then looked back at me.

"Thigpen said he was going to nail you this time, and twice made the point I wouldn't be around to protect you."

I briefly thought about the situation four years ago when Thigpen had constantly threatened me with arrest, and Harte had protected me. "I appreciate the heads-up," I said. "I'll watch my back."

"Don't underestimate Thigpen," Harte said. "He's vindictive and dangerous. He's got resources you don't. I doubt you're a match for him. Few people are once he gets them in his cross-hairs."

"I'll keep that in mind," I said. I didn't like the feeling of *déjà vu* that welled up inside me.

Harte looked at his watch. "Damn," he said, "I'm late to

meet my daughter." He pushed his chair back and started to stand up.

This was the second time in five minutes Harte had referred to a daughter. I'd never thought of Harte as a family man.

"My advice to you, Cheng, is keep clear of Thigpen. Every time he sees you, it's a reminder how much you piss him off. If you're not careful, he'll hurt you bad, one way or another."

CHAPTER 21

E UGENIA MEANDERED ACROSS THE PARLOR in a daze, barely aware of her surroundings, shuffling her slippered feet as she roamed forward. She wiped her eyes with the back of her hand in a futile effort to clear away the translucent film that obscured her vision.

She closed her eyes, tilted her face upward, and inhaled deeply, pulling the melded fragrances of basil, incense, olive oil, and ventilated air deep into her lungs, all sustaining her euphoria.

She walked to the book shelves and checked the knickknacks. Nothing appeared to have been moved. She glanced along the walls at the hanging ikons. All seemed normal. It had been that way for days, since before Selena's clandestine entry into her home.

Perhaps, she thought, *with Selena's death, the danger has passed.*

She walked to the piano and picked up a framed photograph. She stared at the faded silver image of her dead husband, then inadvertently let the frame slip through her fingers, as if her hand were greased. She watched as the framed photo bounced along the floor. The glass protecting the image cracked. Eugenia giggled like a young schoolgirl and covered her lips with her fingers.

She turned away from the piano and walked over to a traditional three-legged stool, called a Tripod stool, sitting in the corner of the parlor. She had been introduced to the Tripod stool by the sisterhood of Apollo when she was in training to become the Pythia.

She carried the stool to the center of the room, then climbed up onto its saddle-like seat, mounting it with deliberate, almost theatrical care. Once seated, she closed her eyes and sat still, awaiting the coming of a revelatory vision.

———————

Eugenia sat stone still, her eyes closed, her mind open to whatever the gods might send her way.

One hour passed, then another. She continued to sit and wait.

Her eyes remained closed until well within the third hour, when she abruptly opened her eyes, wrapped her arms around herself, and hugged her shoulders. She shivered in the warm, humid room.

CHAPTER 22

MILOS' PROVOCATIVE STATEMENT INCITED PANOS' curiosity.

The two strands of the collecting helix — the thrill of the hunt and the gratification of possession — again gripped Panos as he contemplated Milos' bold assertion. He could feel his collecting throttle slip back into the on position.

Milos had fed Panos just the tease he unknowingly craved to revert to his collector's state of mind.

"What's that mean, you might have a solution for me?" Panos said.

His heart beat more quickly than usual. Suddenly he had no interest in giving up his passion. He tried to mask his excitement by frowning and slightly, almost disdainfully, shrugging as he asked the inevitable question, the question Milos had intentionally seeded and whose harvest he now would reap.

"There are ways, my friend," Milos said, "for serious collectors like yourself, collectors with absolute discretion, collectors who are constrained by a limited budget, to acquire the finest objects available, museum quality objects, not seconds as before. But this is not for everyone, only for the select few we invite to partake in it."

The raw meat had been set in the trap.

Panos nodded cautiously and sniffed the bait. "How?"

"First, you must give me your word. If you decide not to participate in this opportunity, you will say nothing about this conversation to anyone. Not ever."

Panos nodded. "Agreed."

"Good," Milos said. "Come with me to the back room. We will eat some *Tsoureki* bread, drink coffee, and smoke cigars. Then we will talk. I will tell you what we offer, and you will decide if it is for you or if it is not.

"Come," Milos said, and with his arm he motioned Panos toward the curtained doorway at the back of the gallery.

CHAPTER 23

A FEW DAYS AFTER MY MEETING with Harte, I was at home putting the finishing touches on a marketing plan to generate new PI business, when my cellphone rang.

I checked the CallerID, and said, "Good morning, Ma."

"Come over here, Socrates, we have a problem, Eugenia and me."

"All right," I said, "but what's up?" She wouldn't tell me over the telephone.

Twenty minutes later I settled into a chair in my mother's living room.

My mother told me that Selena's son, George, had brought Eugenia the news that the official conclusion concerning his mother's death in Eugenia's apartment was that she had not had a heart attack as originally thought, but that she had committed suicide by poisoning herself.

"We don't believe it," she said. She looked over at Eugenia, who was sitting on the sofa, and nodded once. Then my mother turned back to me. "The police are wrong. Selena wouldn't poison herself."

Eugenia said, "She would not. Selena was a pious woman."

"Ma," I said, first looking at her, and then turning toward Eugenia, "it happens sometimes. People kill themselves, and those who knew them are shocked and find it hard to accept. You can't always know what goes on in the mind of another person, not even someone you think you know well."

"Not Selena," my mother said, "she wasn't the type." She paused, and then looked at Eugenia. I thought I saw Eugenia nod once, but I wasn't sure until my mother turned to me and said, "We want you to find out what really happened."

I should have seen that coming. "I need to think about it," I said, looking first at my mother, and then at Eugenia. "It won't be easy since the official ruling on her death is closed."

I wanted time to think about the likelihood I could find some answers before I committed my time. "I'll let you know tomorrow."

Selena's official cause of death ruling raised several questions for me: If I assumed the ME's conclusion was correct, why did Selena kill herself in Eugenia's apartment rather than in her own home? And, less important, perhaps, had Eugenia predicted Selena's death when she gave Selena her most recent reading? Was that why Selena had been agitated when I saw her?

My mother said that the authorities had released Selena's body to George so she could be dealt with by her mourners and by the Church, and could be promptly buried in accordance with the customs and rules of Orthodoxy. According to George, the fate of his mother's soul had already been compromised by the authorities because they had not allowed him to promptly sanctify and then bury her after her death. George had told Eugenia, however, that he had acted as if he was able to follow the requirements of his Church by covering all the mirrors in Selena's home, placing black borders around photographs of Selena, and by placing a plate on the floor as if it was under the casket on view in his mother's home.

The ME's conclusion that Selena had killed herself offered me a measure of comfort. Assuming the conclusion was correct — and I had no reason to think it was not — it meant I did not have to worry that my mother might be in some danger living in the building.

CHAPTER 24

P ANOS FOLLOWED MILOS THROUGH THE gallery and
into a small backroom filled with unmarked cardboard
boxes stacked almost to the ceiling. At Milos' direction,
he seated himself on an old sofa, the only piece of furniture
in the room other than a gun-metal desk, with a folding chair
behind it. Panos turned down Milos' offer of a snack. He
accepted Milos' suggestion that they smoke the Cuban cigars
Milos offered, and he fired one up while Milos poured coffee
for them.

"There are ways," Milos said, "to acquire the finest Greek
antiquities available," he repeated, as before. Then, to set
the trap he'd already twice baited, he added, "It is not for
everyone, my friend, only for those few people my brother
and I invite to participate, only for serious, trustworthy
collectors." He lifted his cup to his lips, and looked at Panos
over the cup's lip as he sipped his coffee.

Panos nodded. He could feel the parasitical collecting-
bug nibbling.

"There are rules you will be required to follow," Milos
said.

"Rules are not a problem," Panos said. He didn't wonder
what those rules might be because he didn't care. He rarely

followed rules unless he had no choice or the rules worked to favor him.

Milos smiled. "Good. I anticipated so." He leaned across the table and poured more coffee into Panos' demitasse cup. Then he walked across the room, and returned carrying two glasses of water.

"You have been acquiring interesting seconds from my brother and me to build your collection. We understand this. Many collectors who aspire to greater collections accumulate seconds as a compromise rather than not collect at all. Others, such as yourself, use their acquisition of seconds to educate themselves and to train their eyes."

Panos remained silent. He drew heavily on his Cohiba, held the smoke in his mouth, then reluctantly let it escape. He raised the coffee to his lips, sipped it, and waited.

"Should I go on?" Milos said.

Panos nodded. "Yes, by all means," he said, his masked excitement now evident to Milos.

Milos smiled. "If you agree to our terms, first we will liquidate your existing collection, holding back any pieces you choose to keep. We will turn the proceeds over to you, less, of course, our customary transaction fee.

"Thereafter, from time-to-time, we will offer you antiquities you may purchase for prices that will not be subject to negotiation or change. You won't be obligated to acquire anything we offer, but you must make an irrevocable decision within twenty-four hours."

Panos briefly thought about this. His inborn instinct was to demur, to resist agreeing in advance that he would not attempt to bargain about the offering price. For Panos, as for most indigenous Greeks, the price offered was never the right one, never the ending point. Bargaining over the price was as natural as breathing, and Panos had always thrived on it. But he said nothing. This was new territory.

Milos continued. "If you purchase our offering, you must pay twenty percent of the price up front. The balance will be paid in equal installments over twelve months. There won't be any finance charges, and you will have possession of your object in the meantime." He paused, lifted his cup and drained the coffee. For a few seconds he stared at the dark grounds accumulated at the bottom of his empty cup. Then he took a swallow of water.

"In place of a usual security interest in the object, for reasons that will be clear to you in a minute, should you miss a payment or be late, even one day late, we will have the right to reclaim the object, cancel the sale, and keep all payments you had made so far with respect to that object."

Panos nodded once. *I'd like to see you get away with that,* he thought.

"In addition," Milos said, "and this part you must weigh carefully before you agree to journey down this road, as a penalty for missing a payment or being late, we will also select any object from your collection, of any value, with no exceptions, and will confiscate it from you for our own account. This means, my friend, you could lose your most prized possession you have already completed paying for if you are late with one payment for some other object." He paused, then said, "Are you still interested?"

Panos nodded. "Of course. You said something about a rule?"

"Ah, yes, the Rule, Milos said. "If you participate, you must never disclose the existence of our arrangement to anyone or ever permit anyone to see your collection. The collection you build will be for you, and for you alone, to know about and enjoy."

"I can do that," Panos said. "What's the catch? There must be one." He drew on his cigar and then expelled the smoke. He picked up the coffee cup and drained its contents.

"The objects we will offer you, as I said, will be museum quality, the best of the best, but they will be artifacts that were stolen from their owners or custodians."

Milos paused to watch Panos as he absorbed this statement and its implications. "Can you deal with that?"

Panos never hesitated. "Of course," he said. *You young fool*, he thought, *I couldn't care less how you obtain the objects. They are better off in my collection than in someone else's or in some museum.*

Panos smiled with his lips, but not with his eyes. *What pisses me off is you should have offered me this arrangement ten years ago, you son of a whore, and not sold me inferior objects all that time.*

Panos said, "I have no problem with this arrangement. But no fakes. I will not accept fakes under any circumstances. Understand?"

"Of course," Milos said. "Understood. No fakes. And the payment and non-disclosure rules?" he said. "You will honor them?"

Panos stabbed out his cigar in the ashtray, and said, "It will be my pleasure. Let's get started. What do you have for me?"

Milos beamed. "You just wait and see, my friend. You just wait and see. I have something very special to show you. Something just for you. I get it right now."

CHAPTER 25

R ALPH HARTE MISSED BEING A COP.

He missed the action that came with the Job, and the accompanying adrenalin rush that had fed his days and nights as he and Thigpen consistently achieved the highest clearance rate in the 2D's homicide squad. Most of all, he missed the camaraderie that accompanied the knowledge you were all in it together, for better or for worse, with or without danger at any given moment, as part of the life. He hadn't been prepared to give it all up when the hammer had unexpectedly dropped.

Even so, Harte wasn't bitter about the situation he'd found himself in. Not like many retired cops who were forced to leave the Job before they were ready to opt out on their own. Harte figured being wounded on the Job, even when off duty, and then being put out to pasture, came with the territory, so why resent it.

As a cop, Harte was unusual in other ways, too. Unlike many cops, he hadn't resented his superiors, and always got along with those above him in rank, rarely made waves, and never made bitching and moaning about the cop's plight his way of life.

There were other ways, too, he broke the mold. Harte wasn't divorced or on his third or fourth marriage. He still was married to his high school sweetheart, Rose Baron, the woman he'd married when they both were eighteen. And unlike many cops who gave in to the temptations offered them by Badge Bunnies or by prostitutes who traded free sex in return for a *get-out-of-jail-free* pass, Harte had never cheated on his wife, except one time that eventually came back to visit him.

All in all, Harte was a well adjusted ex-homicide detective who accepted he had landed in the correct place at this time in his life.

The only problem Harte had to face was boredom, day in and day out, because he had nothing to look forward to. No new challenges. No new adrenalin rushes. Nothing to dilute or break through the ennui that wrapped itself around him like a giant boa and squeezed the energy from him, making it difficult some days for him to drag himself out of bed. Nothing to look forward to except more of the same, every single day. Nothing, that is, except for Clotille.

Clotille Harte, age 32, was the apple of her father's eye. Harte worshiped her. And she reciprocated.

Clotille was the product of Harte's only deviation from his marriage vows, long ago, when he was twenty years old, and had attended a police convention in New Orleans, where he met and, unknowingly, impregnated Clotille's mother, a Cajun prostitute working the Bourbon Street bars. Harte spent two nights with her at his hotel, and then never heard from the woman again, not for ten years, at which time she came calling on him from among the dead.

Clotille's existence had been kept secret from Harte for the first ten years of her life, a secret maintained until Clotille's mother was knifed while visiting a crack house in New Iberia, Bayou Têche, Louisiana. The Parrish cops contacted Harte because they found Harte's expired driver's license in the woman's purse where she'd placed it after stealing it from Harte ten years before. Harte vaguely remembered replacing his license when he returned to Washington because, he'd thought, he'd lost it in some New Orleans saloon. The New Iberia cops traced Harte through the help of the 2D.

Harte claimed the body of the woman he hadn't seen or thought about for a decade, and arranged to have her buried along with almost all thoughts of his one-time dalliance. Ten year old Clotille, who had been living with her mother, moved north to live with Harte and his wife.

It required three years of intense marriage counseling to save Harte's marriage. It took another two years of fostering Clotille, under the benign supervision and neglect of the DC Department of Child Welfare Services, before Harte and his wife were permitted to legally adopt her. Harte and Rosie gave Clotille their last name, encouraged her to learn about and to honor her Cajun heritage, and enthusiastically welcomed her into their lives.

Clotille responded positively. She learned to love Harte and Rosie, and eventually considered herself to be their daughter. She studied her heritage, as Harte and Rosie encouraged, and was proud of her Cajun culture. She adamantly clung to traces of her remembered or reconstructed past, especially in her manner of speech, even as she was teased about it in school. To this day, Clotille continued to speak with the idiosyncratic cadences and idiomatic phrasings native to Bayou Têche.

CHAPTER 26

PANOS WAS NOT A MAN easily seduced, but the first time he saw *The Mourning Woman* he was overwhelmingly smitten.

When Panos first set eyes on her, Milos held *The Mourning Woman* in his arms, cradled like a newborn. She was wrapped in swaddling bands and a light-weight pink blanket.

Panos had to have her.

Panos promptly accepted the price Milos required for this 9" tall, early sixth century BCE terra cotta figurine. He wrote out his check for the initial payment, then cheerfully carried his seductress home to his Treasure Room.

With this acquisition, Panos enthusiastically joined that club of collectors who knowingly acquired stolen art and antiquities, and neither showed their possessions to anyone nor disclosed their ownership of the objects. It was a netherworld of collectors for whom the possession of the objects was as important as the objects themselves.

Panos took perverse pride in his membership in this club, and enjoyed a private smile on those occasions when he recalled the persistent rumor in the art world — always officially denied — following the theft and subsequent anonymous return of Leonardo's *Mona Lisa* to the Louvre, that the thieves had actually returned an expert copy of the painting, not the original masterpiece. According to the legend, rather than admit this, the Louvre authorities hung the clever forgery in place of Da Vinci's original, correctly trusting that the viewing public would never know the difference. According to the rumor, the genuine *Mona Lisa* had been sold by the thieves to an undisclosed member of Panos' new club, and hangs somewhere in private for that collector's sole enjoyment.

CHAPTER 27

TUESDAY NIGHT. THE NIGHT OF my mother's biweekly
support group meeting.

My mother had asked me to speak to the group,
to describe my life as a private investigator. I'd reluctantly
agreed.

I entered the condo's common room to fulfill my
commitment to give a short talk. I intended to briefly describe
the routine aspects of PI work in the District of Columbia,
offer a few humorous anecdotes — some of which I would
make up — then duck out early.

I wanted to make a good impression so I dressed up for
the occasion, putting on a tie, freshly pressed beige slacks,
and my best sports jacket.

As I entered the meeting room, I looked around for my
mother, but didn't see her.

The room fell silent as I walked in. There were about
twenty-five people standing around. It seemed as if all eyes
had turned to look at me.

I walked to the lectern and dropped off my file folder
containing the outline for my talk, then turned away to
again look for my mother. I spotted Eugenia heading toward

me, boldly tapping her walking stick on the floor as she approached.

"Hello, Mr. Cheng," she said. She still was about ten feet away. She was followed by a man in his early 40s, who seemed imprinted on her. He wore a scowl on his face.

I smiled and said, "Hello, Eugenia. Nice to see you." I turned my smile toward her duckling. "Hello," I said to him.

"This is Selena's son, George," Eugenia said. "He wants to talk to you."

George looked as if he'd been around the track a few times or, more accurately, around the boxing ring. He had the artificially asymmetrical face of a prize fighter at the end of an infelicitous career.

George didn't greet me or even smile. Instead, he gestured abruptly with his chin, jutting it out toward me as if daring me to take a swing at it, and said, "I understand you're looking into my mother's murder."

I hesitated. I didn't want to offend him after the loss he'd just suffered, but decided it would be best to establish a baseline for dealing with one another in case we ever were to meet again. I took his bluntness head on.

"The ME called it suicide, not murder," I said. When he said nothing in response, I continued. "I'm not looking into it, but I was there with Eugenia after she found your mother."

"My mother wouldn't kill herself," he said. "No way." He made the sign of the cross.

I suppose all children want to believe that about their parents, even when it might not be true, but I had no interest in convincing him. I fanned out my hands in a *what-can-I-say* gesture, and looked at Eugenia for reinforcement. She didn't respond and rescue me from this awkward spot she'd placed me in.

I waited a few more seconds while George and I stared at one another across the sticky silence. When I started to turn toward the podium, George put his hand on my shoulder, holding me back. I turned and looked hard at him, waited for him to remove his hand from my shoulder, and when he didn't, I deliberately and slowly lifted his hand off me and let it drop to his side.

"Nice to meet you, George," I said, intentionally lacing my voice with sarcasm, and brushing off my shoulder with my palm as if to rid my shoulder of an insect. "I have to go get my talk organized. Perhaps we can—"

"My mother wouldn't kill herself," he said again. "It would be against her religion, against everything she believed in."

"Maybe she was depressed," I said, regretting my statement the minute it slipped my lips because of the opportunity for discussion it invited.

"She wasn't depressed," George said. "My mother was murdered, and nobody in this building will be safe until her killer is caught, including your mother." He placed his hand on my forearm as if to restrain me. Some people never learn.

If he intended to grab my attention by grabbing my arm and if he wanted to provoke a response, he had pushed the right button. I felt my neck and face grow warm with anger. I didn't like attempts to intimidate me, especially attempts that used my mother as bait.

I took hold of George's arm above his wrist and slowly, as if to say, "I didn't give you permission to touch me, not before, not now," lifted his hand from my arm, then dramatically let it drop. He had crossed the line again. Now I would cross back.

I stepped in close to him, less than a foot away, intending to make him uncomfortable as I invaded his personal space. I never took my eyes from his.

"Are you threatening my mother?" I said. "If you think—"

He quickly stepped away from me, raised his palms in front of his chest and shook his head. I could smell garlic on his breath.

"No threat intended," he said. "Sorry you thought so. I was just saying I know my mother. She wouldn't kill herself. Not under any circumstances. And that should worry everyone who lives at this condominium."

I waited a few seconds and continued to look hard at him to underscore my point and allow things to settle. I looked at Eugenia, nodded, then turned back to George. "Okay," I said, speaking softly, "no offense taken, this time."

I again looked at Eugenia. "I better review my outline now," I said. "Nice seeing you." I turned back to George, raised both eyebrows briefly and nodded once. I turned away without another word and walked toward the podium, a grin on my face.

I'd traveled about five steps when I heard George say to my back, "Denying it won't change anything. My mother was murdered. Yours could be next. You can't hide from it."

CHAPTER 28

PANOS ENTERED HIS TREASURE ROOM, muscled the vault door closed behind him, and set the security lock. He settled into his bolted-down swivel chair and looked around at the mostly empty shelves and pedestals. He hadn't yet restocked them with newly collected artifacts after the sale of his former collection to the Theodoros brothers.

The room felt unnaturally denuded, as he imagined it might after a burglary — an impossible scenario given the sophisticated security systems he had in place. Yet the room suffered from a sense of trespass, just as if it had been thrown on its back, ravished, robbed of its coin, and then cast aside.

Panos was suffering from seller's remorse. The seven objects Panos had retained seemed diminished by the emptiness surrounding them.

But Panos smiled his *I got you, sucker* smile. He had possession of *The Mourning Woman*. She would be the cornerstone of his new collection, an assemblage that would be without the contamination of inferior seconds.

Panos cast his gaze across the room and fixed his eyes on *The Mourning Woman*.

He had placed her on a five foot high white enamel pedestal, posed under her own spotlight. She was deliberately set four feet away from the wall so Panos could indulge his inclination to walk all around her, circling the figurine whenever he looked at her.

She is perfect, a masterpiece, he thought. *The ideal size and shape to convey the anguish over the loss she mourns.* He resisted for now the temptation to walk over to her, reach out, and gently stroke her cheek.

He could never do better than this, he knew, no matter how many other antiquities he might acquire under the new purchase arrangement.

CHAPTER 29

I WAS GLAD TO GET AWAY from Selena's son and to briefly lose myself in my lecture notes. I quickly read through my outline. It was short because I intended to speak for only fifteen minutes or so, then take questions.

I closed the folder and scanned the room again looking for my mother. I still didn't see her. I was mildly worried now because her absence was entirely out of character. My mother prided herself on her punctuality, a constant source of bemused conflict between her and my father, who believed punctuality was only for meals, for ones appointment with the Grim Reaper, and for people immersed in the philosophy of the industrial age. My mother, of course, thought otherwise, and took great pains to notify people on those rare occasions when she would be late for or had to miss an appointment.

A movement caught my eye and diverted my attention. *Uh, oh*, I thought, *here we go again*. I spotted Eugenia heading toward me, working her way through the rows of chairs, this time with a woman in tow.

Relentless old busybody, I thought. When she came within ten feet of me, I said, not smiling this time, "Hello again, Eugenia." I wanted her to know I didn't appreciate the last meeting she'd orchestrated, the one with George. I turned toward Eugenia's companion. "Hello," I said, then I turned back and faced Eugenia, a large *Now what?* question etched on my face by my conveniently converging eyebrows.

"This is Toula," Eugenia said, turning her head briefly toward the woman. "Toula Xandereas. Toula lives here with her mother, Arête."

An awkward silence followed. I felt like shrugging my shoulders as if to say, *Is this supposed to mean something to me?*, but I didn't say it. Instead, I turned toward Toula, smiled, and said, "Nice to meet you." I extended my hand to shake hers, and tried not to stare at the black eye patch she wore over her left eye.

Eugenia must have picked up on my confusion concerning her statement and on my ambivalence concerning this woman because she said, "I guess you haven't met Arête yet, Toula's mother. Well, you will soon enough."

I nodded, and said to Eugenia, "Looks like Selena was the one causing the problems when you were out walking. Any idea why?"

She shook her head. "I don't believe Selena was the one who entered my home before," Eugenia said.

So much for making polite conversation, I thought. "Perhaps," I said.

"Not perhaps," Eugenia said. "I know, because ever since Selena's murder, someone has started coming into my home again."

Before I could respond, Toula looked at me, then at Eugenia, and said, "If you don't mind me sticking my two cents in, what are you both talking about?"

I looked at Eugenia for permission to answer or for some

sign she didn't want me to. She gave an almost imperceptible nod.

I turned back toward Toula, and said, "It seems Selena might have been sneaking into Eugenia's apartment for several weeks while Eugenia was out walking, although Eugenia doesn't think it was Selena who'd been doing that."

Toula shook her head. "I don't see Selena doing anything like that. She wasn't that kind of a person. You must be mistaken."

As she said this, Toula stepped in close to me, too close, I thought, closer than any stranger or recent, casual acquaintance should. I reflexively stepped away from her and watched a wry smile slowly overspread her face. She locked her single-focus gaze onto my eyes.

I excused myself from the conversation, saying I wanted to look at my notes one more time before I spoke to the group. As I said this I felt a hand lightly touch my shoulder from behind me. I turned. It was my mother.

I took a quick deep breath and sighed it out. Tension leached from my body.

"Where've you been, Ma? I've been worried."

"I'll tell you another time," she said. "It's complicated. You're better off not knowing right now."

I opened my mouth to protest, but she shook her head and raised her palm, stopping me. "I said, not now, Socrates."

CHAPTER 30

TOULA WAS INTRIGUED BY SOCRATES.

She thought about him the next morning as she finished wiping the rim of her hollowed eye socket, using an astringent-laced cotton pad. She tossed the used pad into the wastebasket and fit the black patch over the empty socket. Even after forty-three years of this, she still was not used to seeing herself in the mirror looking like the consort of one of the Barbary pirates.

Toula had been three, and her brother eight, when the soldiers representing the new democratic movement in Greece, the group who overthrew the Colonels, came crashing through the great room's windows, commando style, to arrest her father. As Toula and her brother stood terrified and looked around for their mother, a shard of glass pierced Toula's left eye. The pain had been unbearable.

All the medical attention Toula received, first in Athens and later in Washington, had been for nothing. Eventually, Toula's eyeball was surgically removed and a prosthetic glass eye fitted for her. She hated the device.

Toula suffered years of skin irritation and associated pain — some real, some phantom, but real to her — as well as minor infections and ongoing general discomfort from ill fitting prosthetics that left her with socket shrinkage and which provided a nesting site for invading dust, dirt, cigarette smoke, and assorted particles and micro-organisms. This ultimately led Toula to the pirate patch.

Toula's affliction had brought with it the usual stew of ills attendant a child's handicap. As a youngster, Toula had been teased by her classmates and was called, pirate lady. As a teenager, she was never asked out on a date or asked to dance at the school functions she occasionally attended alone. In college, her professors and classmates tiptoed around her affliction and dealt with it by ignoring both it and Toula. She'd had no social life at college, no friends, and no incentive to engage in any activity. Instead, Toula's life revolved around her participation with her mother in the apotheosis of Petreus Xandereas, Toula's home-martyred father.

That is, she had no other incentive to broaden her interests until she met Socrates.

CHAPTER 31

T HE DAY AFTER I DELIVERED my talk at the support
group meeting, I stopped by my mother's apartment to
have coffee with her. I wanted to eliminate any tension
that might still have lingered between us from the night
before when she wouldn't tell me why she'd been late for
the meeting. I never liked leaving disagreements between us
hanging unresolved, hovering in the background to grow and
work their internal poison.

I knocked twice on her door, then used my key and
entered.

I called out from just inside the entryway, "Ma, good
morning. It's me."

I waited.

No answer.

I called out again. Still no response. She wasn't home. I
scribbled a brief note asking her to call me when she returned,
and left it on the kitchen counter next to the stove where she
was sure to see it.

Since I was in the building, I decided to visit Eugenia.
I wanted to find out why she thought someone was again
entering her apartment. Maybe she would say something this
time that would give me a lead to investigate.

I headed for the stairwell, but changed my mind. My knee had been bothering me even though I hadn't jogged regularly these past few weeks. The pain was the result of a long-term injury, the byproduct of my running days when I was in my twenties and just knew, with all the certitude of youth, that I could ignore my knee pain and run through it because any possible long-term effects were too far out in the future to then worry about. Now, at age forty-two, I was paying the price. I had been forced to drastically cut back my weekly running mileage and, sometimes, to take off a week or two to rest my knee.

I turned away from the stairwell door and walked over to the elevator. I watched the lighted floor indicator above the twin doors as it clocked its progress up to the sixth floor. The polished metal doors slid apart revealing a black wrought-iron gate which Nikos pulled aside for me.

"Morning, Nikos," I said. I smiled, nodded, and stepped to the back of the cab.

Nikos rarely spoke. He mostly grunted, if he said anything at all. Rumor had it he did not speak fluent English even though he had immigrated to the United States many years ago. The only thing the building's pundits agreed on concerning Nikos was that he ran the elevator, day-in-and-day-out, as smoothly as anyone could hope. He never gave anyone any trouble, and could be very helpful when he was in the right mood.

"Fourth floor," I said. I could see his eyes dart over and look at me, then flick back to stare straight ahead, as if to ask: What business do you have on a floor other than your mother's?

Nikos stood up as we approached the fourth floor and

pulled aside the iron gate when we stopped. He immediately dragged it closed behind me after I stepped out.

Eugenia opened the door as soon as I knocked. It was as if she'd been standing there waiting for me.

"Oh, it's you," she said, slurring her words. "I was expecting a client for a reading." She languidly motioned with her hand for me to enter.

I stepped in, moved aside, and waited while Eugenia passed by me heading in the direction of the parlor. I watched with interest as she shuffled forward, tapping her cane on the floor as she walked.

She seemed drunk or stoned, or maybe just medicated. Some prescription meds caused that effect in the elderly. She weaved slightly like a tacking sailboat as she made her way along the hallway and into the dusky parlor. I followed her in.

"Sorry to bother you," I said. "I have a question, then I'll go."

She didn't say anything, nor did she indicate she wanted to hear my question. Instead, she turned away and walked deeper into the gloom.

She suddenly stopped walking, turned around, and then walked back toward me. She stopped to my left and lowered herself onto the over-stuffed sofa. She pointed her finger at a chair she wanted me to sit in.

"Your question, Mr. Cheng?" Her voice was husky.

I cleared my throat. I wasn't comfortable going behind my mother's back to get this information, but I wasn't just curious; I also was worried.

"Do you know where my mother was before the meeting last night, why she was late arriving there?"

"You should ask your mother," Eugenia said.

I nodded and frowned. "All right," I said, as I stood up from my chair. "Thanks for your time. I'll see myself out. Sorry I bothered you."

As I turned to leave, Eugenia said, "I saw you this morning."

I turned back. "What's that supposed to mean? I wasn't here this morning."

"I saw you in a vision."

"And?"

"Be careful, Mr. Cheng"

"Meaning what?"

"Be wary," she said, "of where you choose to venture and who you choose to venture with."

I hated mind games. "Can you be a little clearer?" I said.

Eugenia stood up, but said no more. She had delivered her cryptic message in the manner of the ancient Oracle, and would say no more to me today about it.

CHAPTER 32

THREE WEEKS AFTER *THE MOURNING Woman* successfully captured his heart, and Panos had installed her in her place of honor in the Treasure Room, Panos' infatuation with this Siren hadn't flagged. If anything, he found himself more enamored with her with each passing day.

His enchantment with this seductress lured Panos into a new routine he slavishly followed every morning. After taking care of his personal, home-related, and business needs — paying bills, organizing for his once-a-week cleaning woman, writing clients' checks, and the like — Panos would glance through the sales catalogs for upcoming antiquities auctions as part of his continuing self-education, and also would look at advertisements for upcoming antiquities exhibits he might want to attend in Washington, New York, Boston or Philadelphia.

Each day, after he completed his research, Panos entered the Treasure Room and took his seat facing *The Mourning Woman*. He usually did no more than stare at her and imbibe her grace and integral beauty as reflected in her terracotta pathos and grief. On other occasions, he meditated, losing all awareness of the unglazed lady's presence and radiated power over him. On those occasions, Panos' thoughts usually focused on the collection he'd sold back to the Theodoros brothers.

His thoughts were not warm, nor grateful.

Even though Panos knew the sale had been the right thing for him to do since the objects in the collection had become an enervating distraction for him, he nonetheless suffered mixed feelings because of the many years he'd devoted to purchasing defective objects from Aristides and Milos.

It didn't bother him that he'd spent twelve years buying seconds since he had knowingly entered into that arrangement for what he then believed to be a good reason. Nor did it surprise him that he eventually grew disenchanted with his ownership of seconds. That, too, was predictable. What bothered him was that he had wasted so many years buying seconds when he could have used that time and his limited, purloined funds building a first-rate collection under the present arrangement, if only Milos had brought him into the fold sooner. It wasn't, after all, as if the brothers had had any reason to think that buying stolen art might bother him. It did not. *No*, he'd decided, *the enormous delay in introducing him to the new arrangement existed so the brothers could wring every last dollar from him before Panos became unhappy with his purchases, at which time the brothers would start him buying objects all over again under a new purchasing plan. In other words*, Panos decided, *the Theodoros brothers had played him for a sucker and might be doing so again.*

Panos sat at his kitchen table and turned the pages of the Sunday *New York Times* Arts & Leisure section looking at gallery exhibit notices. One posting caught his attention. If it proved to be as advertised, Panos would catch a bus to New York one morning, visit the gallery and see the exhibit. Afterward, he would run over to the Metropolitan Museum and wander through its antiquities section, then catch a bus back to Washington around dinner time.

Panos clipped the ad from the newspaper and called the gallery. He ordered a catalog and paid extra for overnight delivery so he could familiarize himself with the exhibit before he went to New York.

THE MAURICE DALVEEN COLLECTION
OF
ANCIENT ART AND ANTIQUITIES:

**An exhibit of
Objects from the Greek, Roman and Byzantine
Civilizations**

Works on public view from January 2 - April 1

Full color catalog available

**HELLENE Gallery
366 Madison Avenue
New York, NY 10019
212.367.1425
hellenegallery@aol.com**

The catalog arrived the next day.

Panos was enjoying himself immensely. He poured himself a glass of Ouzo, which he mixed the traditional way with water until it turned milky white, and fired up a Cohiba he'd taken from Milos. He settled into a chair with the exhibit catalog on his lap, and turned the pages slowly, taking the full measure of each full color illustration and, for now, skimming most of the textual captions describing the ancient wares. He intended to go back to the catalog another day and to carefully read the descriptions of the art objects that would be on display.

The exhibit catalog was even more interesting than Panos had hoped. The hardbound book was beautiful, itself a work of art, attractively displaying the well known and very important Dalveen collection.

Panos had just started looking at page 164 when his stomach knotted and his chest suddenly constricted. His palms became so wet from perspiration that he refused to continue holding the catalog for fear the moisture would stain or wrinkle the pages.

Panos could not believe his eyes as he stared at Object 528.

Object 528 was an Attic red-figured *krater*, circa 300-320 BCE, depicting a male human figure said to be modeled after the Socratic student, Plato. The catalog description called the object the *Plato Krater*, and stated that Object 528 was the only known vase of this type that could be attributed to the archeological dig at the home-site of the philosopher. The attribution of the image, the cataloger wrote, was based on ancillary findings also made at the Plato-site dig.

Panos' initial adverse response quickly abated, and he calmed down. He had over-reacted, he decided. The explanation was clear. The Theodoros brothers obviously had taken the *krater* he'd sold back to them and then offered it to Dalveen, in whose collection it now resided. He gave no thought to the improbable timing such an otherwise creditable explanation would require of such a sale and purchase.

Panos carefully read through the catalog's description of the *Plato Krater*. The catalog's describer offered all the important details about the artifact: its measurements; its history; and most of its provenance. Panos was pleased that neither he nor the Theodoros brothers was mentioned in the provenance paragraph.

He closed the catalog, mashed out his cigar in an ashtray, and swallowed the last of his Ouzo. An uneasy feeling writhed within his spine. Something was not right. Something about the catalog's description bothered him although he had no idea what it was. Yet he felt instinctively that something was out of kilter.

Panos returned to his chair, closed his eyes and leaned his head back. He pictured the *krater* as illustrated in the catalog. It was his, all right, but obviously spruced up for the exhibit.

He reopened the catalog to the page showing Object 528, and studied the illustration.

All Panos' instincts silently screamed alarms he couldn't ignore, but also couldn't interpret.

What was it?

The image looked correct.

The lot description seemed accurate. The—

Oh, sweet Jesus! he thought. *That was it! He'd almost missed it?*

The object's describer had lied in the description, and that was what Panos had subconsciously glommed onto. The catalog description never mentioned the repair to the *krater* that had caused it to be classified as a second. The description stated that the vase was museum quality, free of any major flaws or repairs. Panos knew better.

He set aside the catalog, leaving it open to the page showing Object 528, and dialed the long-distance telephone number of the Hellene Gallery listed in the front pages of the catalog. He would let them know he was on to them, had spotted their false description of the *krater*, and would insist they withdraw the object from the exhibit or amend the description.

As Panos waited for his call to be answered, it occurred to him that the gallery might be an innocent party. It was conceivable, he decided, that the Theodoros brothers might have repaired the *krater* and then hidden the repaired defect from Dalveen. He wouldn't put it past the brothers.

Panos waited for his call to be answered.

CHAPTER 33

I WAS IN MY OFFICE, LOCATED on the corner of Q Street and Connecticut Avenue, on the second floor above the restaurant, *Circa at Dupont*, when my cellphone rang. It was my mother.

"Socrates, I'd like you to come to another support group meeting. There's one tonight."

"Why? Am I suddenly in demand as a speaker on the Hellenic toastmasters' circuit?"

"I don't need your sarcasm, Young Man. It doesn't become you."

I realized when she said this that I'd been angry with my mother and had just succumbed to that anger by using sarcasm. I decided to face this again with her.

"Why won't you tell me where you disappeared to before last meeting?" I said. "At least tell me *why* you won't tell me."

"You don't need to know. Not yet. Maybe later, maybe never," she said.

I sighed. My mother was a stubborn woman. "So why do you want me there tonight?" I asked, my plaintive tone revealing my capitulation.

"Because we plan to discuss Selena's murder."

"How does that involve me?" I said, although I really

didn't want to know. I had a bad feeling where this might go if I didn't immediately put my foot down and stop it.

"Because being there and hearing people express their opinions might help you when you try to solve the killing."

I sighed again. If I were paid to sigh, this could prove to be a lucrative conversation.

"Ma," I said, "let's get this settled once and for all. I'm not working on Selena's murder, I mean, on Selena's death. It wasn't murder; the police ruled it a suicide."

"I don't care what they said. The police don't know everything. It was murder, no question about it, everybody knows it, and I want you to catch Selena's killer. I won't be able to relax until you do."

She paused, probably to give me time to capitulate. I stubbornly held my tongue. I definitely was my mother's son.

"Who knows who's next?" she finally said. "It could be anyone, even me."

That did it. My mother hadn't just daintily placed her finger on my button and lightly pressed it; instead, she'd curled her hand and smashed her fist on my button.

"Okay, you win," I said, my surrender again evident in my voice, as well as in my words. I took a deep breath and sucked in my defeat. I knew when I was beaten.

"I'll come by tonight to see what's up, but I don't promise anything. I don't plan to investigate Selena's suicide. Understand? I'm not committing to anything."

"Of course not, Socrates. We'll see," she said, "we'll see."

I had no doubt I was going to have to work hard not to waste my time pursuing this dead end.

I arrived at the meeting at 6:10, about twenty minutes before the scheduled time. I saw my mother across the room talking with Eugenia, Toula, and a man I recognized from the last meeting, but hadn't met and couldn't identify. I walked over to join them.

I acknowledged everyone, kissed my mother's cheek, and reluctantly made room for Selena's son, George, to join us. I had watched him make a dash for me as I crossed the room to my mother. I deliberately ignored his frantic attempts to arrest my attention by waving at me and calling my name. I continued to ignore him even as he snaked his way between me and Toula. I turned to face the stranger in the group.

I smiled and reached out my hand to shake his. "Hi," I said. "I'm Socrates Cheng, Sophia's son." I tilted my head toward my mother.

As he took my hand in his and opened his mouth to say something, Toula said, "This is Uncle Panos, Socrates. Well, not my real uncle, not a blood relative, but Uncle Panos is a longtime family friend, and I have always called him Uncle."

Panos bowed his head slightly, smiled, and looked in my eyes. His smile was broad, but there was no conviviality in it, nor in his flat, gray eyes.

I looked hard at Panos. He seemed to be about my mother's age, although he clearly had taken a more difficult route getting there.

I said, "Do you live here, too, Uncle Panos?" As soon as I called him Uncle I felt silly, and could feel myself blush.

"Just plain Panos will be fine," he said. "You don't have to call me 'Uncle'." He said this without smiling, as if he was stating an obvious fact to a child.

"Yes, I live on the fourth floor, down the hall from

Eugenia," he said. He looked over at Eugenia, then turned back to me. "We were talking about Selena before you joined us." He pulled a face like a predator who has sighted its prey. "I'm afraid I cannot shed any light on her death. The poor woman."

"I can shed light on my mother's death," George interrupted. He stepped in closer to the center of the circle.

"She was murdered, and I intend to hound the police until they reopen the investigation. If they refuse to reopen it, I'll do my own investigation. My mother did not kill herself! She wouldn't."

As he said this, George reflexively reached over and touched the black arm band he'd been wearing and would continue to wear for the balance of the forty days since Selena's death.

I stepped back half a step as George made his statement, placing Toula between me and his line of sight. I felt like a target and thought it prudent to operate on the time-tested principle of *out of sight, out of mind*. I looked across the group and saw my mother watching me. I had the feeling she was about to say something, was about to offer my services to George. I stared at her and subtly held up my palm and shook my head once to head her off.

"Did you want to say something, Socrates?" my mother said. "We would all like to hear from you, wouldn't we?" She looked at Toula, George, Eugenia, and Panos, one-by-one, pulling each into her gravitation field. Everyone assented with a grunt, a nod, or by mumbling, Yes.

"Socrates will help us, won't you?" my mother said,

I was roped, thrown down on the dirt, and hog-tied. She had me.

"Do I have a choice?" I said, fanning out my palms and smiling feebly as if my statement was an in-joke. "I'll spend a little time on it, but don't get your hopes up. I don't see what I can do that the police haven't already done. I'll look through the police file and get back to you all."

I assumed doing this would lead nowhere and would be the end of it.

How naïve of me.

CHAPTER 34

THE MORNING AFTER THE SUPPORT group meeting, Panos found himself again thinking about the *Plato Krater* and the telephone conversation he'd had with the woman at the HELLENE Gallery. He reread the *krater*'s description in the catalog and studied the catalog's photograph.

The catalog's image certainly did his krater justice, he thought. *In fact, it looked even better than he remembered. But there was no mistaking the misleading description.*

There were several possibilities. The cataloger might have made an innocent error and simply missed the repairs because the flaws were no longer visible to the naked eye. It also was possible there was more than one example of this *krater* known, that the *krater* up for sale, although very similar, was not the same vase Panos had resold to the Theodoros brothers. And there was a third possibility, but Panos dismissed it from his mental catalog of possibilities. The brothers would not have dared done that to him.

He decided to call the gallery again but this time be more specific. He dialed the number.

"Hello, I would like to speak to someone in authority with respect to an object shown in the Dalveen exhibit catalog."

Panos' call was routed to the telephone of the HELLENE specialist in charge of antiquities.

"Antiquities Department, Ms. Bernlimmer speaking. How may I help you?"

Panos hesitated, briefly put off by subtle hints of a Brooklyn accent in the woman's otherwise patrician voice. He had expected someone with a Mediterranean accent or, at least, a condescending British accent, real or contrived. But, Brooklyn? It momentarily knocked him off stride.

He recovered quickly and introduced himself as he had in his previous call. He said he was interested in the *Plato Krater*, but believed it had been incorrectly described in the catalog. He explained his reason for thinking this. Ms. Bernlimmer thanked him and said she would call him back within the hour.

Panos' phone rang twenty minutes later.

"Mr. Makeresos, this is Lydia Bernlimmer from HELLENE. I have some information for you." She hesitated. "I checked our files, then talked with others at our gallery familiar with this lot. I even called a colleague at the Metropolitan. They all agreed on one point: the *krater* we're offering is the only one known with the Plato-site attribution." She waited for some response, then continued when none came.

"Not only that," she said, "our records indicate that the *krater*, like every object we exhibit, was carefully inspected by two experts looking for damage, flaws or repairs. Every flaw or repair or damage, if any, would have been meticulously described in the catalog, but there were none.

"Furthermore," she said, "because of its singularity and substantial value, the *Plato Krater* underwent a CT scan looking for repairs or flaws or damage invisible to the naked eye. The vase is perfect. This was not the *krater* you described in our earlier conversation."

"Then you people are wrong," Panos said. "There must be more than one *Plato Krater* known. Mine was another example."

"I'm afraid that's not possible," the woman said, "not according to our records, which are quite thorough. The Dalveen *Plato Krater* is the only one of its design and attribution known, and has been part of the Dalveen collection for more than thirty years."

Panos felt his stomach tighten. "Perhaps your records aren't up to date."

"No, Mr. Makeresos, that was one of the points I checked. Even the Metropolitan records the Dalveen *Plato* as the only one known."

"You're sure?"

"I'm sure."

"I know I'm right," Panos said.

"Well," she said, a harsh edge creeping into her voice, "we do not make such elementary mistakes at the HELLENE. We are very careful."

"I didn't say you people made a mistake," Panos said, "but believe me, someone did." *And that someone will pay for that mistake*, he thought.

Panos sat in his Treasure Room, his eyes fixed on *The Mourning Woman*, but not seeing her. To all outward appearances, had someone observed Panos at this moment, he would have appeared to be in a state of deep meditation. But he was not meditating. His mind was not settled and contemplative. His mind was in a state of deep turmoil, fixed on his memory of his *Plato Krater*, and locked onto the information the gallery's woman had passed along to him.

Assuming the HELLENE woman was correct, there was only one possibility. His Plato Krater was not a second, not a defective ceramic that would not be qualified for acquisition by a museum, as the Theodoros brothers had led him to believe. His Plato Krater had been a fake knowingly sold to him by the Theodoros brothers.

Panos brooded about this. He stewed over how for twelve years he'd been made a fool of by the Theodoros brothers, how he had likely been tricked into believing he had built a collection of genuine and desirable antiquities seconds, but actually had built a collection of deceptive, overpriced fakes.

If so many of the objects in his former collection were fakes, what about the objects he now was buying under the new arrangement? He had no choice but to assume the worst. No sane man could do otherwise.

All that remained to do now was to decide how he would exact his revenge against Aristides and Milos, and for him to determine if *The Mourning Woman*, his beloved terracotta, was genuine, but stolen, or was just another fake.

CHAPTER 35

I HAD PROMISED MY MOTHER I would look into Selena Kostas' death, so it was time to acquit myself of that undertaking. I would read the police file and ME's report, and then advise my mother and her neighbors why I believed the ME's conclusion was correct, that Selena had committed suicide in Eugenia's apartment. This, of course, assumed that nothing untoward would come to light when I read the reports.

I knew from past experience not to think I could just waltz into the 2D station house, ask for the file, and have it handed over to me. But if I followed MPD protocol, I would have to wait until the final police report — called the PD 251 Report — had been written, vetted, edited, and finally released to the public. Depending on the case loads of the cops involved, it could be weeks or even months before the report would be available.

I decided to call Ralph Harte and ask him to help me. Doing so was a long shot because Harte had no reason to help him, but I had nothing to lose by asking. I was prepared to read the PD 251 now, whatever its current stage as it headed toward its final production.

"Harte," I said into my cellphone, recalling his admonition

not to refer to him as Detective, "it's Socrates Cheng. I need a favor."

"What's that?" His tone did not sound inviting.

"I need to read the ME's report and police file on the Kostas woman I reported dead."

"I'm retired, Cheng. Remember?"

"I know, but I'm doing a favor for my mother. She was a friend of the DOA. I want to be able to tell her I looked at the file, and that the ME was right, that it was suicide."

"Isn't that how you got in trouble a few years back, snooping where you didn't belong?" Harte said.

I couldn't argue with that. "I just want to put the matter to rest for her, then I'm done." I paused, then said, "I'd really appreciate your help."

"You can have the PD 251 when it's ready. You don't need me for that."

"No, but I need you to expedite this. I want to report back to my mother as soon as possible, and move on."

He said nothing.

"Listen," I said, "I know this is an imposition, but my mother will drive me crazy until I get back to her." I paused. Time to humble myself. "Please, Detective, I mean, please, Harte."

A few seconds of silence followed, then he said, "Sit tight. I'll get back to you."

CHAPTER 36

HARTE CALLED ME A FEW hours later to say he had copies of the ME's report and a draft version of the PD 251 for me. He said he wasn't able to copy the entire file, but hadn't seen anything in it that would contradict the ME's finding. We agreed to meet at the Dupont Circle Starbucks.

As before, Harte was already there and seated on the patio when I arrived.

"Hey, Harte," I said, as I walked up to him. I saw a large manila envelope on the table.

"Cheng," he said, and nodded his head.

I went inside and bought us each a Vente-size bold coffee, then settled into the chair across the table from him.

"That it?" I asked, and pointed my chin at the envelope.

Harte nodded. "Don't expect much. There aren't no landmines in there. The ME and cops were thorough, the suicide routine. Routine from a cop's point of view, that is. The only wrinkle was she offed herself in that other woman's apartment with an unusual poison — Succinyl Choline."

Although I was puzzled by the selection of the poison Selena had used and would have to research it, I didn't say so since the ME and cops didn't appear to think its choice by Selena raised any questions.

"I don't expect anything at all," I said, "so I won't be disappointed. This is strictly a courtesy review to appease my mother and her neighbors." I smiled and raised my eyebrows as if to say, 'You probably had a mother once. You know how it is.'

We drained our coffee cups, and I started to gather up the envelope so I could leave, when someone said, "Hi, Daddy. Sorry I'm late, me."

I'd never heard syntax quite like that, but before I could turn around to see who had spoken, I watched Harte undergo an immediate transformation. He suddenly sat up taller, sucked in his gut, raised his head up, and lost his distinctive, dispirited expression. Now he smiled big and started to get up from his chair to greet the speaker, when she said, "Sit, Daddy. No need to get up, you."

Harte plopped back down into his chair and offered his cheek to the young woman. She bent over and kissed it, then straightened up and turned to face me.

The woman aggressively thrust out her hand to shake mine.

"Hi, I'm Clotille Harte, the number one Harte daughter, me. The only Harte daughter, in fact, as far as we know, 'though with my daddy's history, we can't be too sure."

Her smile revealed two rows of very white, very straight teeth, and much warmth. What struck me most of all about her looks — and they were very good looks — was her skin and hair. Her face was white, much like Harte's, but not pasty white like his. Her skin was white like day-old dairy cream, not quite white, but not quite yellow, either. She had a sprinkle of light freckles running across the bridge of her nose and down both sides of her face, stopping where her cheeks began. Her features, unlike Harte's, were soft and girlie-delicate.

But it was her hair that got to me. Her hair, like her father's probably had been long ago, was red, just like Maureen O'Hara's red hair in the Ted Turner 1940s and '50s colorized movies now on TV. Not orange-red, not brassy-red, and definitely not bottle-red. Instead, her hair was deep, luxurious red, so sumptuous red that I was tempted to reach out, wrap a strand among my fingers, and place it under my nose to inhale its fragrance just before I leaned in and kissed it.

Before I made a fool of myself by staring too long at Clotille, I stood up, stuck out my hand to take hers, and said, "I'm Socrates, Socrates Cheng, a friend of your father's." I tilted my head toward Harte as if Clotille otherwise would not know to whom I was referring. She definitely had me off-balance and flustered.

I held onto Clotille's hand a millisecond longer than a handshake with a stranger should allow, just long enough to cause Clotille to look into my eyes, hold my stare for a few seconds, then look back down at our joined hands and nod once before she gently let go.

"I'm Clotille, Harte's daughter," she said, introducing herself again. She realized what she'd done and blushed, then moved away to the other side of the table.

I stood up. "I'll leave you two alone," I said. I turned to Harte.

"Thanks, I appreciate this." I held up the envelope to indicate what I'd referred to. "I'll be in touch." Then I turned toward Clotille.

"Nice meeting you, Ms. Harte. It is still Harte, isn't it?"

I said, knowing from her introduction she still used Harte's surname, but also hoping she wasn't married and she would use this question as a smooth way to let me know. I didn't see any rings on her fingers, but who knows these days.

"Oh, yes, still just plain old single Harte, me," she said, obviously picking up my thought.

"Good," I said, then blushed when I realized how I'd responded.

"Nice meeting you, Clotille," I said. "Hope to see you again." I glanced over at Harte. He was looking hard at me and frowning.

I turned and left, ready to kick myself for having acted like a tongue-tied, love-starved schoolboy, and for not sticking around long enough to make some civil conversation with Clotille.

CHAPTER 37

ANOS SAT IN HIS TREASURE Room and stared at *The Mourning Woman*, breathing in her emoted grief. After several minutes, he stood up, walked over to her, and lifted her off the pedestal. He caressed her lovingly, his fingers gently stroking her head, neck and shoulders. He sighed.

Try as he might, Panos could not avoid thinking about the *Plato Krater*. His mood abruptly changed, more accurately mirroring his dark thoughts, spiraling down into a deep, dour pit. He looked hard at the grieving woman in his hands, and inhaled slowly and deeply. He kissed her forehead, then placed her back on her pedestal.

He returned to his chair, settled in again, and cast his gaze across the room at *The Mourning Woman*.

This time he did not see her, although he looked directly at her. Instead, he visualized glimpses of the collection he'd sold to the Theodoros brothers, and wondered if everything he'd bought from them, just like his *Plato Krater*, had been bogus.

He shook his head hard to rid himself of this corrosive thought, stood again, and walked over to an Eighth Century BCE, 4½" tall bronze female figure, one of the seven seconds he had held back from the sale. He considered the armless female figure, and smiled. She was absolutely magnificent, even with her visible shortcomings.

Panos smoothly pivoted ninety degrees away from the bronze woman and swept his eyes around the room, pausing his gaze briefly on each of the other six objects just long enough to contemplate the possibility that each also might be a fake. Then he turned back to the small bronze figurine and again picked her up and held her in his open palm.

She was indeed beautiful, he thought. *In her own way, as lovely as The Mourning Woman.*

He turned the statuette over in his hands and looked closely at her, admiring her from every possible angle.

She is one of my best, he thought.

He raised the figurine to his lips, lightly kissed her once on each nipple, then knelt and placed her on the floor, positioning her gently to avoid scuffing her.

He looked down, pursed his lips, and floated a kiss to her.

He slowly raised his foot, paused, sucked in a deep breath, and then stomped down on the figurine with all his power and weight, crushing her under his twisting heel, as surely as if he was smothering out a cigarette on the concrete pavement.

Panos looked down at the twisted bronze scrap metal and shook his head. He left the ruined statuette in her repose, then walked to his chair and sat.

He again fixed his eyes on the treasure arrayed around the room, then fastened his concentration on *The Mourning Woman* as he weighed the likelihood she, too, might be a fake.

CHAPTER 38

A s I WALKED AWAY FROM Starbucks, I left all thoughts of Harte and Clotille behind me and cut through Dupont Circle. I used my cellphone to call my mother, but didn't reach her. I wanted to ask her to leave me out of future meetings of the support group. That would have to hold for another time.

Since I was unable to reach my mother, I called Selena's son, George, and asked him to meet me. Then I sat down on a bench on the south side of Dupont Circle, away from Starbucks and my office, and read the draft versions of the reports Harte had given me.

I looked at the autopsy report first, aware that the ME's report always reduced the human victim to clinical kilograms, centimeters, and glass slides, with a dollop of test results thrown in.

The opening of the report set the tone. It stated that Selena Kostas — not using her name, but referring to her using a number that had been assigned to identify her — was a Caucasian female of approximately seventy years of age, measuring a certain number of centimeters, and weighing a certain number of kilograms.

The report stated that there was no indication of external

trauma on the subject's body. There was, however, evidence of a foreign substance in her bloodstream, that substance being the highly toxic poison, Succinyl Choline. By all appearances, the report concluded, the subject had died from the self-administration of this poison. Conclusion: The cause of death was suicide.

It wasn't clear to me from the ME's report how Selena was supposed to have administered the poison to herself, but my mother and her neighbors wouldn't care about that detail, so that could hold for another time.

The draft PD 251 Report was a single page form which, in this case, revealed little I didn't already know from having seen Selena on the floor in Eugenia's apartment. The Report stated the time and date the call had come in to 911, named me as the caller, and stated that officers had been sent to the scene at a specified time. The also Report indicated that the named patrol officers had found the body where it was said to be, that there was no obvious evidence of a fight, break-in or other crime, and that the officers had secured the scene while awaiting the arrival of the ME and detectives.

The PD 251 was accompanied by photographs that were typical of the type taken at a death site where there was no obvious evidence of a crime. Each shot was made from a different angle as the photographer walked in a circle around the body, stopping every few feet to snap a picture. There also were photographs of the kitchen and two bathrooms.

All in all, if you ignore that Selena died from ingesting a highly toxic and scarce poison while in an apartment she wasn't supposed to be in, the ME's report and the police report were plain vanilla routine.

I checked my watch and saw it was time to go to Zorba's Café at R Street on Connecticut Avenue, north of Dupont Circle — near the west side of Sunderland Place — to meet Selena's son.

George was seated at a table when I arrived. He had a small pot of Nescafé Greek coffee and a glass of water in front of him.

I ordered a double cup of espresso, and said to George, "I've reviewed the medical examiner's report concerning your mother's death. I thought you might want to know what it said or want to look at it yourself. I have it here." I nodded at the envelope.

George frowned and started to drum his fingers on the tablecloth. "Of course I want to know," he said. "What do you think?"

I think you're an ass, is what I think. But I didn't say that. Instead, I said, "The report's straight forward, George. The ME concluded that your mother took a poison called Succinyl Choline. I didn't see anything in the ME's or cops' report to contradict the findings."

"You a doctor?" he asked.

I leaned toward him. "You don't have to be a doctor to read and understand what's in the report. I don't know how a wrist watch works, but I can look at one and tell the time. I know you're upset, George, but it's not complicated. See for yourself." I picked up the envelope and held it out for him. He ignored my gesture.

He shook his head and glowered. "You can believe what you want," he said. "My mother did not kill herself. If you think otherwise, then screw you. I'll find someone else to help me."

With that, he threw a ten dollar bill down on the table, stood abruptly, and said, "Keep the change. Consider it your unearned fee." He stormed out of the taverna.

I was counting out a generous tip for the waitress, leaving five on eight, when my cellphone rang. I checked the readout and saw it was Toula, the woman I'd recently met, calling. I connected the call.

I'd barely said, hello, when she interrupted me.

"Your mother's been hurt," she said. "Eugenia, too. They're in the hospital."

I could feel my heart race. "What happened? How serious is it?" I said. "Which hospital?" I said all this as I ran outside to grab a taxi.

I questioned Toula as I rode to Georgetown University Hospital.

"Your mother had invited me and my mother to have tea with her and Eugenia," Toula said. "When I arrived at Sophia's apartment, she and Eugenia weren't there, although the door was partly open. I called out thinking they might be in the back. When no one answered, I let myself in." She paused.

"Go on," I said. "Please—"

"Your mother and Eugenia were in the kitchen, unconscious, lying on the floor. It was awful. I've never been so scared in my life."

My hands were shaking. I reached into my pocket and pulled out two twenty dollar bills and threw them onto the front seat as we headed toward the hospital.

"This is an emergency," I said to the driver. "Don't stop

for lights. Get me to the Emergency Room fast. I'll take care of any tickets."

I switched my cellphone to speaker mode and laid the phone on my lap. "What did the paramedics say? Will my mother be all right?" Rivulets of perspiration ran down my back and soaked my shirt.

"The paramedics wouldn't give me any information," Toula said. "But I could see both your mother and Eugenia had bruises on their faces and necks. And they both were alive, moving a little and moaning. That's all I know."

I took a deep breath. We were entering the hospital's parking lot and angling over toward the ER entrance.

"You did fine, Toula, just fine. Thank you . . . . I'm just arrived at the hospital so I'm going to hang up. I'll call you later," I said. "I have to go."

As I hurried from the taxi to the ER entrance, my heart raced, and I sweated heavily.

I needed to know what had happened to my mother and Eugenia, then try to convince my mother to sell her condo apartment and live elsewhere. I doubted she'd agree, but I'd try.

The one thing I did know was this: It was not safe for my mother to continue to live at the Mount Parnassus, not as things stood right now. Whatever was going on there, she somehow was caught up in it. That being so, I decided, I needed to become involved in finding out what had happened. I also had to rethink George's position concerning his mother's death. And, as much as it pained me to admit it, I also had to reconsider Eugenia's belief that someone had followed her, and that someone other than Selena had entered her apartment when she was out walking.

There was a whole new universe of possibilities for me to consider now, none of them good.

PART TWO

CHAPTER 39

A FTER I ENTERED THE HOSPITAL'S Emergency Room I learned that my mother and Eugenia had been transferred to semi-private rooms on the sixth floor of the hospital's Bles Building. When I arrived at their floor, I spoke to the duty nurse who told me my mother was very banged up and bruised, but her wounds were not life threatening. She refused to give me any information about Eugenia because of the federal privacy act — HIPAA.

My mother and Eugenia were in separate rooms. I first walked to my mother's room. The door was open and the lights out. I knocked, waited a few seconds, then knocked again when she didn't respond. After a few more seconds of silence, I cautiously walked into the room and said Hello as I came into view of two beds.

The bed closest to the door was unoccupied and stripped of its bedding. My mother laid on her side on the other bed with her back to the room. Based on her deep rhythmic breathing, I assumed she was sleeping.

I walked over for a closer look. Her eyes were closed, her lids swollen and red, the area around her eyes and nose black and blue. She had two stitches on the side of her head where her left eyebrow ended.

She was hooked-up to an IV drip, which ran under the blanket. She also was attached to a monitor which fed information into terminals located on the wall behind the head of the bed. She was covered up to her neck by a sheet and a lightweight blanket. I couldn't see any injuries to her arms and legs because of the blanket.

I didn't want to wake her, so I stood alongside the bed and watched her sleep. After a few minutes, I quietly left the room.

I followed the same entry routine when I arrived down the hall at Eugenia's room. This time I received a response to my knock.

"What?" a weak voice asked when I knocked. I recognized Eugenia's voice.

"Hello," I called out. "I'm here to see Mrs. Stamos." I thought perhaps church-Orthodoxy decorum required that I approach Eugenia this way.

"Come in."

I entered the room, nodded, and smiled at a woman in the bed closest to the door, then headed for the other bed where I could see Eugenia staring at me.

"Oh," she said, as I came close to her, "it's you."

"How are you doing?" I asked.

As far as I could see, Eugenia's injuries appeared to replicate those I'd observed on my mother's face and head. In addition, Eugenia's arms were outside the covers revealing a cast on her left arm and a bandage around her right wrist. An IV tube led to her right forearm.

Eugenia didn't answer my question, so I said, "I wanted to stop by to say, Hello, and see if you need anything."

She shook her head, then stared at me. She didn't say anything.

"I'm going to leave you now," I said. "If you want something, tell a nurse. I'll leave my cell number at the desk so the duty nurse can call me."

I turned to walk out when Eugenia said, sotto voce, "I saw something no person should ever see."

I stopped walking and turned to look back at her. "What's that?"

"Who will murder me and how."

CHAPTER 40

'D JUST SETTLED INTO THE backseat of a taxi, and was heading to my office to regroup and think about the implications of the assaults on my mother and Eugenia, when my cellphone rang. The LCD readout didn't identify the caller because the caller wasn't listed in my contacts list. I answered the call because I thought it might be from the hospital.

The call was from Toula.

I thanked her for calling me earlier to tell me about my mother and Eugenia, and brought her up to date on my visit to the hospital. Then Toula said, in her usual low-pitched, raspy, smoker's voice, "My mother wants me to ask you to come over for dinner."

"Your mother?" I said, warily.

"Well . . . me, too. We both would like it if you would come."

This set off alarm bells. It seemed like a classic matchmaker's invitation.

"When?" I asked, trying to keep the cynicism out of my voice.

"Tonight will be good, if you can," She said. "If not, another night. We're always here."

I thought about it. I wasn't anxious to have dinner with Arête and Toula, but I also didn't want to insult them. I probably owed Toula at least that much for tracking me down to tell me about my mother and Eugenia. Beyond that, I'd probably run into them at the condo from time-to-time and didn't want to insult them by not accepting their invitation. I decided I'd think about the invitation as if it were a business requirement rather than as a social or personal situation.

"Tonight will be good for me," I said. "What time?"

CHAPTER 41

ARRIVED AT ARÊTE'S AND TOULA'S apartment a little after
7:00 p.m. Toula answered my knock, smiled, and motioned
me into the foyer. Arête was sweeping the hallway between
the foyer and the distant room that, like Eugenia's room
located at the same place in her apartment, probably was used
as a parlor. She looked up as I approached, kept on sweeping,
and said, "*Kalispera*! — Good evening!"

I nodded and smiled. "*Epsis* — And to you, too."

Toula motioned to me with her head, indicating that I
was to follow her. She led me into the living room and over
to a dry sink. She poured two glasses of chilled Retsina. Even
though this wine had lost popularity with my generation and
the younger generation, I still loved it and was glad Toula had
selected it for us.

We touched glasses. "*Siyiam* — Your health."

"*Siyiam, re* — And you," Toula answered.

Toula led me on a tour of the apartment. Except for
the peculiar shrine Arête maintained in the parlor for her
dead husband, and the nearby ikon shrine dedicated to Saint
Pareskavi — the saint who heals those with eye problems —
the apartment seemed fungible with others I'd seen lived in
by elderly Greek immigrants.

Dinner consisted of *tiropita* — an appetizer of Greek cheeses rolled between layers of buttered filo dough and baked golden brown — salad, roast leg of lamb, and *tsoureki* — a sweet, moist Greek bread. The food was delicious.

While we ate, Toula talked about the break-ins at Eugenia's apartment, and asked about Selena's death. She also engaged me in small talk about my PI business. Otherwise, there was little said across the table, and the gulfs of silence were uncomfortably vast. I tried several times to bring Arête into the conversation, but she resisted participating, and for the most part remained quiet throughout the meal, stuffing food into her mouth and hungrily puffing on one cigarette after another between bites.

The meal was topped off with the ritual cup of Greek coffee, with a back of water, and a tiny serving of peach quince preserves that Toula told me she'd put up this past summer. The quince was absolutely delicious, slightly smoky, and wondrously exotic, its syrup almost unbearably sweet.

Arête said goodnight to us immediately after dinner, and started to shuffle off to another part of the apartment.

I said, trying to be polite, "*Kalf sas* — The meal was delicious."

Arête turned and looked at Toula with a panicked expression. I realized my attempt at good manners, and especially my compliment, had backfired. Arête evidently thought I was giving her the Evil Eye. I looked at Toula, who had a wry grin on her face as if to say to me, "Let's see how you get out of this one."

I turned back to face Arête.

"*Panayia mazi tou* — May the Virgin Mother be with you," I said, making the sign of the cross as I spoke. Then

I turned one palm upward and dry spit into it three times, making the sound *ptu, ptu, ptu,* to remove any evil spell I might have cast on Arête by praising her.

This apparently satisfied Arête because she looked briefly at Toula, then left.

I made a mental note to stop at a church store to buy a *Mati* — a glass necklace with a flat pendant, guaranteed to ward off the Evil Eye — as a gift for Arête, to apologize for my social *faux pas.*

Toula and I cleared the table, but left the dishes soaking in the sink while we settled in the living room. Toula lit a cigarette. I lit a *Romeo Y Julieta* cigar I'd brought along with me.

"Your mother didn't have much to say to me during dinner," I said, "not even when I tried to talk to her. Is there some reason she doesn't like me?"

"Don't take it personal," Toula said. "It's because your people are *xeni,* foreigners, not *Sparti* like my mother's people."

"My mother's from a village near Sparta," I said.

"If she's not actually from Sparta," Toula said, "my mother doesn't count it. Your mother might as well be from Athens or from Mars."

I thought about that and shook my head. "Of course," I said, "the indomitable *Sparti,* their *xorio* — their villages — and their lives of conflict and unending vendettas. I should have realized. The rest of Greek culture pales beneath their contempt."

I drew deeply on my cigar, held the delicious smoke briefly in my mouth, then streamed out a thick, fragrant cloud. "Some things never change," I said.

Toula shrugged her indifference. "*Dhén pirazi* — It doesn't matter. Anyway, our mothers aren't so different."

I thought about Toula's statement. It had no meaning for me. I nodded.

"How's your mother like living here?" I said, trying to make conversation.

"If you mean living in this condominium," Toula said, "she likes it fine. It connects here with her past. She's glad Eugenia lives here because they knew each other when they were girls. And she's happy to be with other Greek women her age."

I nodded again.

"So," Toula said, "would you like to have dinner with me?"

I must have looked confused because Toula immediately added, "Alone, I mean. Just us, out at a restaurant."

I hesitated. "You mean like on a date?"

"Don't be so shocked, Socrates. This is the twenty-first century. Even Greek women sometimes ask men out on dates now." She smiled ambiguously.

This put me in an awkward position. I didn't want to date Toula. For one thing, I wasn't ready to date, not even after the passing of almost four years since Jade. For another thing, I didn't find Toula particularly attractive, either in her looks or her personality. She wasn't bad looking, but she wasn't very good looking either. Perhaps it was her age — she was about four years older than me — because I could see that she might have been attractive at one time, but not now. Not to me. More importantly, I found I constantly had to resist the urge to stare at her eye patch when I was with her, making me self-conscious in her presence.

I composed my thoughts so I could decline her invitation without insulting or hurting her. I'd respond by being passive-aggressive, a common way of dealing with people I usually despised in others, but occasionally employed myself because it could be very effective. Now would be a good time to use it.

"That's fine," I said. "We can get together sometime, if you'd like." I hoped my lack of enthusiasm hadn't slipped through.

Toula squinted. She was nobody's fool. "When?" she said. "I mean, if you don't want to, you don't have to. Just say so. I don't care." She seemed a little miffed as she backpedalled from her request.

"I don't need you or nobody else doing me any favors," she said.

Then her face softened. "It's just I thought I would like to see you again, but only if you want." She shrugged, fixed her gaze on my eyes, and slowly licked her lower lip.

I paused again, forced a small smile, and said, "How about if I check my schedule when I go to my office tomorrow. I don't carry my calendar with me. Then we can set a time."

I watched Toula's face contort through several responses: disappointment, then puzzlement, then anger, and finally resolution. She settled into a twisted smile. I wasn't sure which emotion that represented. She looked like a cat that had just figured out how to talk a mouse into coming out from its hole.

"I have a better idea," she said. "Forget about dating. Let's have an arrangement based just on sex. We'll hook-up once in a while and do it. No dates and no commitments. Just sex."

If I said Toula had caught me off guard, I'd be too subtle.

I stared at Toula for a moment and resisted the urge to break into a big smile.

"You're kidding, right?" I said.

"Do I sound like I'm kidding?"

"Well, no." I smiled. "*Vevayos* — Of course," I said. "I'd like that. I'd like that very much." I could feel my face grow warm with blush.

"Good," Toula said. "Then it's settled."

"It is," I said, and thought, *it's settled as long as you don't take off your eye patch when you take off your clothes.*

CHAPTER 42

THE HOSPITAL DISCHARGED MY MOTHER and Eugenia two days after their admission. I drove them home in a car I rented for this purpose. Both women were still badly bruised from the beatings they'd received and were not easy to look at. Their black and blue blotches had started to change from dark Rorschach inkblots to irregular yellow and green smears.

I wanted my mother to move out of the Mount Parnassus and move into my condo with me until the police caught the assailant, but she insisted on going home to her own apartment. I engaged a nurse to stay with her 24/7. I also wanted to hire a bodyguard, but she wouldn't have it.

Hiring the nurse being the limit of what I could accomplish with my mother right now, I set out to find who had done this to her and Eugenia.

I began by calling Ralph Harte. I asked to meet with him again. I hoped he could steer me toward a productive investigative path and warn me away from any approach that might be time and resources dead ends.

Harte joined me an hour later in Georgetown at *The Guards* bar/restaurant on M Street, between 28th and 29th.

I hadn't been to *The Guards* in about two years because four years ago I'd been banned from there — 86ed, it's called in the bar world — under penalty of arrest if I entered the premises again. This was because one night, when I'd had too much to drink, I'd gotten into an argument at the bar with another customer, and then refused to leave when Boxer, the tender at the time, told me to leave. Boxer finally called the cops, and I was arrested for criminal trespass. Boxer then publicly banned me from *The Guards* for as long as he tended bar there.

Now Boxer was gone. He had left the city altogether, I learned, and he'd been replaced by another tender with whom I'd made my peace. I had privileges again at *The Guards* as long as I behaved myself.

Harte walked up to my table, pulled out a chair, and sat down. He didn't smile, didn't shake my hand, and didn't offer any greeting. Instead, he brought an anomalous wariness with him that set up shop in the space between us and hovered over our table. Since I had mentioned in my call the purpose for getting together, his mood puzzled me.

"Cheng," he said, after he settled into his chair. "How's your mother doing?"

I described my mother's visible injuries, and said, "That's physically how she is. I don't know how she's really doing. Inside, I mean. She pretty much keeps her feelings to herself."

"Okay, you called this party. What can I do for you?" Harte said.

"I'm going to investigate the break-ins at Eugenia's place, Selena Kostas' death, and the assault on my mother and

Eugenia." I lifted my cup of coffee, took a sip, and watched Harte over the cup's lip.

When he said nothing, I continued. "I'd like to run what I know by you and get your thoughts how to proceed."

"Let's hear it."

I spent the next fifteen minutes describing my understanding of events, then said, "What problems do you see for me?"

Harte leaned forward and placed both elbows on the table. He rested his chin on his intertwined fingers.

"First off," he said, "don't do anything to piss off the cops investigating the assaults, especially if one of them turns out to be Thigpen."

I nodded my understanding, then said, "I'm leaning toward believing someone did enter Eugenia's apartment and maybe even followed her, just as she said, but I have no idea why."

"What else?" Harte said.

"Given where Selena Kostas died, I have to consider the possibility she was the one entering Eugenia's apartment. If so, I want to know why."

Harte sat back in his chair and crossed one leg over the other. "It's strange she chose her neighbor's place to off herself," he said. "I don't think I ever heard anything like that before."

"If she *did* kill herself," I said, "and wasn't murdered."

"Right," Harte said, stretching the word out into a three-second word, "if she wasn't murdered. The big, if."

"There's another possibility," I said. "What if Selena was murdered, but wasn't the target? What if the killer thought Selena was Eugenia?"

"Then I'd say Selena was one very unlucky lady," he said. "Real unlucky."

I didn't care for Harte's wise-ass remark. It made me feel he wasn't taking me seriously, that he still saw me much as he had four years ago, as a meddling amateur playing at being a private eye. I decided to let my feelings pass without comment because I needed his help.

"So," I said, "how should I move forward on this?"

"Careful," he said, "real careful. You're probably going to piss off everyone and wind up in deep shit. If that happens, Thigpen won't be your only problem."

"Noted again," I said. He must have picked up on my frustration with him because he dropped the subject and moved on.

"Probably the first thing to do is find out why the Selena woman was in Eugenia's apartment, then prove the ME wrong about the suicide, if he was wrong. That should keep you busy for a while and should lead you naturally to your next steps. If not, give me another call and you can buy me another cup of coffee. We'll talk."

CHAPTER 43

P ANOS SPENT SATURDAY AND MOST of Sunday after
church pouring through his accumulation of auction
catalogs and art books, researching the six objects he had
held back from the sale of his collection to the Theodoros
brothers. He regretted having destroyed the beautiful figurine
before he knew for sure if she was genuine or not. Soon, he
hoped, he would either justify or condemn his impetuous
action by proving once and for all that the six survivors were
frauds or not. He would deal with *The Mourning Woman*
after that.

Late Sunday afternoon Panos closed his last art book,
reshelved the auction catalogs, and poured himself a small
glass of Retsina.

He was in a quandary. He had not proven that the
six objects were fakes, but he also hadn't eliminated that
possibility. He had not been able to find any reference to the
six objects in any catalog or art book he owned. His attempts
to find out something online also had come up empty.

He wasn't sure how to interpret this, but he was grateful
he had not come across any other examples of his so-called *one
of a kind* antiquities. It was possible the six artifacts were *sui
generis*, genuine one of a kind objects, not fakes; seconds, to

be sure, but all as represented to him by Milos and Aristides. *They better be*, he thought.

Panos finished his drink, poured another, and carried it with him to his Treasure Room.

He strolled around his vault and stopped before each of the six objects. He picked each up and examined it closely, slowly turning each over and over in his hands. He was conflicted. His gut told him these might be fakes, that the Theodoros brothers had deceived him with these as they had deceived him with the *Plato Krater*, yet he so much wanted these objects to be genuine.

He made a logical leap and had an even more disquieting thought: If these six objects were fakes, then it was likely *The Mourning Woman* also was a fake. This insight caused Panos to break out in an unnatural sweat.

CHAPTER 44

TWO NIGHTS AFTER OUR DINNER with Arête, Toula and I hooked-up under our new arrangement. She had called me earlier in the day, and we arranged to meet at my place at 10:00 p.m.

Toula arrived on time. I helped her off with her coat and turned to put it in the closet when she asked me for a tour of my condo. I gave her the 50¢ special — a quick walk-through the living room, kitchen, office, my bedroom, and the second bedroom — all accompanied by some inane commentary by me.

When we returned to the living room, I said, "How'd you know I was single or not involved with someone?"

"The old ladies at the condo said so. Someone must've asked your mother."

I nodded, and believed her.

Although it had been Toula who suggested our special arrangement and who had kicked it off tonight by calling me, I sensed she was even more nervous about our plans than I was, and I was pretty nervous.

When we finished our walk about, she asked me for a drink. I poured us each a large McCallum single malt Scotch.

I sipped mine; Toula said, "*Yasou* — Your health," and inhaled hers. She immediately asked for a refill.

She quickly drained her glass again, set it down on an end table, and stepped close to me. I put my hands on her hips and pulled her in closer. Our bodies softly touched.

We kissed, gently at first, then more forcefully as our tongues dueled for domination.

We were ravenous, both starved for sexual contact, our stored-up heat palpable. I could feel Toula's small breasts pressing against my chest, and I immediately became aroused. Our tongues relaxed, but we held our kiss until Toula pulled away and stepped back one step. She began to unbutton her blouse from the top. I smiled and followed her lead, working my way down my shirt. When my last button fell free, I angled my head in the direction of the bedroom door. Toula nodded and turned away from me. We quick-stepped to the bedroom, molting the rest of our clothes along the way.

It was just after Midnight, and we sat in the living room. Toula had dressed in a white terry cloth robe she found hanging behind the door of the guest bathroom. I was dressed in a pair of baggy gray sweats and a Redskins T-shirt. My feet were bare.

Toula sat in the corner of the sofa with her legs curled up under her. I sat in my overstuffed reading chair, facing her. Toula held a McCallum in one hand and periodically sipped it. I held a beer and sipped from the can.

"We'll do this again," she said.

It was a statement, not a question. "I'd like to."

"I'll call you."

"Mind if I ask you something?" I said.

Toula gave me a suspicious look as if she was trying to read my mind. Her elevated tone belied her hard facial expression. "Ask away."

"I'm curious. I don't know much about you. How long have you lived with your mother, for example?" This was my polite way of asking, *Why* does a forty-six year old woman live with her mother?

"Two years. Since my divorce," Toula said. "My ex and I had a house I was supposed to get as part of our settlement, but his lawyer and my lawyer colluded behind my back and screwed me out of it."

"Divorces can be rough," I said. "At least that's what I hear."

"They suck," Toula said, "especially when your own lawyer messes you over."

This should have been a clue.

I decided not to touch that one. I changed the subject. "Do you work?"

"More or less. At a woman's clothing boutique at Pentagon City Fashion Mall. Part-time now, although I want to work fulltime. The problem with the job is the two other saleswomen are jealous of me because most male customers want to deal with me, not them. It's because I'm attractive and they're not. Unfortunately the store manager's been sleeping with both them, and he cut my hours to part time to appease the bitches and make me quit."

Another missed clue.

Toula finished her drink, dressed, and left without so much as a Goodbye.

There was no question about it. Toula was strange.

Probably a little paranoid, if nothing else, maybe worse. But I enjoyed the sex, which had been excellent, and anticipated it would get even better with time, so I would stick with our arrangement as long as it worked for me.

CHAPTER 45

M Y RINGING CELLPHONE WOKE ME the next morning. I hadn't been able to fall asleep until after 3:00 a.m., but when I did finally go out, I slipped into a coma-like state.

I reached for the cell on my night table, where I usually keep it while I sleep, but it wasn't there. I followed the sound into the bathroom and found the phone sitting on the sink. The call broke off before I could answer it, but the resulting voicemail was from Harte. He said he had obtained a copy of the draft police report concerning the assaults on my mother and Eugenia. I could meet him and pick it up.

I promptly called him and arranged to meet for lunch at the Greek deli on 19th Street, between L and M, a takeout hole-in-the-wall that served wonderful food. We agreed that whoever arrived first would stand in the ordering line that usually extended out from the deli onto the sidewalk.

Harte and I retrieved our lunch orders and walked over to the Duke Ellington pocket-park a few blocks away from the deli, where M Street, 21st Street, and New Hampshire Avenue intersect. We grabbed the last available bench and spread out our meals on our laps. Harte sat on a large brown envelope he'd been carrying. I assumed it contained the PD 251 he'd brought me.

"I'm looking forward to reading the preliminary report," I said. I tilted my head in the direction of the brown envelope, then looked up at him. "I'm anxious to know who the authorities think assaulted my mother and Eugenia."

"It's not preliminary anymore," Harte said.

I must have frowned because he added, "The case's closed, Cheng. That's the final report, not the draft."

"Closed? It's too soon. How can it—"

"There's nothing more to investigate," he said. "That's reality. Thigpen's closed the file. They're moving on to other cases. Unless something new turns up to light a fire under Thigpen, it's officially over."

We finished lunch without saying much more. I had the feeling Harte was pissed at me for not showing him due gratitude for having brought me the report, but my mind now was tied up with possible avenues of investigation to follow since the cops had given up on the case. I knew I should have been more sociable and engaged Harte in small talk, or maybe I should have run the possibilities that occurred to me by him, but I didn't do either, so he was pissed.

We finished eating, stood up, shook hands, and went our separate ways.

I walked over to the Mad Hatter, a bar/restaurant on Connecticut Avenue, a few blocks south of Dupont Circle, and read the report while I sat at the bar and nursed a beer. Harte was right. If the report was correct, there was nothing more to investigate and find. The police had been thorough, but had reached a dead end.

But I hadn't. Not as long as my mother continued to live at the Mount Parnassus.

CHAPTER 46

AFTER I DOWNED A SECOND beer, I left the Mad Hatter and headed home. Once there, I polished my shoes and changed into a suit and tie in an effort to mime a professional look, stuffed some business cards into my jacket pocket, and headed to the Mount Parnassus.

I spent the next forty minutes going floor to floor knocking on doors, asking if anyone had noticed anything or anyone unusual the day my mother and Eugenia were assaulted. Except for the commotion when the police arrived, no one had noticed anything.

I was able to cover about one third of the apartments; the others were vacant for the time being, their occupants probably at work. I decided I'd come back after dinner tonight and again tomorrow night, and hit the remaining fifty-five or so units. Except for one, that is. I wouldn't stop by the apartment below Eugenia's unit. No use asking for trouble from the filthy young man I had nicknamed the Tweaker.

Then I had a thought. Maybe I would stop at the Tweaker's apartment after all. He might have been the source of the beat-down on my mother and Eugenia. It might have been his vengeance against me for my knee in his groin. If that was the case, he'd have more to worry about from me than my knee.

I also decided I would have to pay more attention to that apartment and its curious occupant. Maybe the Mount Parnassus was not as benign as my mother suggested, but was a more hostile environment than it seemed to the casual observer.

———————

As I walked in my front door, my landline was ringing and my answering machine's message button was furiously flashing red. I had at least five messages waiting, if the speed of the flashing light was any indicator.

I rushed over to the phone and answered it midway through a ring.

"This is Socrates," I said.

"Socrates, it's mom. Where have you been, I've been trying to get you?"

I let out a long breath and relaxed. "As a matter of fact, I just came home from your building," I said. "I was just walking through the door when I heard the phone. It would really help if you would call my cell when you want me, not my landline. I—"

"We can talk about that another time. I need you here right away. Someone just threatened my life."

———————

My mother was alone in her living room when I arrived. She had a cup of coffee and glass of water sitting on the table in front of her. We hugged, then I took a seat.

"I don't know who it was," she said. "He told me if you don't stop nosing around the condo asking questions, and don't mind your own business, I would be sorry."

My stomach roiled. "What did you say?"

"I said, "How dare you threaten my son." But that wasn't what he was doing. He was threatening me, if you continue your snooping, not you."

That gave me pause. I didn't want to do anything that would endanger my mother. I was prepared to drop the investigation.

As usual, my mother read my mind.

"*éla* — No way," she said, as she wagged one finger at me. "Don't start thinking you should walk away from this, Socrates. Eugenia and I now need your help more than ever."

"I don't want to have to worry about your safety," I said.

As I expected, my mother did not roll over so easily.

"You listen to me, Socrates," she said. "If you stop and think about it, you've got to keep on. How can you let me live in a building where a murderer might be living?"

I noticed she'd changed the subject from the assault against her and Eugenia to Selena's death. My mother always was good at knowing which of my buttons to push.

"The cops called it suicide," I said, knowing she would not let it end there.

"*Ach!* — Nonsense," she said. "Of course it wasn't suicide. It had to be murder. Why else would the caller want you to stop snooping around?"

I couldn't argue with that. I'd been thinking the same thing, but it wasn't that simple. If it was murder, what was the motive and how did it tie in with the assaults against Eugenia and my mother?

The FBI's statistics say that people usually killed one another for one or more of three reasons: money, sex, or power. I thought I could rule out sex in Selena's case, but did money or power enter into the equation? And, if so, how?

"Let me sleep on it," I said. "In the meantime, I'd still like you to move in with me until all this is over."

"Go home and get some sleep, Socrates," my mother said, using a tone I'd heard often enough from her, especially when I was in college and convinced I had all the answers. "Call me in the morning to tell me you're still on the case." It was not a request.

With that, she stood, led me to the door, and kissed my cheek before showing me out.

When I arrived home, I poured two fingers of Metaxa, straight-up, and called Harte. I glanced at the answering machine. Its red message light still blinked rapidly. I hadn't checked my messages from earlier tonight.

"There's been a new development," I said, when Harte picked up. "A caller threatened my mother if I don't drop the investigation."

"Which investigation?" he said. "The suicide, assaults, break-ins?"

"I assume all of them."

"You probably should listen to the perp," Harte said, apparently not fazed by the threat against my mother.

"Why would somebody want me to quit looking into a suicide?" I said. "It doesn't make sense." Although I wasn't sure that the suicide was all the threat covered, I limited my question to that.

This, apparently, was the right question because Harte

said nothing in response. It was as if this thought hadn't occurred to him.

When he finally spoke, he spoke more deliberately than I'd ever heard him speak before. It was as if he was carefully formulating each word, and mulling it over, before setting it loose. He seemed pensive.

"I don't know," he said, "but based on what you told me, you should back off for the sake of your mother. Not every crime has to be solved."

Harte coughed, then said, "One other thing, you need to call Thigpen, and tell him. He's still the lead even though the cases are closed."

I thought about that. It wasn't something I wanted to do, although I understood what Harte was telling me.

"Would you mind making that call for me?" I asked.

Harte chuckled. "No can do. You need to man up."

I ended the call with Harte, and dialed Thigpen.

———— •••• ————

Thigpen picked up on the second ring and was his usual charming self once I identified myself as the caller.

"Hell you want, Cheng?" he said.

I told him about the call to my mother, and my suspicion the call would not have been made if Selena's death had really been a suicide. I added that I thought the call included the other crimes at the Mount Parnassus, too.

"Still think you know more than the pros, don't you," he said.

I let the remark pass, and said nothing, but I could feel the heat building in my neck and face. Thigpen's attitude really rankled. I worked to modulate my tone.

"I just wanted to report this, Detective, seeing as how you're the lead on the closed cases. That's all."

As I contemplated hanging up on him up, I heard Thigpen say, "Watch yourself, Cheng. I still have you in my sights."

With that cryptic remark, he ended the call.

CHAPTER 47

WHEN I WOKE THE NEXT morning, my thoughts focused on Thigpen. I knew I would have to tread carefully with him and heed Harte's warning that I was no match for his former partner.

I walked out to the kitchen and put on a pot of coffee. Afterward, as I passed the answering machine, I noticed the blinking red light and realized I still hadn't listened to my messages. I assumed some or all were from Toula. I decided I would play the messages later, and then call her back if I was right.

Harte called while I was drinking coffee and reading the morning paper. He said he had obtained some supplementary materials that had been placed into the police file concerning the assaults on my mother and Eugenia. He warned me, however, that the new material was not game changing. The case was still classified as closed.

We agreed to meet for lunch to talk generally about all the happenings at the Mount Parnassus. Harte asked if I minded if he brought his daughter along. *Was he kidding?* I thought about how good she looked when I met her last week, so I gladly consented.

We met for sandwiches at *Pot Belly* on the corner of L and 19th. Harte was already there when I arrived, but Clotille was not. Before I could ask if she still planned to join us, Clotille walked in and came over to our table. I hadn't realized until I saw her walk in how disappointed I'd been when I momentarily thought she might not make it to lunch with us.

Harte reintroduced me to his daughter, as if that was necessary, then we all got in line and ordered our lunches. I made a point of sitting across from Clotille when I arrived back at our table. I wanted to be able to look at her throughout lunch without being too obvious.

"Before I forget," Harte said, "here's the other file material we talked about. It's no big deal." He handed me a sealed manila envelope. "Now your file's up to date."

I watched Clotille look from me to her father and back at me again. Our eyes met, and she smiled. I think I blushed.

"Daddy," she said, as she turned again to face Harte, "you promised y'all wouldn't talk business during lunch, you."

She turned and looked back at me. "Daddy just lives for chances to talk shop, Mr. Cheng, ever since he retired." She smiled again at me.

This time I'm sure I blushed.

"Call me Socrates," I said. "We won't talk shop anymore, not if you prefer we don't." I looked over at Harte for his assent. He had a smirk on his face as he stared back at me.

"So, Clotille," I said, turning back to face her, "you're not from DC." I was always good at small talk.

"Oh, no, mercy me," she said, "didn't daddy tell you?" She looked over at Harte, as did I. He looked at Clotille, then at me, raised both eyebrows, and shrugged as if to say, *mea culpa*.

"Haven't gotten around to it yet, Sweetie," Harte said to Clotille.

"I'm from Louisiana, me," she said. She pronounced it with three or four 'o's as in, Loooosiana. "New Iberia on Bayou Têche, to be exact."

I nodded. I looked at Harte, who had a twisted grin on his face, then looked back at Clotille.

"Actually, Clotille, I could tell you're not from around here," I said. "I'm a detective, remember?"

"You mean you noticed Clotille talks funny?" Harte said.

"I mean," I said, "Clotille has a different way of expressing herself than I'm used to hearing in Washington. No offense meant," I added, looking over at Clotille, and directing the last part of my comment directly to her.

"In that case, Mr. Cheng — Ah mean, Socrates — I'll re-introduce mahself."

"I am the happy result of mah daddy's journey with mah natural mama along the primrose path of dalliance a long time ago in a New Orleans whore house.

"I am Harte's illegitimate daughter, me, raised by my Cajun mama until twenty-two years ago when my birth-mama died, and Harte here learned about me and took me in."

She paused, took a breath, and said, "Whew. That was a mouthful, wasn't it?"

"Oh," I said. I was at a loss for words. I'd never heard anything remotely like that since *Gone With the Wind*.

Harte stepped in. "Clotille speaks the truth, Cheng," he said. "Although Clotille's mother frequently told her about me, without using my name, I didn't know about Clotille for the first ten years of her life. When I finally learned about her, Rosie and I decided to spring her from foster care in New Iberia and adopt her as our own daughter. Best damn decision we ever made." He smiled at Clotille.

"Daddy and Rosie, they're mah real parents now," Clotille said. "Ah've lived with them longer than with mah first mama. I even went to court, me, and changed my last name from Berenson to Harte."

"That's very nice," I said. "Thanks for telling me." It was clear Harte and Clotille shared a strong, affectionate bond.

"One other thing, Socrates," Clotille said. "You've been polite. Most people here in Washington ask why Ah talk so funny, why I drop pronouns into the middle and ends of mah sentences, but y'all haven't said nothing about that, you."

"I have to admit I was curious, *me*," I said, emphasizing, both verbally and with a big grin, my contrived inserted pronoun.

Clotille laughed and faked shaking her fist at me. "That's good, you," she said. "Ah like y'all's humor."

"Well," I said, "I think your accent and syntax are cute, refreshing, in fact. I reached over and patted her forearm as I said this.

"What's a sin tax?" Clotille said. She wrinkled-up her forehead. "I'm not like my birth mama in that way."

Ooops, I thought. *I put my foot in my mouth with that one.* I swallowed my emerging smile.

"Syntax," I said, then spelled the word for her, is the use of words and phrases in writing and speech. It means their structure and placement. It's not a tax on sin."

Harte had a huge grin on his face as he stepped in to bail me out.

"Like I said, Rosie and I encouraged Clotille to pay

attention to her Cajun heritage," he said, "including her Cajun speech patterns. We think it's important she knows her roots and preserves them."

I had to admit I'd now formed a new image of Harte. He definitely had gone up several notches in my hierarchy of former members of DC's finest.

"Enough about me," Clotille said. "Tell us about you, Socrates. Ah'll just bet y'all have had an interesting life, you."

I thought about that. I had lived an interesting life, but interesting does not necessarily correlate with positive, with good.

"My life isn't all that interesting," I said, looking at Clotille, smiling. I turned my head and glanced at Harte in time to see him cock one eyebrow. "Perhaps another time I'll bore you with some details of my life. Not today."

I decided then and there I wanted to see this woman again, but without Harte present.

CHAPTER 48

A FTER PANOS' SECOND TELEPHONE ENCOUNTER with
the HELLENE Gallery, he sat in his swivel chair in the
center of the Treasure Room and thought about the
artifacts arrayed along three walls surrounding him. If the
remaining six objects were fakes, then he had to assume *The
Mourning Woman*, too, was a fake, not stolen art as he had
been led to believe. Certainly his research concerning her
hadn't eliminated the possibility she was bogus.

He mulled this over. In a sense, he had to admire the
Theodoros brothers for their cleverness and temerity in
telling him that *The Mourning Woman* was stolen. If Panos
believed this, he would abide by his agreement not to show
her to anyone, thereby reducing the likelihood someone
would recognize her for the fraud she was. And, too, under
that scenario, were Panos somehow to learn she was not
stolen, but was a fake, as he now suspected, he would be less
likely to report this to the police because to do so would be
tantamount to admitting his participation in a conspiracy to
traffic in stolen antiquities.

The concept was foolproof. The Theodoros brothers were
protected whether or not Panos discovered the swindle.

Or were they?

If they believed that, they didn't know Panos.

Panos passed the next two hours futilely researching *The Mourning Woman*'s provenance using the Internet. Afterword, he reentered his vault and walked over to the statuette. He stared at her briefly, then picked her up and examined her. He shook his head.

Why can't I find out anything about you? he said, silently. *Are you genuine, but stolen, as Milos and Aristides said, or are you, too, a fraud inflicted on me?*

In the end, it wouldn't matter what the answers to his questions might be or if he never even learned the answers. Panos could not accept uncertainty.

Krimá — What a pity, he thought.

CHAPTER 49

I LEFT HARTE AND CLOTILLE AFTER lunch, and walked directly home. I was anxious to read the new material Harte had given me. As I walked into my condo, I again noticed the answering machine's rapidly blinking message light. I went into the kitchen and opened a Coke, returned to the living room, and pressed the Play Messages button.

The first message, as I expected, was from Toula.

"Hi, Socrates. It's me. I have a nice unopened bottle of Retsina with our name on it if you want to get together tonight. Call me."

I erased the message and hit the Play Messages button again.

"Hi. It's me again. Guess you didn't have time to return my call from yesterday. My offer still stands. Call me."

I pushed the erase button again, then the Play Messages button once more.

"Listen, Socrates. I don't know why you're ignoring me, but I don't like it. Pick up your damn phone and call me."

I deleted the message, then played the next one.

"Damn you, Socrates. Who the hell do you think you are? You're happy to return my call when you want me to get you off, but not otherwise. You better call me soon."

The red light blinked slowly now. Only one message left. I went to the kitchen, made a cup of green tea, and returned to listen to the last message.

"Grow yourself a pair of balls, Socrates. If you don't want to see me, return my call and tell me. You owe me at least that much, you piece of shit." She slammed down the phone.

Toula was right. I should call her.

———————— ••• ————————

She picked up on the fourth ring. At first, once she realized I was the caller, she was ice cold. I apologized, made a lame excuse, and asked if she still had the Retsina.

"Half of it," she said, "but I can get another bottle. Why?"

As if she didn't know. "I have some work to do this afternoon, but why don't you bring it over tonight," I said.

"You sure you want me?" Her tone had mellowed.

"I called, didn't I."

"I'll see you about 10:30 tonight," she said, and ended the call.

I spent the next few minutes thinking about Clotille. Then I put that aside and got to work.

I reviewed the additional file material Harte had given me. Then I turned back to the original report trying to wade through the bureaucratic mud the cops call Report Speak. When I finished, I called Harte.

"Just finished reading the rest of the file," I said. "I don't see anything in it that will help."

"Told you it was no big deal."

"I'm worried the assault cases won't get solved," I said.

"Probably won't, Cheng. Like I said, the cases are closed."

CHAPTER 50

AFTER HARTE RANG OFF, I made myself a cup of tea, carried it to my reading chair, and sat there for twenty minutes mulling over the implications of his statement. My mother called at 3:00.

"I'm glad I caught you at home, Socrates," she said, before I could say, Hello.

"You don't know I'm at home," I said. "You called me on my cellphone this time, just like I asked. I could be anywhere."

"Don't be fresh with your mother," she said. "You're at home."

"Sorry. What's up?"

"I'm going to the meeting of the support group tonight. Eugenia will be there. We thought you might like to come with us."

I thought about my plans with Toula for later tonight. I could probably do both, but didn't want to take a chance something might come up at the meeting to make me have to cancel with Toula. I was just getting back in the groove of having good sex, and didn't want to mess it up by pissing her off.

"Can't, Ma, not tonight. I already have plans. Maybe next time."

Toula knocked on my door at 10:30. I couldn't shake the feeling she had arrived early and stood outside until exactly the time we'd agreed to meet.

She held a bottle of Retsina by its long neck, as if she planned either to hand it to me or whack me with it, depending on how my greeting to her went. I took the safe approach.

"Hi," I said. I smiled big. "You look terrific. Nice dress. Come on in and take it off."

Toula smiled, then giggled like a school girl, and swept right past me into the foyer and on to the living room. I closed the door, then followed her.

She walked over to the dry sink near the bank of windows, and filled two wine glasses with Retsina. All this without yet having uttered one word.

She turned around and walked across the room toward me, a glass of Retsina in each hand. She stopped so close in front of me that if either of us leaned slightly forward, our foreheads would touch. I could feel heat radiating from her body.

I took one of the glasses from her, held it up in front of my mouth as if I was about to lip it, and said, "*Náse kalá*" — Cheers."

Toula looked into my eyes and said, "Enough small talk. Let's do it."

That's my kind of woman, I thought, then nodded as I took a long pull on the wine and followed her to the bedroom.

Toula and I returned to the living room a little after Midnight. I poured the last of the Retsina for us and sat down on the couch next to her. She sat in the corner facing me.

She again wore my white terrycloth robe, this time with nothing under it. Most of her important body parts showed. I was struck by the contrast between the white robe, her crow-black hair, and her black eye patch.

We sat silently at first, content to drink our way to the bottom of the Retsina glasses, while we basked in the redolent musk of our spent bodies.

After a while, Toula said, "I don't know why you refused to return my calls. What did I ever do to you to make you treat me so bad?"

"I had work priorities."

"I thought you liked me," she said.

"It had nothing to do with me not liking you. We agreed our arrangement meant no ties, no strings. That's the beauty of it."

"The beauty of it," Toula said, "is you can get your rocks off whenever you want."

She was right of course. That was the beauty of our arrangement, but for both of us, not just for me.

"Are you unhappy with our arrangement?" I asked. "I didn't think you were suffering from it." *I knew this had been too good to last,* I thought.

At first Toula had been undemanding, exactly as we'd agreed we would be. There were no requirements that we spend time together when we weren't in bed. No need for chatty telephone calls late at night; no demands whatsoever. Just uninhibited, mutually satisfying sex. Friends with benefits. But lately, especially if I wasn't available when she called me, Toula became petulant, saying she made no demands on me even as she peevishly demanded my prompt response to her calls.

I looked away to gather my thoughts, then turned to face her. "Wait a minute, Toula," I said, "you called me this week, not the other way around. I'm not the one who initiated being bedded."

"You bastard," she said. "I thought you were different. I should've known."

I said nothing. I wanted to see where this would go, how far she would push it.

Suddenly she screamed, "Stop trying to control me!" Her face had twisted almost beyond recognition. "I don't have to do what you want, be at your beck and call whenever you want me. You're no better than all the others."

"The others?" I asked, deliberately speaking softly. "You've had this arrangement often?"

"No, you prick. I don't mean getting laid. I'm talking about the other men who always tried to control me, always made me do what they wanted, when they wanted it. Just like you, like my ex-husband, like my asshole divorce lawyer. Just like my boss and the other men at his store. You're all bastards, trying to control me."

As I listened to her recite her collection of injustices that had been perpetrated against her, I realized there was nothing I could say that would appease her. I wasn't even sure I wanted to appease her. I was tiring of having Toula scrutinize everything I said or did, looking for some hint she was right about me and all the other male dispensers of iniquities against her, confirming her mistrust and doubt about all of us, including me.

I realized that Toula's continuous scrutiny of my actions and motives created a self-fulfilling prophesy: the more she became suspicious or hostile or angry toward me, the more she questioned my motives. And the more she attributed her actions and words to me, the more I became secretive and hostile and angry, confirming her suspicions.

The irony of this was that to anyone observing Toula, she appeared to be normal and well-integrated within her own cosmos. Toula's outward personality was intact. Her emotions appeared to be intact. But inside, Toula was entirely different, a bubbling cauldron of anger and distrust.

I decided the time had come to ease Toula out of my life even though our special arrangement had barely gotten off the ground. I would follow the First Rule of Holes: When you're in one, stop digging. I would have to return to the old fashioned, tried and true, single man's method of having sex — which meant hardly ever — but the trade-off would be worth it for the peace of mind I'd have.

"It's getting late," I said, speaking softly. "I have a full day tomorrow. You probably should go."

"If you want me to leave, just come out and say so. Don't bullshit me like everybody else. Don't act like your having me leave for my own good."

She paused as if waiting for me to deny her accusations. When I did not, she said, "You're an ass, Socrates. Don't expect me to come around again when you're horny. You really blew it, you fool."

I didn't say anything. I didn't want to provoke her any more than she already was, but my silence seemed to fuel her anger.

She stomped off to the bathroom and loudly locked the door behind her.

I poured myself a Scotch and waited in the living room while Toula dressed in the bedroom. After ten minutes, she rushed from the bedroom, past the living room, into the foyer, sounding all the way like an angry, recalcitrant child banging its feet. She never said a word to me or even acknowledged my presence as I followed her to the edge of the foyer. I didn't exist for Toula at that moment. Or so I thought.

She opened the front door, then turned back toward me. Her face was contorted and flushed. She looked briefly into my eyes, then turned again to face the door. She took a step to leave, but stopped and looked down at the narrow sidetable that stood along the length of the foyer wall. She leaned forward and, with one swift gesture, used her forearm to sweep everything from the top of the table, causing it all to crash to the floor. Then she left, slamming the door behind her.

I was left with my mouth wide open, looking down at the dozens of shards that once had been part of my father's most prized possessions — a *Jia Jing* period ginger jar and other period Chinese ceramics. All smashed beyond repair.

I balled my fists in anger, sucked in a deep breath, and groaned it out in despair. I looked down at the pieces of broken memories. *At least,* I thought, foolishly as it would turn out, *Toula's out of my life.*

CHAPTER 51

P ANOS FINISHED STRIPPING HIS MONTHLY stipend from his clients' accounts and closed the ledger.

His decision early on to use a hacker-proof hardcopy ledger instead of a vulnerable computer program to maintain his clients' accounts was a stroke of incalculable, laughable irony. Who would have thought that he, of all people, trained at the Athens state academy to be an expert hacker and COBOL programmer on behalf of the government would now resort to hard copy to maintain the books he kept, books that could not be accessed by anyone using a computer.

He poured himself a glass of Metaxa, then jumped a cigarette from his soft pack to his lips, and fired it up. His take from his clients this month had been smaller than usual, a reflection, he assumed, of the still-struggling economy. *No problem*, he thought. *He'd made up his losses by selling his clients' personal information to hackers and to others who engaged in identity theft.*

He finished his drink and stubbed out his smoke in a crystal ashtray. He'd been thinking a lot these past two days about the Theodoros brothers and the scheme they'd been running on him.

It was not in his makeup for Panos to consider the

possibility that the brothers might have made an honest mistake with the *Plato Krater* or that the brothers, themselves, might have been victimized by some grifter when they acquired the artifact. There was no room in Panos' universe for honest mistakes by other people. *After all,* he thought, *he would gladly defraud the brothers if he could. Why should he think they would act any differently toward him?*

For days now, Panos had considered how he would exact his revenge on Aristides and Milos. At first he considered hiring someone to kill them, but decided that would be a waste of a good opportunity for him to vicariously enjoy the sweet, succulent taste of revenge as he watched them suffer. *He could always arrange for their assassinations later,* he decided.

CHAPTER 52

TOULA WAS AT IT AGAIN. She kept calling me even though I didn't pick up since I was able to use CallerID to identify her each time as the caller. I also didn't return her increasingly strident voicemail messages. The woman was wearing me out.

The next time Toula called I did pick up.

"It's about time you took my call," she said. "I know you've been avoiding me, checking your CallerID."

What could I say? She was right, so I said nothing.

"I want to come over."

"That's fine," I said. My voice didn't betray my mixed feelings. "Anything special going on?" I asked.

"You'll see," she said, and laughed.

I wasn't sure I liked the sound of that.

Twenty minutes later we were in bed, and all seemed right with the world. Toula's intensity during our coupling was excessive, aggressive, and, to put it mildly, wonderful. I guess that's what she meant by something special. I hoped that's what she'd meant.

Later that evening, after we'd showered together and

dressed, we went to *Stan's Restaurant and Lounge*, a pub located one level below the ground where L Street and Vermont Avenue come together, a few blocks from the White House. *Stan's* is known for drinks poured to the lip of the glass, with a free beer back on the side. *Stan's* was a true neighborhood bar, one of the few still found in the Northwest quadrant of Washington.

The tender behind the stick when we walked in was a woman named Danika. She and I used to date occasionally at the front end of the '80s. She either didn't recognize me or chose to ignore me. Either way was all right with me while I was with Toula.

I looked around for an empty table. I saw a table for two in a dark corner. We settled at it.

"I don't remember my father," Toula said, without so much as a preamble, "except what my mother told us when my brother and I were little."

I wondered why she'd raised this out of the blue and where she was going with it, but I didn't ask.

"He was a great man, an important man, my father. Did you know he worked for King Alexander until the Colonels took over? Then he went along with the Colonels for the good of our country. He didn't care who was in power. He did his job. That's the sign of a great patriot."

That's one way of looking at it, I thought. My curiosity continued as to why she'd raised this in the first place and where she planned to take it.

"I noticed a shrine for your father in your home, in your mother's home," I said. "That's unusual."

"No it's not," Toula said, a little too quickly and sharply for my taste, as if she'd been anticipating some negative comment from me. "Not if you love and respect your parent. What's wrong with showing respect to your father who gave his life for his country?"

"How'd your father die," I asked, trying to reverse the hostile turn the conversation had taken.

"He was murdered by the democratic government that overthrew the Colonels. They said he was a war criminal."

"Oh," I said. That was the first I'd heard that. I sure was glad I asked. "I'm sorry. I didn't know."

"When the Colonels fell, the group who took over arrested him and put him on trial. They condemned him for organizing the notorious April 21 round-up of 10,000 people who had been traitors to Greece. He died in prison of a broken heart," Toula said.

I nodded. What could I say? It seemed to me Toula was a bit too long-in-the-tooth to be talking about her father with such adoration and reverence after all these years.

She must have read my mind, my face or my body language because she said, "Do you think I'm weird because I love my father so much?"

"That doesn't make you weird."

I wondered if Toula even remembered her father or was reacting to the memory of him implanted by Arête. I didn't say this, of course. Instead, I said, "I admire my father, too."

"It's not the same," she said. "Men like my father come along only once in a lifetime. Such men are never appreciated for their greatness."

Toula drained her drink, put the empty glass down on the table, and signaled for another.

"Do you think it's strange for me to admire him so much?" she asked again.

Before I could respond, she said, "Is that why you've been avoiding me?"

The woman is certifiable, I thought.

"Why don't you say something?" she said, spitting out her words in rapid fire. "Do you think I'm strange because I revere my father? Go ahead, say it, if that's what you think. I don't care. He was a great man, whatever you think."

"I don't want to argue with you, Toula," I said quietly. "I'm just listening, is all."

"Then say what you think. You owe me that much."

I took a deep breath and let it slowly seep out. Time to wrap this up and cut my losses, once and for all. I had learned my lesson.

"Okay," I said. "If you really want to know, I don't think anything about it, one way or the other. Like I said, I was just listening. No need to argue about it."

"Is that because you don't think what I said was important enough to argue about?" She shook her head and narrowed her eyes. "I know your type, Socrates. You pretend to listen and agree, but behind that façade you say to yourself, "What a fool." You think I don't know?"

"Frankly, Toula," I said, "I don't know what I'm thinking half the time you're talking. You're either lecturing me or accusing me of something I didn't think or do, or testing and challenging what I said or didn't say, always looking for some dark meaning. The fact is, you're wearing me out." I kept my voice soft and non-threatening, hoping that might avoid an outburst by her.

"You're jealous of my father, so you want to control me," she said. She laughed a terse laugh that had no mirth in it. It really creeped me out.

"Do you think you're the first man who tried that with me?" She laughed again. "I've got your number, Socrates. You're as easy to see through as anyone I've ever met."

"I think it's time to call it a night," I said. I signaled the waitress for our bill.

Toula put her half-full glass down on the table. She looked into my eyes the whole time. "Let's go back to your place for a little while," she said, as she smiled and fluttered her eye lashes. There was no trace of anger in her voice now. It was as if the past five minutes hadn't occurred.

"That's not a good idea," I said. "Let's split here. I'll put you in a cab and call you tomorrow."

"No you won't, you sonofabitch, you won't call," she said. Her voice was loud enough now to turn heads. I noticed Danika watching us from behind the stick.

Toula's voice increased in volume. "You think you can have sex with me, then ditch me, you've got another thing coming."

I felt my face turn warm.

Toula stood and grabbed her purse. "You don't get rid of me that easily. No one does." With that, she picked up her glass and threw her drink in my face, covering me with watered-down Scotch. Then she turned and marched out of the bar.

I took my time gathering my composure. I wiped myself with napkins brought over by our waitress, then picked up the check and looked at it. I put it down on the table and left twenty on twelve, the excess tip being my compensation for the unsolicited and probably unwelcomed entertainment we'd provided. As I was leaving, I glanced over at the bar and saw Danika staring at me. She raised her eyebrows when our eyes met and cocked her head, calling me over. I walked to the bar.

"That the little woman?" Danika said. She smiled.

I shook my head. "Uh, uh. Still not married," I said. "How are you? It's been a long time. You still look good."

I first met Danika when she was struggling to make it as a professional artist. She needed a lawyer to negotiate a license agreement for a logo she had created for one of Washington's syndicated television shows. A mutual friend had put us together. I completed the legal work she needed, then a little later on we dated a few times. Neither of us particularly enjoyed the company of the other so we parted amicably.

CHAPTER 53

DECIDED TO ATTEND THE NEXT support group meeting with my mother and Eugenia. It seemed important to them that I do this.

I arrived a few minutes early and stepped onto the elevator to ride up to the condominium's meeting room. My mother said she would meet me there because she'd be helping set up chairs.

I stepped onto the elevator and looked around. The cab was empty except for its operator.

"Good afternoon, Nikos," I said.

"Meeting room?" he said.

"That's it," I said.

Nikos made a snorting sound.

"What?" I said.

Nikos didn't respond except to shake his head. "Eighth floor," he said, when we arrived there.

———————————————

I entered the meeting room and looked around. I saw my mother across the room standing with Eugenia and two women I didn't recognize.

I quickly counted thirty-four people in attendance, not

including me. Everyone seemed to be late middle aged or elderly. They were standing around in small groups talking and smoking cigarettes, waiting for the meeting to be called to order.

Folding chairs had been set up in a large circle. It looked like it had been organized for an AA or drug recovery group meeting.

I crossed the room to my mother. She looked up and smiled as I approached.

"I'm glad you're here, Socrates. We need to talk before the meeting starts. I'll get Eugenia. Wait here."

She left before I could say anything. Within a minute, she returned with Eugenia following close behind.

"Let's go to the hallway," my mother said. "Eugenia wants to say something to you."

I followed them out into the hallway. I was curious about what Eugenia would say to me in the hallway that she wouldn't or couldn't say to me privately in the meeting room.

"Eugenia had a dream this morning," my mother said, "I mean a vision. Tell him, Eugenia."

Eugenia seemed uncomfortable. I wondered if this reflected her response to her vision or her reaction to my mother pushing her to tell me about it.

"I prefer not to talk about it," Eugenia said, facing my mother first, then turning to look at me. "Telling you will not change anything."

"Does it affect my mother or me?" I asked. "Will you tell me that much?"

"I have nothing more to say," Eugenia said. She furtively glanced at my mother.

"Then I'll tell," my mother said. "Socrates should know."

Eugenia slowly shook her head, but made no move to quiet my mother.

"Eugenia saw a dead woman, someone she knows."

That wasn't what I expected. "Who was the woman?" I asked, turning to face Eugenia.

My mother answered for her. "She won't tell me."

I looked at Eugenia, then back at my mother. "Will you leave us alone for a few minutes?" I said to my mother. "I'd like to talk with Eugenia alone."

My mother frowned, opened her mouth to say something to me, then turned her head away and looked at Eugenia. "I'll be in the meeting room if you need me." She threw me the *we'll settle this later* look I'd hated ever since I was a teenager.

"What's going on, Eugenia," I said, when we were alone. "Why won't you tell me who you saw in your vision? Was it you again?"

Eugenia stared at me, but didn't answer.

"If telling me won't change anything, then how can it hurt to tell me?"

Eugenia still remained silent.

"Was it my mother?" I asked.

"I have to go into the meeting now," she said, and walked away without another word.

CHAPTER 54

R ALPH HARTE AND CLOTILLE HAD developed the practice of meeting once each week for lunch now that Harte was retired. Rosie occasionally joined them, but not too often. At her suggestion, this time was set aside for father/daughter bonding. Harte and Clotille didn't object.

They varied their meeting places, depending on their moods. Today, they sat in a restaurant in Chinatown, *The Golden Dragon*, owned by a local Triad leader named Li Bing-fa, and ordered dishes to share.

"Tell me about your friend, Socrates," Clotille said. "What's he like, him?"

"He's not my friend. I knew him from years before, from the Job. Why do you wanna know?"

"He's interesting, " Clotille said, "and good looking, him." She blushed.

"Stay away from him, Clotille. You'll be better off."

"Why do you say that, you?"

"People around Cheng have a way of turning up dead."

Clotille took a mouthful of food she's selected from the dim sum offering, and stared across the restaurant while she chewed, as if trying to make sense out of what her father had just said. She shook her head sharply once and turned back to face Harte. She put down her chop sticks.

"Ah don't see it. What are y'all talking about?"

Harte sighed. He put down his chop sticks and wiped his mouth with his napkin. "Okay, if you really wanna know, here's what I'm saying about Cheng."

He signaled the waiter, then pointed to the pot of tea and made a circular motion over it with his finger.

"I met Cheng when I was investigating that burglary at a Chinese art gallery in Georgetown. He got involved as an amateur PI to help his future father-in-law, a Triad crime boss living in Chinatown, the owner of this restaurant we're in right now, matter of fact."

Clotille's eyes widened. "He married into a Chinese Triad? Ah thought he was single, him. Ah didn't know—"

"No. He is single. Let me finish," Harte said. He gently patted her hand and smiled. "Down girl."

Clotille smiled back. "Ah'm sorry. Go on, you." She blushed again.

"He was involved with a woman named Jade Li. She was popped before the case was all over. A couple other people were also wacked." Harte paused and sipped his tea.

"I'll say this for Cheng," he said. "He solved the case. Thigpen and I, we weren't doing squat on it, going nowhere fast. But the price Cheng paid to solve it was high."

"That doesn't sound like he did bad," Clotille said. "It sounds to me like Socrates did good, him."

Harte wagged his head. He knew he was fighting a losing battle against Clotille's young, nature-programmed hormones.

"Okay, you win," he said, holding up both palms in

surrender. "Cheng's a saint." He smiled and lobbed a kiss across the table.

"Mama's right," Clotille said, "you can be unnecessarily sarcastic sometimes, even when you're trying to be nice, you. But Ah love you anyway." She took a sip of her tea, then put down the cup, and asked, "Does Socrates seem the same now as before when y'all knew him before?"

Harte wrinkled his forehead as he thought about Clotille's question. "A little older, as he should be. A little more mature, as he should be, too, but also harder, not as friendly as before. He has an edge now I don't remember from before." Harte paused to consider his next statement. "He doesn't seem as naïve and innocent as before."

Clotille smiled from one corner of her mouth.

"He's cynical now," Harte added, "probably jaded from his experience back then. I don't want you around him. It's too risky. As I said, people around Cheng have a way of turning up dead."

Clotille pushed her plate away from her. She looked into Harte's eyes and smiled.

"Interesting, him," she said, then smiled once again.

CHAPTER 55

I T WAS TIME FOR ME to get back to the investigation.

But the investigation of which crime? The break-ins at Eugenia's home? *If there had been any other than Selena's entry*, I thought. The death of Selena? *If it wasn't suicide*. The assault on my mother and Eugenia? *Definitely that one, at the very least*.

Were they all crimes? The police didn't think so.

Were these events even tied together? I thought so, my gut told me they were, but I didn't have any evidence yet to support my gut.

I decided I had to make certain assumptions to avoid the *chicken or egg* conundrum. I would treat all these events as if they were crimes and deal with them as if they were one, or, at least, as if they were related by some as yet undetermined nexus.

The next step in my investigation would be to figure out who had a motive to break into Eugenia's home, murder Selena, and assault my mother and Eugenia.

The *chicken or egg* quandary soon reared its ugly head in spite of my efforts to avoid it: I would likely know *who* committed the crimes as soon as I knew *why* they'd committed the crimes; And, I would know *why*, as soon as I figured out *who*.

I hadn't taken away much information from the physical crime scenes (my walk around Eugenia's apartment on several occasions; the room in Eugenia's apartment where Selena died, or, my mother's apartment after she and Eugenia had been assaulted) nor had I learned much from the police report Harte obtained for me. For now, I would not be able to rely on physical evidence to guide my investigation. I would have to focus on possible culprits, without the benefit of forensics.

I began by listing those people I was familiar with at the condo building. There was Selena's son, George; there was the old man named Panos; there was Toula; and, there was Toula's mother, Arête. None of these people seemed to be a good candidate for perpetrator. It was obvious I didn't know many people in the building. I also realized I was assuming the villain was someone who lived at the Mount Parnassus, not someone from elsewhere I hadn't met.

I thought about who else lived in the building I hadn't yet considered. It came to me there was someone who had a reason to be angry with Selena, with Eugenia, and with my mother, although I'd forgotten about him. The Tweaker. The sleazebag who lived below Eugenia, and who'd had several noise complaints filed against him by Eugenia and Selena.

Why would I suspect Tweaker of having a motive to harm these women? For one thing, I didn't like him, so, all other things being equal, he fit my criteria for being a suspect: I didn't like the fact he ignored his neighbors' requests to stop making noise; I didn't like the obscenities he'd called Eugenia when I tried to talk to him about her complaints; and, I didn't like the way he physically looked and smelled. And, of course, I didn't have any other suspects at the moment. So, Tweaker would have to do for the time being.

To get started again, as before, I went to the fourth floor and knocked on doors. I wanted to find out what Tweaker's neighbors knew or thought about him.

Over the course of two hours and only a few interviews, since most apartments were empty while their occupants were away from home, I learned very little I didn't already know. I learned Tweaker's real name was Xeno Papadopoulos, and learned that in addition to complaining about the frequent noise coming from his apartment, people also complained about noxious smells coming from there. This was repeated often enough that I noted it as more than an isolated or random comment. I wondered, though, why Eugenia hadn't mentioned the odors when she complained to me about Tweaker's noise problems?

Several of Tweaker's immediate neighbors also mentioned that he frequently paced the hallway outside his apartment for hours at a time, at all hours of the night when his elderly neighbors (who required little sleep) were awake to hear him. They also said that the floor of his living room (the only room in his apartment neighbors could see from the hallway) was littered with candy bar wrappers. Another neighbor mentioned what I had observed when I stood outside his door, that he reeked from body odor and looked like the living dead, having angry, swollen bumps on his face, hair like matted straw, eyes that blinked without cessation, black teeth, and scabrous skin.

After my last interview, I left the Mount Parnassus and headed over to my office to use my computer to check out Tweaker. I would mine several databases I subscribed to. I wanted to learn if he owned the condo unit he was living in or, if not, who his landlord was. I also wanted to see if he had a criminal record, and where he'd worked and lived during the previous ten years or so.

Tweaker owned the condo unit he lived in. According to the Office of the Recorder of Deeds, Xeno Papadopoulos had inherited the apartment under the Last Will and Testament of Athena Papadopoulos. I assumed Athena was Tweaker's mother. Why else would anyone leave him property? The fact that he owned his condo unit would explain why he might have thought he could ignore his neighbors' complaints and not have to worry about being evicted by his landlord.

In the last twelve years, Tweaker had lived in Washington, DC, Salisbury, Maryland, Philadelphia, New York City, and Charleston, South Carolina. I didn't see any pattern among the cities he'd lived in, so I moved on.

My database search for criminal records proved more fruitful. Tweaker had been arrested twice for DUI violations, once eight years ago in Salisbury, Maryland, and once in Huntsville, Alabama. He'd served four months in lockup for the Salisbury conviction, but no time for the Huntsville conviction. However, there was a fugitive warrant out for him from Huntsville because he had jumped probation, a six months' condition of not serving jail time.

More research disclosed that Tweaker also had been arrested on other occasions although none resulted in jail time. Those charges were the result of his possession of marijuana, loitering, driving without a license, and, most serious of all, attempted assault and battery.

I decided I'd keep my discovery about the fugitive warrant to myself for now. If Tweaker turned out to be implicated in the crimes here at the condo, the authorities would discover the outstanding warrant themselves. If Tweaker was not implicated, but continued to disturb his neighbors, I'd drop the dime on him. If he was not involved with the crimes at the Mount Parnassus, and if he became a better neighbor, I'd forget I knew about his fugitive status. It was all up to him.

CHAPTER 56

P ANOS DECIDED THAT HIS REVENGE against the Theodoros brothers would be severe, prolonged, visible to them (but unfathomable as to the reason for its being), and unrelenting in its total destruction of their lives as they've known their lives to be.

Just thinking about this brought a rare, unfeigned smile to Panos.

He poured another Ouzo and booted up his computer. He couldn't stop smiling. He felt like a school kid about to play a serious prank on his teacher.

Panos spent the next four hours implementing his revenge. First, he hacked into the Experian, Equifax and TransUnion databases. When he finished with those repositories of our lives, he entered the FBI's trusted network and roamed around the National Crime Information Center database. He made some record changes among the millions of records, and finally signed off, totally undetected in his afternoon's adventure.

The only part of the whole scenario Panos regretted was that he had once again arrived back to his original decision to no longer collect antiquities.

CHAPTER 57

I WAS SITTING IN MY LIVING room reading when my landline rang. I looked at the CallerID and debated letting it go to voicemail, but then decided to face up to the call.

"Hello, Toula," I said. "I'm surprised to hear from you."

I might as well have said nothing for all the effect my statement had.

"How about I come over tonight to talk and catch-up?" she said.

"It's not a good idea," I said. "I thought we resolved that."

Was I really suppose to believe she just wanted to talk as she now said? Was I really to believe she wasn't trying to rekindle a dead paradigm?

"Please," she said. "Just talk, nothing else."

I knew I shouldn't agree, but I did.

"If talk is all you want, then all right," I said. I was skeptical, but thought I might be better off in the long run if I humored her.

Toula arrived twenty minutes later.

I no sooner opened and closed the door, then turned to face her, when she was all over me, kissing my lips, neck and cheek; pressing provocatively against me; holding me in a vice-like grip so I could not pull away.

"Come with me," she said, as she moved away, took my hand, and started to lead me toward my bedroom.

I dug in my heals and shook my head.

Toula stopped pulling and turned back toward me.

"What's the matter?" she said. "We can enjoy ourselves first, then talk all you want."

I shook my head again. "Not a good play," I said. "If you want to talk, fine, but no sex."

"Fine, we'll talk," she said, in a voice that could chill out an ember. "Your loss."

We went into the living room and settled on opposite ends of the sofa, facing one another. I felt awkward as I twisted to face her, so I stood up and headed to the dry sink to pour myself a glass of Zinfandel.

"What can I fix you?" I asked.

I handed her the glass of wine she asked for, then settled into a chair facing the couch. I felt safer having the coffee table between us.

"I've been thinking," she said, "I don't want us to end. We have something special here."

"No," I said, "it's over for us. It's best that way. We had an understanding going into this. Now it's time."

I watched Toula's expression morph from that of a cajoling young girl to that of a puzzled, then furious adult.

"What's the problem, Socrates. Didn't you like the sex?"

"It's not that," I said. "The sex was great." I decided to lie now. "But it was becoming more than just sex for me." *It was becoming fear*, I thought, but I wouldn't tell her that. "I was beginning to develop feelings for you." *Negative feelings.*

"That wasn't supposed to be part of our arrangement. I'm not ready for that."

"So go with it," she said. "You're not a child. Plans change."

"I'm not ready, not after my situation a few years ago," I said.

Toula stood up. "You've got to be kidding," she said. "You want to give up the greatest sex you've ever had and ever will have just because you're beginning to be attracted to me?"

I shrugged. "It's not really that simple, but I'm afraid so," I said.

"You're really calling it off?" she said, her tone reflecting her incredulity.

I nodded. I was amazed at Toula's capacity to ignore facts to suit her inner truth. It was as if I'd never called our arrangement off a month ago.

"Don't do it," she said, speaking softly, as she stepped over to me.

She put her arms around my waist and moved in close. I strained to keep from taking her in my arms.

"Hold me," she said. "It's the least you can do."

I shook my head and lifted her hands away from my waist. Then I stepped away.

"Let's do it one more time, something to remember later on," she said.

"No," I said. "There's no later on for us. You should go."

Toula narrowed her eyes and became rigid.

"Okay, Socrates, have it your way. You'll be sorry, that much I promise you." She strode toward the foyer, then stopped and faced me again.

"You think you can take advantage of me, then just shut

me out of your life when it's convenient for you. Well, you're a fool if you think that. Nobody messes with me that way. Not you, not anyone."

CHAPTER 58

MILOS THEODOROS LOOKED ACROSS THE dinner table at his date for the evening. He loved the perquisite's of his new wealth — the expensive meals at four-star Washington restaurants, the fine wines he did not appreciate, but knew were good because of their cost, and the beautiful women he dated and bedded now, women who had never given him the time of day before he'd publicly demonstrated his financial *bona fides*.

Milos blew a kiss across the table to his dinner companion, then raised his arm and caught the waiter's attention. He made a writing motion with his hand to signal for the check, read over the check when the waiter brought it, and blanched when he saw its bottom line. The meal was outrageously pricey, he decided, but definitely worth the cost in order for him to have his way with his companion.

He placed his VISA card in the folding leather case with the check, and waited while the waiter disappeared into the back of the restaurant to process the charge.

When the waiter returned a few minutes later, Milos reached out to retrieve his plastic and the credit slip, but was met with a cold stare.

The waiter stepped in close to Milos, pulled the leather

case holding Milos' card close to his chest, and leaned over to whisper into Milos' ear. He spoke softly enough to suggest he was concerned to protect his customer's privacy, but loudly enough so everyone in the immediate vicinity would know that Milos' credit card had been rejected.

"I'm sorry, Sir," the waiter said, "there's a slight problem."

"A problem?" Milos said, speaking in a louder than normal voice, "What problem?"

"Your card is not going through. Do you have another?"

"That's nuts," Milos said. "It's a mistake. Put it through again."

"There's no mistake, Sir. I tried three times." He handed the card to Milos.

Milos handed over his MasterCard, and sulked while the waiter headed to the backroom to resubmit the charge.

The waiter returned within a minute. This time he had a scowl on his face. He shook his head as he closed in on Milos. He made no effort to speak softly.

"Sorry, again, Sir, but—"

Milos cut him off. "This is bullshit. My cards are all paid up current. You're not putting them through right or something." He looked hard at the waiter, and said, "Try the God-damned card again, and do it right this time."

Heads turned to see who was arguing with the waiter.

"Get it done," Milos said.

Twenty minutes later, on the drive back to his 6,000-square foot McLean, Virginia, house, Milos said to the quiet woman sitting to his right, "I don't understand it, the cards are both good." He paused and tried to smile at his sullen companion. "Lucky for us you had your VISA card with you," he said.

"Sure it is," the woman said, her sarcasm wrapping itself around her words and hovering over the car. "Lucky for us."

"I'll pay you back as soon as we see an ATM. I'm watching for one."

A few minutes later, Milos stood at the cash machine outside the Wells Fargo Bank branch on Route 123, and stared in horror at the message on the machine's screen. The ATM had twice rejected his debit card before it, after Milos' third attempt, swallowed his card and advised Milos to talk to a bank officer during regular business hours if he wanted his card returned.

"Hell's going on?" Milos said to no one. He knew he had approximately $21,000 in his checking account, yet the screen showed his balance to be zero, and informed Milos that he was attempting to complete a transaction using a debit card that had previously been canceled, a federal felony.

Milos looked at his dinner companion who stood next to him at the ATM. She had one hand on her cocked hip and a skeptical frown on her face.

"What's happening to me?" Milos said to no one in particular as he stared at the screen. "I didn't cancel my debit card. I have plenty of money in this account."

The woman rolled her eyes.

Milos and his dinner companion, whose mood had turned noticeably frigid, were two blocks from his home when Milos looked in his rear view mirror and saw the flashing red lights behind him.

"Jesus, now what?" he muttered, as he pulled to the curb and lowered his window.

"What's the problem, Officer?"

The policeman looked through the rear driver's-side window at the back seat and floor area of Milos' car; he turned back and looked at the woman accompanying Milos; he gave the front floor the once over; then he turned his attention back to Milos.

"May I have your license and registration, Sir," he said, in a tone that left no doubt this was not a request. "Have you had anything to drink tonight?"

Milos admitted to drinking wine at dinner, described two glasses as his total intake, and reached into his suit jacket to retrieve his wallet. He handed the two documents to the officer.

"Stay in your vehicle, Sir, and wait," the policeman said, as he turned away and walked back to his patrol car.

Milos looked over at the woman riding shotgun. She stared straight ahead through the windshield. Milos remained quiet.

The policeman returned to Milos' car. He stopped approximately four feet from the driver-side door, placed his right hand on his holstered weapon, and said, "Place both your hands on the top of the steering wheel, Sir."

When Milos complied, the officer said, "Now, step out of the vehicle. Keep your hands where I can see them." He then directed Milos' companion to step out, too.

Milos did as he'd been ordered and assumed the position — legs spread apart, palms on the front fender of the car, and a forward lean to keep him off balance. When the cop finished checking Milos for weapons, he told Milos to straighten up and place his hands behind his back. The officer cuffed Milos, and then frisked and cuffed Milos' dinner companion.

The cops processed Milos at the Fairfax Barracks of the Virginia State Police. They did not hold his evening's companion. After Milos had been fingerprinted and briefly questioned, he was locked in a holding cell to await the arrival of his attorney.

"I don't believe this, Constantine," Milos said to his lawyer. "They won't even tell me why I'm locked-up."

"It's serious, Milos, way beyond my experience. I'm going to bring in a criminal defense attorney to help you," Constantine said.

Milos couldn't believe what his attorney then told him: He was under arrest for driving on a revoked license, driving with no insurance coverage, driving with enough unpaid tickets to fill the empty glove box, and for driving a vehicle that had been reported stolen.

Aristides Theodoros pulled to the side of Reservoir Road in the District when he saw the flashing red and blue lights behind him.

In short order, Aristides found himself being held for arraignment by the MPD, based on outstanding arrest warrants from three towns in western Pennsylvania.

It didn't matter that Aristides did not know what the police were talking about or that he claimed he had never been to the towns in Pennsylvania where he was supposed to have committed crimes. The National Crime Center

Information database did not lie. In fact, according to the database printout, not only was Aristides wanted on three outstanding arrest warrants in Pennsylvania, he also was wanted in New Jersey on a fugitive drug arrest warrant, and by the Feds on a warrant recently obtained by the DEA. In this latter document, Aristides was described as an armed and dangerous drug dealer. The printout also contained the notation, Do not try to apprehend alone.

Aristides knew this was some kind of horrible, Kafka-like mistake, but no one would listen to him.

CHAPTER 59

EUGENIA LEFT THE SUPPORT GROUP and was exhausted by the time she arrived at her front door. The meeting had lasted much longer than usual. She made a mental note to cancel two readings scheduled for the morning so she could sleep in before going for her walk.

She opened the front door, stepped into the foyer, and flicked the light switch on the wall to light the lamp sitting on the hallway's side table. The narrow passageway remained dark.

"*Ach! Ti néa?* — So, what's new?" she muttered.

Because Eugenia always left the lamp's switch set at the *on* position so she could light up the hallway from the wall switch as she entered her apartment, its failure to light indicated to her that the lamp's light bulb, the main source of light for this part of her apartment, had burned out.

Eugenia stumbled through the dark, windowless hallway toward the living room so she could throw the light switch near the living room's entrance, and indirectly illuminate the path to the utility closet just off the parlor, where she kept spare bulbs.

A minute later, Eugenia returned to the hallway lamp, unscrewed the lamp's bulb, and replaced it with a fresh 100 watt bulb. She flicked the wall switch again, but the hallway remained dark. She frowned, then walked over to the lamp and tried its switch. The bulb lighted.

She left the hallway and walked toward the parlor to make her telephone calls to cancel tomorrow's readings when she abruptly stopped and slowly turned back toward the hallway she'd just left.

How was the lamp switched off? she wondered. *I've never done that, not in all the years I've lived here.*

"*Ela Panayia mou!* — Come Virgin Mother, and help me!," she said aloud, suddenly afraid. She crossed herself.

Eugenia's years of living alone in the apartment had fine-tuned her radar to the presence of anyone else. She listened for the sound of an intruder, but heard and felt nothing. After a few minutes, she walked deeper into the parlor, taking quiet, mincing steps. She stopped and again listened, trying to sense the presence of an intruder.

Satisfied she must be mistaken, that no one had entered her apartment and switched off the lamp, Eugenia breathed a sigh of relief and attributed her response to the faulty memory of old age. She flicked the parlor's wall switch, but the room remained dark.

"*Kakómiros* — Ill-fated one," she said, just seconds before she felt a sharp pin-like prick in the back of the base of her neck, just before the sheath of the knitting needle pushed through tissue, sinew, and fat to burst from her throat, just before everything went dark and Eugenia dropped to the floor, no longer the prophet.

I was at home using my computer to pay bills when my mother called.

"I told you Eugenia was in danger, but you wouldn't listen. Now maybe you'll believe me even though it's too late."

"What happened?" I asked. "What're you talking about?"

My mother was speaking so quickly, folding deep sobs into her statements, I was having difficulty following her. I took a deep breath, and hoped my mother was not about to tell me what I knew she was about to say.

"Eugenia's dead. Stabbed in the neck," she said. "Murdered in her apartment."

I felt my breath sucked from me. My stomach twisted into a hard knot.

"I'll be right over," I said, and hung up the phone.

All I could think of as I raced over to the Mount Parnassus was that I had failed Eugenia and therefore failed my mother. Now, I worried I would fail again, this time fail to protect my mother, and keep her from coming to harm?

CHAPTER 60

P ANOS SPENT THE MORNING AGAIN looking through his accumulation of auction catalogues and reference books, then searching the Internet, to find any reference to the theft of *The Mourning Woman* from some museum or private collection. He was willing to start with any reference, however oblique it might be, that might offer him hope that the statuette was stolen, and not a fake, as he suspected. He didn't come across a single reference to *The Mourning Woman*. Yet he wasn't ready to give up on his seductress. She existed for Panos beyond the realm of his decision to abandon the collecting of antiquities.

He walked to the kitchen. He was at a loss how to proceed, but he needed to resolve this, one way or the other.

He poured himself a glass of Mythos birá, took the drink to the living room, and sat down to think this through. He closed his eyes as he sipped his beer. He recalled the old adage: that the absence of evidence wasn't evidence of absence. Somehow, though, given the Theodoros brothers' history with him, this offered him no solace.

It took Panos twenty minutes to decide on his course of action. Although it had risk, he would take *The Mourning Woman* to the Sackler/Freer Galleries at the Smithsonian

Institution. He would take advantage of a benefit the museums offered its members to receive an informal, quick inspection of artifacts, and an informal, non-binding opinion about the objects examined. If all went well, he might learn that the statuette was genuine or fake. The risk was that it might be recognized as a stolen object, in which case he would be forced to explain to the authorities how he'd come into possession of it. It was a risk he was willing to take if it would bring him peace of mind.

Panos worked out a cover story that satisfied him if *The Mourning Woman* was recognized as stolen art, then he called the Freer. He made an appointment to bring *The Mourning Woman* in for examination.

As he left the Freer and walked toward the Smithsonian Metro Station on the National Mall, *The Mourning Woman* safely wrapped in a heavy cloth and lodged in his briefcase, Panos thought about the devastation he'd brought upon the Theodoros brothers' lives. In terms of *The Mourning Woman*, it had been for nothing because he still hadn't resolved the issue of her genuineness, but in terms of how the brothers had previously swindled him, it had been worth it to make them suffer. He smiled.

Lucky for them the museum didn't have any negative information about The Mourning Woman, he thought.

CHAPTER 61

I DIDN'T BOTHER KNOCKING WHEN I arrived at my mother's apartment. I used my key and headed straight for the kitchen. I could hear her sobbing as I approached.

She was sitting at the table with a box of tissues in front of her, and half a dozen or so used tissues scrunched up on the floor. She looked up as I walked in, and dabbed her eyes with the crumpled tissue she held in her hand.

I walked right over to her, put my arm around her shoulders, and squeezed, then kissed the top of her head.

"Are you all right?" I said, as I moved around to the other side of the table and sat down.

She shook her head. "Do I look like I'm all right?"

"What happened?"

My mother said she had last seen and talked to Eugenia the night before at the end of the support group meeting, that they had each gone home instead of having tea together because the meeting had started at 8:30 this time, rather than the usual 6:30, and it was after 11:30 p.m. when it ended.

"Those same two police people, the two detectives you talked to from Selena," she said, "woke me this morning, knocking on my door."

I nodded. "That would be Detective Thigpen and his partner," I said. "What'd they say?"

"They asked about Eugenia last night, the meeting, did anyone argue with her, did she seem upset or act unusual during the meeting?" She blew her nose, then wiped her eyes. "I don't think I helped them although I wish I could have."

"Did they say how she died?"

My mother nodded and repeated what she'd been told.

I decided it was time to deal with another issue.

"I know this isn't a good time," I said, "but we need to talk."

My mother nodded and wrinkled her forehead. "What?"

"I no longer think Selena's death was a suicide, not after the assault on you and Eugenia, and now this," I said.

"I told you Selena was murdered," my mother said.

"The upshot is, I don't feel like I can protect you while you're living here," I said. I waited for some response, but getting none, continued, "I want you to come stay with me until the crimes are solved."

My mother shook her head. "I'm not leaving my home. You just put more effort into solving the murders and assaults, then I'll be all right."

"But, Ma—"

She held up her palm. "There's nothing more to say."

Although I grudgingly accepted that I couldn't convince my mother to leave the Mount Parnassus until the crimes were solved, I didn't easily accept that this meant I would not be able to protect her until then, even though I had said that to my mother.

The problem was I had no idea why Selena and Eugenia had been murdered. I didn't know whether my mother's friendship with them was just a coincidence in terms of the crimes, so that she now was in no danger, or, if she was unknowingly part of whatever had motivated someone to take the two women's lives, that my mother still was at peril.

My mother insisted she wanted to be alone to mourn her friend, so I reluctantly left her and headed to my office.

The first thing I did when I arrived there was call Harte, fill him in on what had happened, and ask him to meet with me. He said, No.

"What's the point?" he said. "You're not going to listen to my advice anyway."

I thought about that. He was correct, of course, but that didn't mean I didn't want his advice so I could consider it before making a decision.

"No reason we can't do it over the phone, right now if you want. I have time," he said.

I reluctantly agreed to the phone meeting although I perform best when dealing face-to-face, when I can see the other person's body language as they said things to me or listened to what I said, when I could adjust to the nuances of their physical tells.

Since Harte seemed unwilling to bend on the point, I explained my concerns about my mother's safety and my inability to protect her as long as she continued to live at the Mount Parnassus.

"As I see it you have two choices, Cheng," Harte said. "Either you say whatever it takes to convince your mother to move in with you, or you accept she won't, relax, and keep out of the cops' way while they do their job."

"That's not very comforting," I said.

"Wasn't intended to be," he said. "It's reality. You prefer I sugarcoat it for you? That won't help you.."

I reluctantly nodded over the cellphone. What could I say to that? Harte was right. But knowing he was right did nothing to ameliorate my concerns. Nothing would do that until the killer — or killers — was brought down.

I asked Harte if he knew anything about the state of the police investigation of Eugenia's killing.

"A little. I've talked with Thigpen. He caught the case."

"And?" I said.

"And it's a straight forward homicide unless the DOA figured out a way to drive a knitting needle through the back of her own neck and out her throat."

I wanted to comment on his use of sarcasm, but didn't since I wanted him to bring me up to date on the investigation.

"Any clues?" I asked?

"Two I know of. Some blood spatter and hair at the scene. The specimens have been sent to the lab to see if they're the DOA's or the perp's. If they're not the DOAs, maybe Thigpen'll get lucky and they'll be in the system. If not, then you know the drill: We'll ask everyone who works or lives in the building to give a DNA elimination sample to see if there's a match. Then we'll get subpoenas for anyone who refuses. The usual exercise."

I heard back from Harte four days later. He said Thigpen had told him that the DNA tests from Eugenia's crime scene had come back. The blood was Eugenia's. The hair was not, and was not in the system. Harte said that the cops would be taking DNA swabs from the building's occupants and employees over the next two or three days.

That night I took my iPod and hooked it into the docking station I'd bought for it. I scrolled to a Lester Young collection I'd recently downloaded from iTunes, poured myself a glass of Retsina, and sat back to listen to the music while I considered my options and next move.

As I saw it, I had only a few choices. I could follow Harte's advice, do nothing to investigate and solve the crimes, and just wait for the police to make an arrest and eliminate any danger to my mother. Or I could move in with my mother since she wouldn't leave the Mount Parnassus, although that would do nothing to render her safe when I was away from the condo. The third choice, the one I settled on, was to ignore Harte's advice and investigate the crimes with new intensity, hoping to resolve them before my mother fell victim to the killer.

I would begin in the morning by calling Detective Thigpen to set up a meeting with him and his partner.

CHAPTER 62

THIGPEN AGREED TO MEET WITH me at the 2D.

The 2D Precinct building on Idaho Avenue looked from the outside exactly as I remembered it from four years ago when Harte had interrogated me there.

The inside entryway had changed. Now there was a metal detector I first had to pass through. The yellowed protective Plexiglas shield, behind which the precinct's sergeant previously had hidden himself, was gone and had been replaced by an old-style elevated desk without any noticeable screening protecting its occupant. What hadn't changed was the fish-eyed stare I received from the sergeant on duty.

He looked old-school. He had grey hair, a florid face, and a bulbous nose mapped with thin blue and red gin veins, and a turkey-neck wattle hanging over his necktie's square knot. He raised his eyes when I walked in, stared hard at me as if he was mentally frisking me, and said nothing. If my previous experience at the 2D was typical, he now would deal with me as if I was a civilian nuisance who had to be tolerated, at best, but also intimidated, if not just for sport, then to remind me whose territory I'd wandered into.

"Good morning, Sergeant," I said. I put on my friendliest smile for his benefit. It was wasted.

He nodded, but still said nothing. He left no doubt he was the alpha dog in our crowd of two.

I have an appointment to see Detective Thigpen. Name's Cheng."

He pointed to three molded plastic chairs across the room. "Wait there," he said.

Ten minutes later a side door marked Employees Only opened and Thigpen beckoned me toward him.

Thigpen stepped aside so I could enter the restricted-area hallway. As I approached him I searched his face hoping to read his mood. I didn't see the usual hostility I'd expected to find there. His mouth was neutral; his eyes flat and dead.

I stepped past him, stopped, and turned back so he could walk by me and lead me to where we were going. He took me to an interview room. His partner was standing there waiting for us. She nodded when our eyes met, but said nothing.

Thigpen motioned me to a chair, then sat in the seat directly across the table from me. His partner settled into the chair at the head of the table.

"You called this meet, Cheng," Thigpen said. "What's up?"

"I'd like your advice on something."

Thigpen didn't react. Although he never moved his head and ostensibly focused all his attention on me, I saw him glance at his partner who responded by slightly shrugging her shoulders. I would have missed it if I hadn't been watching for some tell.

"Here's the situation," I said. Both Thigpen and his partner fixed their eyes on me as if I was about to confess to one of the crimes they were investigating at the Mount Parnassus.

I explained my fears concerning my mother's safety, and her refusal to temporarily move out of the condo. I was careful not to suggest, either with my words or tone, that I was saying, "I told you so," with respect to Serena's death. I wanted Thigpen's help, not his continuing enmity.

Because of our checkered history, I expected Thigpen to respond with some sarcastic remark such as, "What do you want me to do, put my weapon to your mother's head and order her to move in with you?" But that wasn't what happened. Instead, he surprised me by offering compassion I didn't know he was capable of. I guess even he'd had a mother.

"I get your concern, Cheng. What do you think I can say to you to make it better?"

"Will you give me a candid read on the cases so I can realistically judge if my mother's in danger?"

He looked at his partner, shrugged, then looked back at me. "We can do that, but I don't see how it'll help you. It won't make her move out."

"I guess what I need to know for my peace of mind is should I be worried about her safety or does it seem the DOAs were the real objects of the crimes, that my mother was just in the wrong place at the wrong time when she was assaulted with Eugenia Stamos?"

"Don't know," Thigpen said. "There still are too many unanswered questions to say that. We've asked the ME to exhume the Selena dame and reconsider his finding of suicide. Her son's agreed to let us have a second look."

"Good," I said. I realized this was a subtle form of *I told you so* so I changed the subject. "What about the murder of Eugenia Stamos?"

"We struck out with the DNA. None of the occupants or employees at the condo match the crime scene exemplar from the hair."

I nodded. "I want to continue my investigation," I said. "I'll share whatever I find with you, and will keep out of your way."

Thigpen turned his head and looked at his partner, then back at me.

"May I go into Eugenia's apartment or is it still a crime scene?" I asked.

"Be my guest, we're done with it," Thigpen said."

I nodded and started to stand.

"One thing," Thigpen said. "Since you spend so much time at the Mount Parnassus, give us a DNA swab while you're here. It'll eliminate you as a suspect."

That briefly stopped me cold. I paused, then said, "Okay, Detective, no problem. Glad to."

Thigpen nodded, which was fine, but I didn't like his feral smile of old that had returned.

CHAPTER 63

F RIDAY MORNING, MY MOTHER AND I attended Mass held at Saint Sophia for Eugenia, then attended her burial. Notwithstanding my mixed feelings for the woman, I felt bad for her.

After I dropped my mother off at her apartment, I went home, changed clothes, and went for a long-overdue run in Rock Creek Park. I'd just finished showering when my cellphone rang. It was Clotille. With just that call, my day immediately seemed better than I had any right to expect it would be.

She invited me to have lunch with her. We agreed to meet at *Stan's* because it was located within walking distance of the Commodity Futures Trading Commission (CFTC) where Clotille worked as a market analyst.

I offered to pick her up and walk with her to the restaurant, but she declined. She wanted to meet me there. I assumed this reflected southern decorum for single ladies. I didn't press it.

I deliberately arrived early so Clotille wouldn't have to sit alone in a strange bar/restaurant waiting for me. Danika was working the stick again so I parked myself on a bar stool across from her and chatted her up while she cut lemons and limes for the lunch crowd.

I was there only five minutes when Clotille walked up to me, kissed me lightly on the cheek, and introduced herself to Danika.

We settled into a booth on the far side of the room, away from the bar. We sat side-by-side rather than across from one another.

Clotille looked beautiful. She was wearing a dark green A-line pleated skirt and a cream colored blouse. She had fixed her red hair so it was up in the back and emphasized her long, slender neck and high cheekbones. Her lipstick was *come-catch-me if you can* red. I had to consciously pull my gaze away from her full, luscious lips.

Clotille looked around, then turned to me and asked if I liked bars.

"I do," I said. "I like bar ambiance, bar solitude, being able to be alone in the crowd."

Clotille nodded. "Are y'all one of them men who thinks he can lose himself in a bar's darkness and recapture something from his youth?" she said.

"Maybe once upon a time," I said, "but not anymore. And you? Do you like bars?"

"Sometimes. Depends who I'm with, me. I like being here with you," she said, "so I like this here bar."

I couldn't help smiling, and said, "Me, too, being here with you." I squeezed her hand.

We made small talk, first-date-type talk, all through lunch. We were drinking espresso when Clotille said, "Tell me how y'all met my daddy. I know you were both investigating a burglary, but how did you become involved?"

This wasn't the topic I would have chosen to break the ice with, but Clotille put it on the table, so there it was. I would tell Clotille an abbreviated version of my tale and see where it would lead.

When I finished, Clotille took my hand and lightly squeezed it.

"I'm sorry y'all had to go through that. I can see why my father admires you."

That surprised me. "He does?" I said. "I thought he just tolerated me."

"He likes you, he told me that, but he worries about the safety of people around you."

A frown crossed her face.

"What's the matter?" I said.

"My daddy said he was concerned his old partner, Detective Thigpen, resented you, and was going to mess with you." She paused as if thinking about something, then said, "Why would he want to do that, him?"

"We got off on the wrong foot during the Mandarin Yellow investigation. He saw me as someone interfering with his prerogatives and territory. Now he's probably pissed because I solved those crimes and showed him up."

"But my father's not angry with y'all for that," Clotille said. "He was glad the crimes were solved. He told me."

"Your father's a decent man," I said. "Thigpen's not."

I wanted to change the subject, move our talk away from me, so I said, "How did your birth mother die, if you don't mind me asking?"

"One of her johns cut her throat."

I sure was glad I'd brought that up. *Open mouth, insert foot.*

"I'm sorry," I said. "I didn't mean to pry."

Clotille shrugged. "That's all right. I don't pay it much mind, not anymore. She was what she was, a good woman in a bad woman's life. She loved me to death, her."

I needed to switch subjects again.

"How's Harte adjusting to retired life?" I asked.

Clotille smiled. "He won't admit it, but he hates it. He's bored and restless, him. Mah daddy's too young to be put out in the bayou with the 'gators."

"He was a good cop," I said. "Always treated me fair, even when we disagreed."

"Mah daddy likes to say he didn't have any of those so-called unsolved *bottom drawer* cases that nagged at him, cases he worked at on his own time on nights and weekends, cases he worried about all his waking hours, him, cases to keep him busy now he's retired."

This all sounded good to me, but I knew that because Harte had been a homicide cop for eleven years, the picture couldn't be as benign as she made it seem or thought it was. I doubted Harte was a saint among cops. It didn't fit the personality profile for any cop in the field for that long.

We finished lunch, and Clotille insisted on paying the check since she had invited me to meet her. We agreed we would get together again soon, and I would pick up the tab.

We left *Stan's* and headed west on L, walking toward 21st Street. I planned to walk Clotille back to her office, then head home to plan the interviews I wanted to conduct with other residents at the Mount Parnassus.

We walked slowly, making small talk, figuratively

dragging our feet to delay the point when we would go our separate ways.

I had no clue that as we headed toward the CFTC, we were being followed.

CHAPTER 64

'M NOT MUCH OF A church goer. I never have been, especially when my father was alive. It's not that I have anything against organized religion or attending services. It just wasn't for me.

But since my father's death two years ago and my mother's return to Greek Orthodoxy, I've made an effort, whenever she asked, to accompany her to Sunday morning services at Saint Sophia. She's always asked me to attend with her on the Sunday that fell in the anniversary week my father died, like today.

Father Demetrius is Saint Sophia's principle priest. He always says a special prayer for the dead, and, in particular, for my father during his anniversary week, even though my father refused to convert to Orthodoxy, and had remained a devout Taoist all his life. I appreciated Father Demetrius' gesture, since a more rigid cleric would have been justified in refusing to pray for my father's soul. Father Demetrius is a good man, not one of those clerics who lauded the virtues of Orthodoxy at the expense of his flock.

I also liked Father Demetrius as a person, and appreciated the comfort he had extended to my mother at my father's funeral-viewing two years ago, even as he politely ignored my father who carefully oversaw his own wake from his open coffin.

———————————— ••• ————————————

I arrived early at Saint Sophia so my mother wouldn't have to wait for me, and stood outside on the front steps, savoring the fresh air and sunshine. I stared north up Massachusetts Avenue to where it intersected with Wisconsin. Ten minutes later, I saw my mother and two other women alight from a bus and start walking toward me. They all were dressed for church, wearing black head scarves, black stockings, and black dresses.

My mother walked slowly, still limping from the injuries she received when she and Eugenia suffered their beatdown. She used a wooden cane now when she walked any distance. It hurt me to watch her, and know I hadn't yet caught whoever had done this to her.

The women laboriously ascended Saint Sophia's outer steps, slowly moving up toward salvation. When they reached me at the halfway point, my mother stopped and kissed me on my cheek. The other women ignored me and continued their ascent toward the entrance doors.

"*Pos eise, pethi mou*? — How are you?," my mother said.

"I'm fine, Ma. *Yasou*? — And you?"

"I'm fine, too."

I kissed her on the cheek, and said, "You look pretty."

She dismissed my compliment with a grunt, and said, "Let's go inside so we're not late for your father's Mass."

We walked into the narthex and were immediately greeted by several of my mother's neighbors and some other people I didn't recognize. I left her standing with them and walked over to the ikon stations set up to honor Saints Michael and Gabriel. I lighted an orange candle in honor of my father, and crossed myself. Then I kissed the tips of my two fingers and placed my slightly damp fingertips briefly on the Saints' cheeks in an act of planting a simulated kiss. I dropped a twenty dollar bill into the Plexiglas box set up near the ikons stations, and walked back to my mother.

Once she finished with the ikons, my mother and I settled into a pew, sitting together since Saint Sophia, unlike most Orthodox churches, did not require the separation of men and women. We faced the alter and listened to Father Demetrius and the cantor perform the liturgy. I particularly enjoyed their fine baritone singing voices and the sound of the choir that overlooked us from the balcony above and behind us, as they sang Byzantine chants.

I closed my eyes and breathed deeply, taking in and enjoying the hovering smell of burning incense.

CHAPTER 65

MILOS AND ARISTIDES WERE RELEASED from jail when they provided the authorities with verifiable alibis for the dates they allegedly had committed crimes in cities they claimed they'd never visited. The authorities promised they would correct the records so neither brother would again be detained on those charges. But Milos knew better. The authorities had better things to do than worry about inaccuracies in federal crime databases. And even if the authorities did follow through and take steps to correct the federal records, there would still be state databases that would have to be checked and possibly corrected, bank accounts to unfreeze, and drivers' licenses to restore. The list was daunting.

Milos and Aristides stood in the back room of a rundown, one story, free-standing wooden hut located on 17th Street, near M, in the heart of downtown DC's prime commercial and office real estate markets. The large painted wooden sign on the front of the building read, George's Flowers.

The owner of the property did sell flowers from this location, and had done so since 1958 when he purchased the property and opened for business. But the owner also transacted other business from this site, specifically, numbers running, and all aspects of his complex criminal enterprise known as *Oikoyennia*, the secret society cavalierly referred to by Interpol as the Greek Mafia.

Milos and Aristides stood shoulder-to-shoulder, their heads bowed slightly, their eyes on the floor in front of them. They stood in front of Kronus Kalakos, the old man they'd come to ask for help. The brothers were flanked on each side by five *adelfia* — soldiers — whose loyalty was to the old man, the head of the *Oikoyennia*.

Kalakos sat at a small kitchen table shelling pistachio nuts and stuffing the marrow into his mouth. He never looked up at Milos and Aristides, or otherwise acknowledged their presence. When he had emptied the bowl, he nodded at one of the *adelfia*, who fumbled a cigarette from a soft pack and placed it between the old man's lips. The soldier then pulled out a Zippo lighter and put fire to the smoke.

Kalakos drew heavily on the cigarette, held the smoke's chemical stew in his lungs and mouth while he thought over some matter, then coughed it up and expelled a long stream of particulates directly at Milos and Aristides. He made no effort either to block the smoke or direct it and his cough away from the brothers.

When his coughing subsided, Kalakos wiped his mouth and nose on his sleeve, dropped the half-smoked butt to the floor in front of him, and watched as one of the *adelfia* used the sole of his shoe to grind the cigarette into the linoleum. Kalakos then looked up at Milos.

"Do I know you? Either one?" he said, speaking in a rasping, high-pitched voice.

"*Patera* — Father," Milos said, speaking softly, his eyes still riveted to the floor in front of him, "you don't know us personal, but my brother and me, we buy the ikons and other antiquities your business creates, to sell them to our customers." He sneaked a quick look at Kalakos, who was not looking at him and his brother.

"We are Milos and Aristides," Milos said, pointing first to himself and then nodding at Aristides, "your loyal compatriots. The Theodoros brothers. We all have done business together, *Patera*, for many years."

"What do you want?"

"We need your help, *Patera*, to get back our lives that have been taken from us."

Milos explained the recent attacks on their credit, the frozen bank accounts, the revoked drivers' licenses, the false arrest warrants, and other matters involving the recent subversion of their lives.

When he finished his catalog of troubles, Milos said, "Only you can get to the bottom of this, *Patera*, and find out who has done this to us, and make it right by us. We beg you, *Patera*, help us."

The old man stared at Milos. After a few minutes, he said, "I will consider your request. You each will bring me $50,000." He paused and reached into his pocket and pulled out a toothpick which he plugged into the corner of his mouth. "That's all," he said, dismissing the brothers with the wave of his hand.

"Yes, *Patera*," Milos said. We will bring the money this week."

Notwithstanding the hold that had been placed on their bank accounts by the Feds, and notwithstanding the authorities' failure since then to follow-up and unfreeze their accounts, Milos and Aristides had ready access to money. Their bank accounts were for show and convenience only, mostly for the benefit of the tax man, who expected to see evidence that the brothers' gallery business was a genuine going concern. The brothers never deposited serious money into these accounts. The cash they needed now would come straight from the hiding places they routinely used for their off-the-books transactions and from other cash reserves.

CHAPTER 66

CALLED THE WOMAN WHO MANAGED the Mount Parnassus and received permission from the unit's owner to inspect Eugenia's apartment. The managing agent agreed to meet me there and let me in. She told me my timing was good since a cleaning crew was scheduled to clean up the apartment in two days to ready it for its next tenant. Apparently, Eugenia hadn't purchased her condominium unit, but had rented it from its non-occupant owner.

I waited in the hallway while the agent removed the last vestiges of crime scene tape from the entryway. When we entered, the woman walked directly to the bank of windows across the living room and opened two windows.

As I entered the foyer, I removed a pair of latex gloves from my pocket and slipped them on even though the apartment would not again be inspected by lab technicians. Habits die hard.

I hadn't walked far when I came to the place Eugenia's body must have fallen. There was a chalk outline on the carpet and a dried blood stain close by.

I watched the management agent look at the carpet, and

then at me as if she expected me to comment on the chalk outline and blood, but I said nothing. Although I hadn't been around many dead bodies in the past two years, I had seen enough of them so that I had taken on their silence.

I walked into the living room, over to the bank of windows, and leaned back against the sill, facing the room. As I glanced around, I thought about Eugenia, the walks we'd taken and the few conversations we'd had, trying now to make sense out of what we'd said, the stories and rumors I'd heard about her, and what I saw now. I realized how little I actually knew about her even though I had learned a great deal of information. Everything I knew about her now seemed out of focus, too general, and very impersonal.

I stayed by the bank of windows and eyeballed the room. Like the parlor and hallway, the living room contained many framed ikons hanging on the walls. From what I could see, there didn't seem to be any missing, no blank spaces within the groupings, but that didn't surprise me. Eugenia had said the ikons all were well wrought copies. But I wondered if a thief would know that.

I walked around the apartment looking for some sign that the apartment had been burgled, but I saw none. I left the apartment convinced burglary had not been the catalyst that had brought about Eugenia's death.

CHAPTER 67

TOULA STOOD IN THE DARK and focused her attention across the street on the entrance to the Pierre L'Enfant Condominium, the building Socrates lived in on 22nd Street, between N and P. She had performed this watch-and-wait routine for almost two weeks, ever since Socrates announced he would not see her anymore.

Most of Toula's time spent so far on this rolling stakeout had been futilely passed. She had sighted Socrates only three times over the entire period she watched. In two instances, Socrates had entered his building and not come out while Toula was still there; in one instance, he emerged from the building, and Toula followed him back to his office where she had originally picked him up to follow him home.

As with most surveillances, Toula found herself spending more time waiting for something to happen than she spent achieving whatever self-fulfilling purpose her stakeout was intended to yield to her. Yet she continued on, night after night.

Toula watched as Socrates stepped away from his building's entryway and walked north on 22nd, heading toward Dupont

Circle. She stayed in her hiding spot, hanging back in the darkness of the entryway, until he had sufficiently distanced himself from her so she could follow and watch him without being detected. Toula fixed her eyes on Socrates as he strolled leisurely along the sidewalk far ahead of her.

To see the bastard, she thought, *you'd think he didn't have a care in the world. Maybe he doesn't, but he will.*

As Socrates approached the corner of P Street, Toula picked up her pace and hurried toward Dupont Circle, keeping out of sight by walking along the street side of parked cars.

When Socrates turned right at P, Toula hurried to catch up so she wouldn't lose him. When she arrived at P, she saw Socrates two streets to her right at the intersection with 20th, standing on the curb waiting for the light to change so he could cross the Circle by walking through it.

Toula hurried over to 20th, turned left, then rushed north, walking parallel to the direction Socrates walked as he cut through Dupont Circle. She used the presence of other pedestrians as cover, arrived at the far side of the Circle, and settled herself in place, out of sight, in time to see Socrates cross the street and walk north on Connecticut.

She watched Socrates enter *Circa on Dupont* restaurant, directly below his office. She settled onto a bench in a nearby pocket park. She had a clear view of the restaurant's entrance.

Toula looked at her watch. She was becoming restless. Forty minutes had passed since Socrates had entered the restaurant.

She stood up from the bench, crossed the small park she'd been sitting in, and strode across the Connecticut Avenue service road toward the restaurant. It had occurred to her that she might not have seen Socrates leave the restaurant, not because he was still eating and hadn't yet left, but because he had spotted her following him and slipped out a back door to elude her.

She was fifteen feet from the entryway when she saw Socrates through the front plate-glass window. He was sitting at a table, but not alone. A redheaded woman sat across the table from him. She had a large smile on her face.

———————————

Toula's emotions raced the entire gamut of responses: *That can't be*, she thought. *This is not happening. Socrates wouldn't be with some other woman. He wouldn't do that to me.*

She abruptly turned away from the restaurant and raced across the street, out of sight of anyone looking from the restaurant's window toward the street. She stopped walking when she reached the bench she'd been sitting on earlier. Now she paced in front of the bench.

Toula fumed. *How can he do that to me? How can he betray me this way?* And soon, *How dare him!*

She lowered herself onto the bench, then immediately stood again.

She took a deep breath, briefly held it, then let it seep out.

He's not interested in that woman, she decided. *He's just trying to make me jealous.*

She collapsed onto the bench and dropped her head into her hands. *Why does he want to make me so miserable? He must know how unhappy I am seeing this.*

Toula wiped her eyes with the back of her hand, then shook her head and stood up. She glared at the restaurant.

I can't make him stop treating me so bad, Toula thought, *but I can make him pay for doing it.*

She smiled and ran her tongue across her top lip.

Toula watched Socrates and Clotille leave *Circa* and walk across Connecticut Avenue to the Q Street Metro Station. She stayed far enough in the background to remain out of sight, but still close enough to see the couple as they paused in front of the station's escalator.

Toula watched the woman laugh when Socrates spoke to her. She felt her neck and face grow warm as she watched the woman smile again and, this time, playfully punch Socrates on the shoulder. She didn't know which made her more furious: the woman laughing at Socrates' comments and bantering with him; or, Socrates playing the fool to entertain the woman at her expense.

The issue settled itself for her when the redheaded woman stood on her toes and lightly kissed Socrates' cheek.

Toula's emotions roiled as Socrates placed one hand on each of the woman's shoulders and pulled her in close, hugging her. The redhead reacted by wrapping her arms around Socrates' waist and turning her face up to be kissed.

CHAPTER 68

FOUND MYSELF THINKING ABOUT XENO Papadopoulos — the Tweaker. I thought about what I had learned from his few neighbors I'd spoken to, from my computer research, and from my own observation of him and his apartment when I stopped by to talk to him. It all added up to one thing: Tweaker was an addict, probably a crystal meth addict. That would explain his hostility when I spoke to him, as well as his physical characteristics, as well as his sleep and sanitary habits.

But did this give him the motivation I was looking for to commit unlawful entry, assault and battery, and murder at the Mount Parnassus?

Under other circumstances — circumstances not involving my mother, and where I was not without any leads — I would say, No. But given the situation I found myself in, I was able to conjure up a motive for him for each of the crimes.

As I saw it, Tweaker broke into Eugenia's condo to find valuables to sell so he could support his addiction. He killed Selena in the course of an assault and battery, I speculated, because she had complained to management about him, then had resisted his attack, either physically or verbally, and the beating went too far, killing her. He assaulted Eugenia, I decided, because she, too, had reported him, and he assaulted my mother, either because she was with Eugenia when he attacked her or to avenge himself for my knee action, or both.

All of these reasons were plausible. Unfortunately, all of them were pretty flimsy, too, as far as motives go. Worse, they also left unanswered other questions such as why Selena was in Eugenia's apartment when she died?

CHAPTER 69

I T WASN'T TOO LONG AFTER my meeting at the 2D with Thigpen and his partner that I found myself again sitting in the interview room at the station house. Thigpen had called and asked me to come in to talk with them.

"Am I a suspect or something," I asked.

"No," Thigpen said, "nothing like that. Just following up on our meeting to clear up a few things and help out each other."

Since I knew we could do that over the phone, I also knew there was more to it than he was letting on, but I didn't see how I could avoid coming in, and I didn't want to piss him off by asking too many questions, so I agreed to meet in an hour.

I turned down Thigpen's offer of coffee or a soft drink so we could get started with the interview. My curiosity was gnawing at me.

"Thanks for coming in," Thigpen's partner said.

"Always glad to help," I said. I glanced at Thigpen, who was staring at me. He had an ironic *don't give us that bullshit* grin on his face.

"What can I do for you, Detectives?" I said, looking first at Thigpen, then at his partner.

"We're tying up loose ends," Thigpen said. "Tell us again about your involvement with the Kostas dame and the lady they called the Oracle."

I walked them through my history with both women. I was as candid as I could be about my doubts and concerns, and the evolution of my conclusions concerning Selena's death and the purported break-ins at Eugenia's apartment. I wanted to rehabilitate myself in Thigpen's eyes and eradicate the ill will that still seemed to linger from four years ago.

"Okay," Thigpen said. "You sure this is all there is? Anything else you want to tell us?"

"One more thing," I said. I proceeded to tell them about the complaints made against Tweaker, and my visit to him on behalf of Eugenia. I even described my assault on his family jewels. Thigpen chuckled. "Ouch," he said.

"Am I in trouble for admitting that?"

"Only if he files a complaint with us," Thigpen's partner said.

They asked a few more questions, then Thigpen nodded at me as I stood up from my seat. I interpreted that to mean he finally was thawing toward me.

Thigpen called me four days later. He told me he'd arrested and charged Tweaker with operating a DMT drug lab, manufacturing a Schedule 1 controlled substance, possession of drug paraphernalia, and possession of a controlled substance with intent to distribute.

"A meth lab?" I said. "I should have picked up on that

from his physical appearance and habits. From the reported odors, too, I suppose. I thought he was just a user, not a manufacturer and dealer."

"It wasn't meth," Thigpen said, "it was DMT."

"What's that?" I asked.

"Dimethyltriptamine. It's similar to meth, but with a slightly different chemical composition," Thigpen said. "It's dangerous, explosive, and puts out some strange smells."

"What's it do?" I said.

"Hallucinations, visions, loss of normal appetite, but a craving for sweets. All while it's rotting your brain and driving you into severe malnutrition."

"Was it a big operation he had?"

Thigpen chuckled into the phone. "Big enough to light up the city for a few square blocks if it went off. This boy'll be going away for a long, hard time."

Before hanging up, Thigpen added that the police and lab reports on the raid at Tweaker's apartment were ready, and he'd like me to come in to the 2D to read them in case they triggered a memory of something I'd forgotten to tell them before. I said I'd come by later in the day. Then I booted up my computer and researched DMT.

I left my office a little after 3:00, and walked the couple of miles to Idaho Avenue and the 2D. On the way I thought about what I'd learned about the drug, DMT. Specifically, I thought about the effects of inhaling the drug's vapors, the proximity of Eugenia's apartment above Tweaker's, and Eugenia's reputation for visions and prophecy.

I spent twenty minutes reading the lab and police reports,

but didn't have any insights to offer them now that I hadn't already shared with Thigpen and his partner. Thigpen wasn't pleased.

Before I left, I decided there were two things I still wanted to do in connection with my own investigation of the crimes at the Mount Parnassus. I turned to Thigpen.

"I'd like to look around Tweaker's apartment," I said.

"Be my guest." Thigpen said, as he shrugged one shoulder. "It's not a crime scene now we've finished with it."

Unlike with Eugenia's apartment, since the landlord had given us permission to enter there, the condo's management agent was now reluctant to let me inspect Tweaker's apartment until I told her that if she didn't, I'd have no choice but to file a hazardous substance claim with the federal Environmental Protection Agency and with city agencies on behalf of my mother and all other occupants of the Mount Parnassus. And that, I told her, probably would require the evacuation of the building if remediation was required. She agreed to let me into Tweaker's apartment.

When we arrived there, the agent removed the yellow crime scene tape.

An odor that reminded me of cheap perfume, but which I otherwise cannot describe, enveloped us. The woman swooned and made preliminary barfing sounds, and said, "Holy Jesus, what died?", then blushed. She said she'd wait in the hall for me.

The apartment's air was heavy with the stench of garbage, old trash, stale cigarettes, and chemicals. Most of the candy wrappers and trash I'd seen from the hallway when I stopped by on behalf of Eugenia were gone, probably bagged and taken as evidence to test for drug residue.

I walked through every room looking around. The exhaust ducts in the kitchen and both bathrooms had been covered over with a heavy, clear plastic sheeting, and taped down along their edges. A similar clear plastic sheet overhung the bottom of the entryway door so no odors could escape under the door. Obviously, based on the complaints of Tweaker's neighbors, this wasn't foolproof. A large exhaust fan filled the bottom pane area of one window in the living room. The fan was set to blow the apartment's air from the apartment to the street outside, not to bring in fresh air.

I spent half an hour looking around, then left. I headed to my office to deal with the second matter that had occurred to me when I read the official reports. I wanted to go online and research the current state of scholarship — the current thinking among scientists, not historians — concerning the possible causes of the visions experienced by the ancient Oracle at Delphi in Greece.

Most of the scientific community involved in investigating this question believed that the ancient Oracle experienced hallucinations induced by the leakage into her chamber of noxious gases located in the peculiar geological setting of the area where her cave — a shrine to Apollo — was located. It was a perfect storm: a cave located above a combination of two intersecting and active geologic fault lines, porous limestone, seismic activity, and an under-layer of bituminous coal.

This suggested that a good part of Western civilization's

ancient history had been driven by women whose senses were distorted by their inhalation of volatile hydrocarbon vapors of methane gas seeping into their chamber from fissures in the floor of the cave — women who, as the Pythias, uttered cryptic and freely interpretable answers to questions of life and death, and war and peace, posed to them by well-paying supplicants.

In light of this, I again researched DMT on the Web and found that it, like meth, induced the same type of euphoric and buoyancy responses when inhaled as did methane and ethylene gases. This meant that the result of any leakage of vapors from the Tweaker's apartment into Eugenia's home through her floor would have resulted in the same type of hallucinatory experience for Eugenia as the ancient Pythias underwent in Apollo's Delphic cave. I wasn't sure what all this had to do with the crimes at the Mount Parnassus, but it was a start.

I called Thigpen and told him what I'd learned.

"So what?" he said.

"Don't you think you should run some tests in Eugenia's apartment to see if I'm right?"

"Nope. We'll use our tiny budget for something useful. Anyhow, the case's closed."

"But—"

"Let it go, Cheng. We got our perp. It's just a matter of time 'til he cops to the assaults and murders. It's over."

I entered my mother's apartment with some trepidation. I didn't know how she was going to take the news concerning Eugenia's prophecies. I found her in the kitchen. She was sitting at the table peeling cloves of garlic. She looked up as I walked in and broke into a big smile.

"*Yiasou,*" she said.

"Good, Ma, thanks. *Ke esí?*"

"I'm good, too," she said.

"I want to talk to you about something. Is this a good time?"

"Sit," she said, pointing to a chair across the table. "I'll put on a pot of coffee."

I explained what I'd learned from walking through Tweaker's apartment and what I had learned in my research concerning the ancient Oracle.

"So what," my mother said, "doesn't mean a thing about Eugenia. She was a true prophet."

"Maybe," I said, "but the evidence suggests otherwise."

"No *maybe,*" she said. "Eugenia obviously predicted her own death that time she wouldn't tell us what she'd seen, and she predicted Selena's death, too. There's no *maybe* about it, Socrates."

I didn't see any point in mentioning that Eugenia's predictions, like those of the ancient Oracle, were sufficiently ambiguous to suit any interpretation.

I also didn't bother to raise the role of coincidence in our lives and perceptions, how we noticed coincidences when they occurred and were significant, but did not take notice of them when they were insignificant — which was most of the time. For my part, I lumped Eugenia's predictions into this latter category.

I called the condo's management agent and said I wanted

Tweaker's and Eugenia's apartments tested for leakage of gases and, in the case of Eugenia's condo, for DMT residue. The agent's immediate response was, No.

I reprised my previous threat to her, and suggested she might want to head off a formal complaint by cooperating with me. To underscore my seriousness, I also asked her for the correct spelling of her first and last names so I could get them right when I filed my formal complaint with the environmental protection agencies. She said she would get back to me.

CHAPTER 70

ARISTIDES WAS SITTING AT HOME alone, smoking and reading the newspaper, when the front door of his McLean, Virginia, home caved in under the pressure of a weighted battering ram. A dozen black-clad federal agents swooped in with automatic weapons raised and voices screaming over and over again, "Get down on the floor, hands behind your head. Down!"

Aristides was promptly cuffed and placed in an unmarked, windowless black van. His home was cleared for other occupants, thoroughly searched, stripped of likely evidence such as his computer, iPad, and smartphone, then abandoned by the special agents.

Aristides was brought before a federal magistrate sitting in Alexandria, Virginia's United States District Court, and held under a fugitive warrant that had been issued by the Commonwealth of Kentucky the year before. The warrant alleged that Aristides had jumped bond while awaiting trial for the possession and dissemination of child pornography. Aristides used his one permitted telephone call to reach Milos.

Milos promptly retained the expensive services of Darius Alexios, Esquire, one of Washington's most aggressive criminal defense attorneys. Milos knew him from Saint Sophia.

At Aristides' bond hearing the next morning, his attorney contended that although logic would suggest that no court in its right mind would grant bail to someone arrested because he had jumped bail elsewhere, the special circumstances of Aristides' case argued for a different result. The attorney then proceeded to walk the court through the recent history of the subversion of Aristides' and Milos' financial and personal lives by some person or persons unknown, and presented much evidence to support the story in the form of affidavits from the FBI, as well as Milos' sworn testimony. The magistrate listened to the presentation, asked several questions, then agreed to set bail for Aristides, but at a level so high as to, in effect, split the baby. Milos then arranged to have bond posted in the amount of $6,000,000.

The brothers left the U.S. Courthouse and drove to Aristides' home. They were furious. They had no doubt Aristides again had been the victim of whoever had hacked into their personal lives. They promised each other that once the *Patera* delivered the person's name to them, they would devote themselves to exacting their revenge against him.

CHAPTER 71

I CALLED CLOTILLE AT HER OFFICE, something I'd been reluctant to do since I had never asked her if she minded taking calls there, but I was anxious to see her and didn't want to put it off. I invited her to meet me for a drink after work, followed by dinner in Georgetown. She accepted.

We met at 5:30 in front of the CFTC's offices, and walked over to the *Foggy Bottom Café*, on 25th Street, near I. We had drinks. After an hour there, we decided we were hungry. I asked Clotille if she would like to go to *Acadiana*, a local restaurant near the Convention Center at Mt. Vernon Square, renowned for its Cajun and Creole food.

"Are you funning me?" she said.

"I'm serious," I said. "It's reputation is good, the food's said to be authentic, and I've never eaten there. I thought it might be fun for us to try."

"Did mah daddy tell you Ah love to cook?"

"No."

"Ah make all kinds of Cajun dishes, and I'm good at it, me, if Ah say so mahself."

I didn't say anything at all for a minute while I thought about what my mother sometimes liked to say about me, that I had a tendency to *open mouth and insert foot*.

"I'm sorry," I said. "I didn't know you cook. I was trying to make you feel at home. I didn't want to insult—"

Clotille laughed and took my hand. "Easy, boy, you," she said. "Ah was teasing." She patted the back of my hand.

I felt myself blush.

"If y'all want me to feel at home with you, Socrates, you should let me make you one of my Bayou Têche Cajun dinners."

I readily accepted her offer, and we agreed to set a date soon for her to cook for me. Meanwhile, we were hungry tonight and agreed to eat Italian this evening. We walked into Georgetown — about one quarter mile from where we were — to *Paolo's* on Wisconsin.

When we finished dinner we caught a taxi to Clotille's place in Arlington, just across the Potomac River from Washington. We left the taxi about two blocks from her apartment so we could walk and enjoy the warm weather. We held hands as we walked.

When we reached her front door, there was an awkward moment while I debated whether I should indicate to Clotille I would like to come in. It seemed to me Clotille was engaged in the same internal debate, trying to decide whether to invite me in.

I took both Clotille's hands in mine and said, "You have to work tomorrow, so I should hit the road." It seemed to me Clotille breathed a quiet sigh of relief.

She nodded and looked into my eyes, then put one hand behind my head and pulled my face down to hers. We kissed long and warmly, and melded our bodies together for a moment. Then Clotille slowly moved away. She stroked my cheek with her finger, smiled, and said, "Thank y'all, Socrates. Thank y'all for everything."

CHAPTER 72

I WAS SITTING IN MY LIVING room later that night smoking a cigar, drinking a beer, and listening to a Bill Evans piano solo on my iPod, when Toula called. I looked at my CallerID, saw that she was the caller, and debated whether or not to talk with her. The alternative, I knew, would be an unending stream of vituperative voice mails.

I had been warned by one of my former law partners, who had been in a hostile dependency situation with his ex-wife after they separated, not to give in to Toula's appeals to get together, not to even take her phone calls, if I ever wanted her to leave me alone. I wasn't sure I agreed with him. I thought that if I acted reasonably in dealing with her, Toula eventually would get the message, give up, and leave me alone. I was wrong. As my former partner was quick to point out to me, you cannot convince a person who was acting irrationally to change behavior or thought by using rational arguments or rational behavior in dealing with them. Nor can you expect them to change and act reasonably toward you on their own as long as you enable them by maintaining contact. That was the lesson of hostile dependency.

My former partner claimed that every time I answered Toula's telephone call I started the cycle over again. As for the hostility part of the equation, Toula's earlier voicemail messages spoke for themselves. The woman definitely was hostile.

Nevertheless, on this occasion I picked up her incoming call.

"Hi, Darling," Toula said. "I thought maybe you'd like to spend some time together tonight. I know I'd like to."

It was as if I'd never broken off our arrangement. "I don't think so."

There was a short pause before Toula slammed down the phone.

I decided it was time to follow my friend's advice — he said it could take a year or more to work — and to accept the concept of hostile dependency. I would wait out Toula and see if she really would move on if I persistently ignored her.

Beginning the next morning, the calls came at fairly regular intervals, spaced in clusters of two or three, then none for a few hours. Occasionally she would skip a day or two before calling me again. I didn't see any lessening of her dependency.

Most of the calls were accompanied by blistering voicemails. I deleted most of them without listening as soon as I recognized Toula's voice or understood the hostile tenor of her message.

There was one message, however, that hooked my attention. I immediately called Ralph Harte. He agreed to meet me.

CHAPTER 73

T HE YOUNG MAN'S LEGS FELT unstable as he stood before the *Patera*, his arms hanging limply by his sides and his head bowed. He stared at the floor directly in front of his shoes. He'd never seen the *Patera* in person before. He had only seen the Father in photographs hanging on the walls of restaurants and other Metro DC businesses. The young man was terrified.

"You found out who did this thing to the Theodoros brothers?" the *Patera* said.

The young man, of course, had never heard the Father's voice before. He was surprised by its high pitch and effeminate rhythm.

"Yes, *Patera*, I know." The young man kept his gaze fixed on the floor.

"Who?"

"His name is Panos Makeresos, my Father."

"You're sure?"

"Yes, *Patera*, I'm sure."

Kalakos turned toward one of his minions. "Who is this Panos?"

The guard shrugged.

Kalakos turned back to the young man. "You tell me, who's this dead man whose name you gave me?"

The young man cleared his throat three times before he spoke.

He described who Panos was, where he lived, and other information he'd acquired using his computer to hack into various databases. His voice quivered as he spoke.

"Leave now," the *Patera* said, looking directly at the young man for the first time. "You will be rewarded for your work."

As soon as the young man closed the door behind himself, the *Patera* turned to one of his minions, and said, "*Lipón* — So, now. Give this information to those brothers. We're done."

CHAPTER 74

STOPPED BY TO SEE MY mother before I headed out to
meet with Harte and discuss Toula's voicemail.

"I told you, Socrates, I won't leave my home and move
in with you. Stop asking."

We were sitting at her kitchen table drinking *ellenikó kafè*
— a brand of Greek coffee. I was halfway through my first
cup; she had just poured her third since I arrived.

I wasn't happy about what I was about to suggest, but felt
I had no other choice.

"All right, Ma. In that case, what if I move in here until
it's all over?"

She shook her head and smiled.

"Thank you, that's sweet, Socrates, but not necessary. You
worry too much."

I nodded. *Of course I do. I'm your son.*

"Ma," I said, changing the subject, "there's something I
want to ask you. It's important to me."

"So, ask," she said, slightly raising her shoulders in a mild
shrug.

"When I went to the support group meeting, you wouldn't
tell me where you'd been and why you were so late. I'd like
to know."

"I didn't tell you then, Socrates, because it was none of your business. It still isn't."

I must've looked upset because she quickly added, "Maybe someday I'll tell you, but not now."

CHAPTER 75

ARTE AND I ARRIVED AT the *M Street Bar & Grill* at the same time. We walked inside together and took a corner table near the back where we would have some privacy. I played Toula's voicemail for him, using my cellphone recorder.

> *Okay, Asshole. I know you're there and avoiding my calls again. That's not going to help you. You owe me and can't treat me like some whore you can use and throw away.*
>
> *If the only way I can get your attention is to go after your redhead bimbo, that's what I'll do.*
>
> *Yes, Socrates, I know all about her. More than you can imagine. I've watched you two play kissy-face and boyfriend and girlfriend together. I even know where she lives and works.*

Harte listened to the recording twice more. I watched his face the whole time. His tension was palpable. His mood darkened with each replay.

I remained silent. This now was Harte's show.

He finally looked away from the table into my eyes.

"Who was that?" he said.

I told him Toula's name, how I knew her through my mother and hers, that we'd had a short but intense physical relationship, and that I had ended that relationship with her, but Toula hadn't accepted that. I told him about the many other voicemail messages Toula had left for me.

"What's her last name?" Harte asked.

I told him.

"Where's she live?"

I told him.

"Do you have a picture of her?

"No," I said. I described her, including her black eye patch.

"Has she made other threats concerning Clotille?

I said No as to Clotille, that Toula had been hostile toward me in other voicemails, but hadn't threatened me directly. Until now it was more her tone, than her actual words, that had carried menace.

Harte nodded. He took his cellphone from his jacket pocket, held up his finger to indicate I should be quiet and sit tight, then pushed a speed dial button.

He spoke briefly with Thigpen, and set up a meeting with him in thirty minutes. When he finished the call, he looked back at me.

"What'd that woman mean when she said you and Clotille played boyfriend/girlfriend?" Harte did not seem curious; he looked hostile.

I explained that Clotille and I had gotten together a few times for a drink or a meal, that I liked Clotille very much and thought Clotille liked me, too, and that we were in the very early stage of getting to know one another.

"It was nothing more than that," I said.

Harte's eyes were hard. I couldn't read anything in them. He was in full cop mode.

"I want you to stop seeing my daughter."

I hesitated, then said, "I don't know. I like Clotille. I like her very much."

"That wasn't a request," he said.

"What if Clotille doesn't agree?"

"I'll deal with her," Harte said. "You worry about you. Stop seeing her and make it clear it's your decision. Understand?"

"I won't do it that way, if I even do it at all." I paused and took a deep breath. "If I stop seeing Clotille, I'll tell her why, including your role. She's entitled to know."

Harte's eyes were flat grey. He said nothing; he just stared at me. I could see his mind working in his contorted face.

He reached across the table toward me. I flinched and sank back in my chair. He turned his hand over and opened his palm.

"Give me your phone," he said.

"What?"

"Give me your goddamn phone," he said quietly. His hand hovered open in front of me. "You can have it back after Thigpen copies the voicemail."

I handed my cell over to him.

"Keep yourself available," Harte said, "in case I wanna talk to you after I'm done with Thigpen."

"But you have my cell," I said. "How will I—"

"Wait for me at your office, Genius. I'll call you there."

I nodded.

"In the meantime, Cheng, don't contact my daughter."

CHAPTER 76

TWO DAYS AFTER I'D FUTILELY asked my mother why she'd been late for the support group meeting, I still felt the presence of an undercurrent of strain between us. I decided I'd make an effort to reduce or eliminate the tension by spending Sunday with her, just having fun together.

I planned to start by going to morning Mass with her. Afterward, I would take her to brunch at *Café Berlin* on Capitol Hill, then we would spend time at the Capitol Hill Flea Market, across the street from Eastern Market. We'd both enjoyed this routine in the past and hadn't spent a Sunday doing it in almost one year.

I spent Saturday morning running my usual weekend errands — going to the dry cleaner, doing my week's food marketing at Whole Foods on 22nd Street, and paying bills online. When I finished, at about 2:30 p.m., I called my mother to set up the date for the next day. She didn't answer so I left a brief voicemail explaining what I had in mind. I said I'd try to reach her later in the day.

I called again at 3:10, but again didn't connect with her. I didn't leave a message this time.

While I waited for her to return my calls, I turned my attention back to the investigation.

Four years ago when I investigated the theft of the historic Mandarin Yellow fountain pen and other Chinese cultural artifacts, I learned the value, as an investigative tool, of creating a written chronology relating to the crimes. The chronology acted much like a writer's plot outline because it gave me the opportunity to see the sequence of events in relation to one another, and, therefore, to appreciate the individual components in their proper perspectives. I decided to apply the same concept to the crimes at the Mount Parnassus.

I started by listing the meetings I'd had with Eugenia related to the break-ins at her home. I added our walks to the document as another category, included the murder of Selena, the assaults against my mother and Eugenia, the murder of Eugenia, and the arrest of Tweaker.

I became so engrossed in this process I lost track of time. When I checked my watch it was a little past 6:30 p.m. My mother still hadn't called so I tried her again. She still was not answering her phone. I left another message asking her to call me. Then I changed clothes and went for a run in Rock Creek Park.

I was cooking dinner for myself — spaghetti with garlic and olive oil — when my cellphone rang.

Good, I thought as I walked into the living room to retrieve my cell that Harte had returned it to me after he and Thigpen finished with it. *She's finally getting back to me.*

I looked at the cell's readout display and saw that the caller was not my mother. The display ID read, Caller Unknown. I pressed the Talk button to take the incoming call, said, Hello, and heard Detective Thigpen's voice in response.

"In the spirit of cooperating we talked about, Cheng, because Harte says you're not a bad guy, I've got something for you," he said. "The perp you call the Tweaker didn't do the Eugenia broad. He alibi'd out. He was in the George Washington University Hospital being treated for malnutrition when the old lady croaked."

This worried me. It meant the killer was still out there. My mother might not be safe at the Mount Parnassus.

"What about Selena Kostas," I said. "Did he have an alibi for her, too?"

"We're still looking at him for that one, but we're not as sure as before. For the time being he's going to be locked down with us while we put together a case against him on his drug lab. When we're done, the Feds want him."

"Good. Anything else?" I said.

"Yeah. His DNA didn't match the DNA at the Stamos dame's crime scene. That's why we have some doubts about him."

I thanked Thigpen, told him I'd been working on a chronology of events, and I'd send it over to him as soon as I finished fine tuning it. We ended the call.

I called my mother again, but still received no answer. I decided three things: I would buy her a cellphone and pay for its monthly plan so we could keep in touch when she was away from home; I would insist she use the cell even though she had resisted having one so far; and, I would go over to her apartment to look around. She'd been out of touch long enough today so that I was beginning to worry.

I entered my mother's apartment with mixed feelings even though none of the lights was on and I wasn't concerned about surprising and frightening her. But it just didn't feel right moving around in her home without her specific invitation, even though she'd given me a key and told me to feel free to use it.

I went from room to room turning on lights and looking for anything that might tell me where she'd been all day and where she was right now. I didn't look in any drawers or go through her snail mail or answering machine messages, so it was possible I might have missed something that could have cleared this up for me. I didn't think an invasive search was required at this point, and I didn't want to embarrass my mother by searching her drawers if it turned out not to be necessary.

I left my mother's apartment after an hour and knocked on all her neighbors' doors on the sixth floor. The few who were home hadn't seen her last night or today.

Her absence was beginning to concern me more than just a little. For the moment, however, I didn't see anything more I could do other than bide my time.

I left the Mount Parnassus and walked into Georgetown to go to *The Guards* to have a beer and think about this.

I drank two beers and decided I could not do anything about my mother's mysterious absence until she returned and we had a chance to talk about it. I left *The Guards* and headed home.

Five hours later, having still not heard from her, I admitted to myself I was worried. I had called her three more times and left more voicemails asking her to call me. It now was 11:30 p.m.. This was not the way my mother conducted her life.

I poured myself a glass of Scotch and quickly drained it. I turned on my iPod to listen to a remastered Maria Callas recital, settled into my reading chair to listen to the music and await my mother's call, and promptly fell asleep. When I woke, my watch indicated the time was 1:40 a.m. My mother hadn't called.

I made my way to bed and had a fitful night's sleep. I awoke at 7:30 a.m., drenched in sweat. I checked my voicemail to see if she had called and I'd slept through the ring tone and message. She hadn't called.

I showered, put on a suit and tie, and headed over to Saint Sophia. I wanted to get there before Mass started. Whatever was going on, as long as my mother had command of her faculties and control over her movements, she'd show up for Mass.

When I arrived at the church, I sought out Father Demetrius and asked him if had seen or talked to my mother in the last day or so. He hadn't, but assured me she would be along in time for Mass. My mother, he told me, has not once missed Mass since she returned to her Faith.

I took a seat inside the narthex where I could see the entryway, and waited for my mother to arrive.

I waited in the narthex throughout the service. My mother never showed. When Mass ended, I watched people file out, hoping to recognize someone who knew her. I spotted the two women who had taken the bus to Saint Sophia with her on the anniversary of my father's death. I caught up with them after they'd descended the front steps and started walking toward Massachusetts Avenue to catch a bus. I reintroduced myself and walked with them as we talked.

"I'm looking for my mother," I said. "She should have been at Mass. Have you seen her or talked to her in the last few days?"

They shook their heads. "We wondered where she was," one of the women said.

"That's not like Sophia to miss Mass," the other woman said.

"Do you know where she might have gone?" I asked.

They looked at one another, turned back to me and again indicated, No.

They turned away as a Metro bus pulled up.

I didn't know where my mother was or why she'd dropped out of sight. What I did know was that her disappearance was not something she was likely to do on her own accord without first telling me. I had no doubt, now, my mother might be in great danger and that I had been unable to protect her from it.

CHAPTER 77

TOULA SUCKED IN A DEEP breath, held it while she silently counted to ten, then let it hiss out between her clenched teeth. It required all her concentration to hide her fury from the two detectives sitting across the table from her. *Socrates would pay for having her dragged in here for questioning.*

She stared at the female detective, then reached up and adjusted the edge of her eye patch, all the while fixing her good eye on the detective's eyes, silently willing the woman to yield the floor. The detective lowered her eyes and looked away.

Thigpen looked at his partner, frowned, then said, "Read Ms. Xandereas her rights."

When Toula had been properly Mirandized, Thigpen said, "Do you know why you're here?"

"Probably because that moron Cheng complained I'm bothering him."

"Why would he do that?" Thigpen said.

"Maybe because he misinterprets my efforts to hold him to his promises as some kind of threat. You'll have to ask him why, not me."

Thigpen glanced at his partner. She raised her eyebrows.

He looked back at Toula, then looked down at a manila file folder sitting on the table in front of him. He opened the folder, took out a sheet of paper with a typed transcript of the voicemail he'd received from Harte, and slid it across the table to Toula.

"Does this look familiar to you?" he said.

Toula didn't touch the paper, but glanced quickly at it.

"Seems like a message I left for Cheng on his answering machine, although I can't say it's right word for word," Toula said. "Close enough, though."

"It's an accurate transcript of your message to Mr. Cheng," Thigpen said. "What do you have to say about it?"

Toula shrugged. "I was pissed, that's what. He knows better than to take it literally. I wouldn't do nothing to his girlfriend. There was no harm meant from it."

"It's a felony to threaten people," Thigpen said.

"*Ksero ego* — How would I know that? I wasn't threatening nobody," Toula said. "I just wanted that asshole to sweat a little for screwing me."

"That not how he interpreted it," Thigpen said. "Me either. Seemed like a threat to me." He looked at his partner. "Seem like a threat to you?" he asked her.

"Absolutely," his partner said.

Toula fanned out her palms. "Well, it wasn't a threat, what more can I say, it was just an angry outburst. If you want I should apologize to that worm or his bimbo girlfriend, I will. It doesn't matter to me."

Thigpen turned to his partner, "You have anything else to ask Ms. Xandereas?"

His partner shook her head. "Not right now, maybe later."

Thigpen pushed his chair away from the table and stood

up. "You can go now," he said. "You might want to stop leaving messages for Cheng and get on with your life."

Toula grabbed her purse from the table and stood up. "Goodbye, Detectives," she said. "Send my regards to Cheng when you report back to him." She nodded once, smiled, and left the interview room.

Thigpen called Harte. Harte was not happy to hear that Toula had skated so easily, but he'd had enough experience on the Job not to be surprised. He had been hoping she would say something in the interview to justify holding her, but she apparently had been too savvy for that.

"What's next?" he asked Thigpen.

"Nothing unless she repeats or escalates. You know that."

Harte admitted he did know that. He thanked Thigpen and ended the call, then called Socrates.

"Cheng, it's Harte. I just talked to Thigpen about your ex-lover."

Harte told Socrates what Thigpen had told him.

"What do we do now?" Socrates said.

"*We* don't do nothing," Harte said. "You stay put, keep out of the picture. I'll deal with your Barbary-pirate lady friend. Meantime, you keep away from Clotille."

CHAPTER 78

T HE TIME HAD COME FOR me to file a formal missing
persons report for my mother. Before leaving for the 2D
station house, I tried reaching her one more time. She
didn't answer. I left another message.

I then called her again before I opened the door and
entered the 2D. Same result as before, with no answer. I
walked into the 2D.

———————

Thigpen and his partner set me up in an interview room.
They were properly courteous and entirely by the book. It was
as if no bad blood had ever existed between me and Thigpen.

We spent an hour together. I answered all their questions
as if this was a preliminary probe into a homicide. When
we finished, Thigpen said he'd have to hold the forms for
another twenty-four hours because she hadn't been missing
long enough, but that he'd put the paperwork in as soon as
he was allowed.

When Thigpen finished with me, I left the 2D and sat
down on a bench out front. First, unsuccessfully, I tried to
reach my mother again. Then I called the condo's management

agent and asked her if she'd gotten back the results from the lab tests run in Tweaker's and Eugenia's apartments.

She said, 'Yes', she had the results. It turned out fumes from Tweaker's apartment had leaked into Eugenia's apartment, and there was DMT residue everywhere, especially in the parlor. DMT had leaked through the floor of Eugenia's apartment, through cracks in the walls, and through light fixtures.

Hmmn, I thought, *Eugenia as prophet? Makes you wonder.*

I left the 2D and walked to my mother's apartment and let myself in. The first thing I did was go to her bedroom and look in the night table drawer for the address book she kept there. I found it buried under her spare eyeglasses and a Chapstick.

I settled onto the couch, opened the address book to page one, and started calling everyone listed to ask if they'd talked to my mother in the past week or had seen her in the last day or so. It required about an hour for me to reach approximately eighty percent of the people listed. No one had had any contact with her recently. I returned the address book to the night table. I would come back tomorrow, I decided, and call those people I hadn't reached.

Next, I started a room-by-room, drawer-by-drawer search for clues to her disappearance. I even looked under the bed, under furniture, and in all the closets. This, too, was a dead end.

PART THREE

CHAPTER 79

HARTE SHOWED UP AT MY condo the next morning. We again reviewed what Thigpen had told him about his interview with Toula.

"You believe her?" I said.

"Not a chance," Harte said. "She's nuts. You don't have to spend much time with her to see that. Besides, I heard the message. It was a threat."

"Now what?" I said.

"You continue to stay away from Clotille so that nut job gets the message and backs off. Meanwhile, I'll talk to Clotille so she knows to be on the lookout for the woman. She shouldn't be hard to miss with her eye patch."

I nodded. Although I wasn't happy with this approach, I couldn't argue with the logic of it, so I let it go.

Harte stood up to leave.

"One more thing," I said.

"What's that?"

"I really could use your help investigating my mother's disappearance and the other crimes at the condo. Please—"

"I thought we put that to bed," Harte said. "I'm retired." He stared at me briefly. He clearly was annoyed I had raised this again. "And like I said, I don't work with nobody's not been on the Job."

"You're also bored," I said. "It doesn't take an oracle to see that."

That was the wrong thing for me to have said. Harte's face darkened.

"I don't do PI work, Cheng. Let it go."

He turned back to the door and left. I wondered what it would take to get him to change his mind.

CHAPTER 80

MILOS AND ARISTIDES LOCKED UP their gallery and entered the back room to talk over and decide how they would deal with Panos now that he had been identified as the person who attempted to destroy their lives.

They didn't ask *why* their good customer Panos had done this; they didn't ask *how* he had done this; they merely asked: now that we know he did do it, how will we destroy him?

The brothers, although not formally educated, were street smart. They read people well, especially adversaries, and homed in on the foibles, weaknesses, and vulnerabilities of their foes.

Panos' chief vulnerability, the brothers agreed, was grounded in his morbid dread of buying fake antiquities. Milos and Aristides decided, they would exploit this fear to bring him down.

———

It took three weeks, and the distribution of much cash among members of the criminal and arts netherworlds, but the day came when Milos and Aristides were ready to deal with Panos.

CHAPTER 81

S ELENA'S SON, GEORGE, CALLED ME. I hadn't expected
that. He had dropped off my radar long
before his call.

"There's a support group meeting tomorrow night," he
said. "I'd like you to come speak to us."

I didn't see any reason why I should do this. "Why?" I
asked.

"After what's happened to your mother," he said, "we
want to know what's going on. We don't feel safe, and the
police don't answer our questions. We hoped you could tell
us if we should fear for our lives."

I understood that all right, but didn't know if I could
answer that question for them any more than I'd been able to
answer it in terms of my mother. But I also realized something
else. If I attended the meeting, I might learn something that
would help me in my investigation. I decided I'd attend.

"George," I said, "all I can tell your group is the little I
know about your mother's death, that it wasn't suicide, and
that Eugenia Stamos was murdered, too. Unfortunately, I
don't know what to say about my mother's abduction, and I
don't know much about the arrest of the druggie living below

Eugenia, except what was in the police file. I don't know how much help I'll be to—"

"Even that will help," he said. "Come and speak to us and answer the group's questions. Tell us whatever you can."

I arrived as the meeting was starting, and was immediately introduced by George to the audience of about fifty people. I spent the next fifteen minutes offering the fullest status report I could. Then the question and answer period began.

"*Kali spéra — Good evening,* Mr. Cheng. My name is Helena Jocasta. I lived here at the Mount Parnassus ever since 1967. I'm sorry about your mother. Sophia is a good neighbor. I hope she comes back soon.

"In the old country, my husband and I supported King Alexander. My question is this: why are people being murdered here. My friend, Eugenia, I know her late husband supported the Colonels, but we don't take sides at the condominium, so who would want to hurt her?"

"Unfortunately," I said, "I don't have an answer for you. I don't know yet why any of these crimes were committed, but I'm working on it."

A man stood up as Helena Jocasta sat down.

"*Signómi* — Excuse me. I'm Achilles Maia. I proudly worked for the Colonels when they deposed the king and saved our country from the Communists."

I nodded at him. I was surprised that the room remained quiet. Perhaps the support group was non-political after all.

"Why were there murders? The police won't tell us."

I could have sworn I'd just said to the woman before him that I didn't know the motive for the crimes.

"I don't know the answer to that," I said. "It's one of the aspects of the investigation I'm still working on. In my experience, if you find who has the most to gain, the identification of the motive usually follows."

I fielded half a dozen more questions without really answering any since I didn't have any answers. The final question came from George Kostas, who now introduced himself to me as a loyal supporter, like his mother had been, of the democratic movement that overthrew the Colonels.

"I don't have no politics," he said, "not since my mother and I came to America. My question is simple, Do you think we are safe here?"

Why did George ask that in a public forum since he already knew I don't know the answer? That was the question I'd been dreading. I said as much in answer to George's question.

I could tell from the sparse applause when I concluded my presentation that the audience was as dissatisfied with my vapid responses as I was. But what could I do? I wouldn't make up information to tell them.

George insisted he buy me a drink afterward to thank me for my participation. I agreed to let him buy me one. Then I intended to excuse myself and head home.

We settled in at *Stan's*.

"I thank you for your help tonight," he said.

"Glad to do it," I said, "but I'm afraid I didn't have much to offer. I doubt I was much help or comfort to anyone."

George nodded. "Did you ever see the revised report they done on my mother after they dug her up?" he said.

"No," I said, "but I was told by the detective the ME

found a pin-prick puncture mark behind her left ear where the poison had been injected."

I switched subjects.

"George, I noticed neither Arête Xandereas or her daughter, Toula, were at the meeting. Any reason?"

"Apparently they heard you were going to speak so they stayed away. At least that's what I heard," he said.

I nodded.

"My mother told me a little about the support group," I said, "that it's non-political, although made up of people with opposing political agendas. Is that right?"

"It's more complicated than that."

"Meaning what?" I said.

"I can't discuss it," he said. "I'm sworn to secrecy.'

I thought that was a strange response. "Is there someone else I can talk to about it?" I said.

George shook his head. "No one who knows will tell you." He paused, then said, "And you really shouldn't ask."

CHAPTER 82

I WAS SITTING IN THE LIVING room drinking Scotch, listening to Miles Davis on my iPod, and worrying about my mother when Thigpen called. It was a little past 2:30 a.m.

"Wake you?" he asked.

"No," I said. "Listening to music. Couldn't sleep."

He told me my mother had been found and was at the George Washington University Hospital. He said the MPD was holding her there in protective custody.

Twenty minutes later, Thigpen and I met in the hospital's lobby.

"Your mother's upstairs being checked by the docs," Thigpen said. "The Feds found her dazed and wandering in Lafayette Park. She seems unharmed, but frightened and exhausted."

I was relieved, but stunned and still worried.

What was my mother doing across the street from the White House in the middle of the night? Where had she been all that time she was missing?

I asked Thigpen what he knew, but he wouldn't say.

"Wait 'til after you see her, then we'll talk," he said.

My mother had been checked into a private room on the fourth floor. When I knocked and entered, I found her lying on her side facing the door. She had an IV running into her arm.

I crossed the room quickly, bent over the side of the bed, and kissed her forehead.

"*Te kánáte?* — How are you?" I said.

"*Ètsi k'étse* — So-so.*"

I took her hand and held it. She squeezed my hand as if she was holding onto the side of a bobbing life raft.

I looked into her eyes. Her pupils were dilated. She was high, other-worldly. She clearly was under the influence of some medication prescribed by the docs.

"I'm here, Ma. Don't try to talk. You're safe now."

She said nothing. She didn't even acknowledge my statement. She just continued to stare at me through frightened eyes.

We stayed this way for almost forty minutes, until she finally fell into a deep sleep, and I was able to loosen her grip on my hand. I pulled up a chair next to the bed, sat, and watched her sleep.

A single sharp rap on the door yanked me from my nap. I turned and saw Thigpen and his partner standing just inside the entryway.

"How's she doing?" Thigpen said, speaking uncharac-teristically softly. There was nothing of his profession in his tone, only earnest concern.

"Don't know yet," I answered. "She seems frightened

— terrified, in fact — but I don't know about her physical condition. I was planning to see her doc when I leave here."

Thigpen nodded.

"Do you know what happened to her?" I asked.

"Not much; not yet. We think she was snatched and held, then turned loose. But we don't know why or by who. We need to talk to your mother so we can get going on the investigation."

"That's up to the docs," I said, "not me, when and how much she can handle." I paused, glanced at my mother, then turned back to Thigpen.

"What *do* you know?" I said.

"Let's get some coffee," Thigpen said.

———————— •·•• ————————

We spread out around three sides of a linoleum topped cafeteria table. Thigpen and I each had a cup of burned coffee sitting in front of us; his partner wrapped her palms around a cup of hot tea.

"Working backwards," Thigpen said, "the Feds found your mother wandering in Lafayette Park. When they approached her, she couldn't ID herself.

"The Feds called for an EMS bus that took her to the hospital. They ID'd her from information in her purse. The ER docs called the 2D, who sent us over to see what-was-what." Thigpen looked at his partner for affirmation. She nodded.

I took a deep breath.

Thigpen continued. "I talked to your mother for a few minutes when I arrived. Seems she was snatched from the street."

I felt my stomach twist. "Did she say why?" I said.

"Wouldn't say. Said she'll only talk to you."

I frowned. I didn't like the sound of that.

"Did the perps ever contact you, Cheng?" Thigpen said.

I shook my head.

"We'll have to wait, then," Thigpen said, "unless she changes her mind when we talk to her tomorrow."

"It doesn't make any sense," I said. "Why would someone kidnap an old women and not demand ransom, then return her after a few days?"

"Maybe they were sending a message," Thigpen's partner said.

CHAPTER 83

ANOS WAS ATTENDING A SOCIAL event at Saint Sophia, trolling for new clients, when across town, at a few minutes after 10:00 p.m., the Mount Parnassus went dark.

All the building's lights and other necessities powered by electricity shut down. The HVAC shut off; the alarm system protecting the building's front entrance stilled; the fire alarm system went into standby; and, the communication systems used for entering and leaving the building fell useless. The Mount Parnassus did not have a backup generator.

At four minutes after 10:00, three men wearing ski masks and dressed in black, bypassed the heavy-metal fire door located on the ground floor at the rear of the building and quickly made their way up the interior staircase, past the now-blind security cameras. They stopped when they arrived at Panos' front door. Within minutes, they entered Panos' apartment and applied their electronic security devices to the dormant security system protecting the Treasure Room.

Five minutes after they'd entered, the three men exited Panos' apartment carrying *The Mourning Woman* with them, but not carrying anything else. They intentionally did not close the Treasure Room door so Panos would become aware of their intrusion when he returned home. One hour later, they delivered their plunder to Milos and Aristides.

At twenty minutes after 10:00, the Mount Parnassus' power fired up.

Panos seethed with fury. Not only had his home's sanctity been breached and his Treasure Room invaded, but *The Mourning Woman* had been stolen.

Panos calmed himself and thought about his situation.

Only two people knew he owned *The Mourning Woman*. *Why would they arrange to steal the statuette?* he wondered.

Panos thought about this, then smiled.

Now it was his turn again. He would have his revenge.

CHAPTER 84

THE HOSPITAL DISCHARGED MY MOTHER the next day. She had no physical injuries but, as I expected, was emotionally in turmoil. I set up a counseling appointment for her for later in the week. She refused to allow me to hire a nurse to stay with her, insisting she was frightened, but not physically injured.

I waited until she was settled in her bed before I entered her bedroom to see her. She was sitting up when I came in.

"This isn't the first time, Socrates," she said, as I walked in.

"What isn't?"

"Not the first time I was taken."

That stopped me. "What're you talking about? When?"

"Before the support group meeting, when I was late showing up, when I wouldn't tell you about why. That was the first time."

"Tell me now."

"*Ach!* There's not much to tell. I was getting ready for the meeting when there was a knock on my door. A man pointed a gun at me and told me to leave the building with him. We went out the back door."

I felt a chill run down my spine.

"I got into a car. They put a hood over my head, and we drove around somewhere. They told me to convince you to stop your investigation, or else. They also told me not to tell you about being taken by them or they would kill you. I was so scared. Then they dropped me off in front of this building."

I put my arm around her shoulders and squeezed.

"What are you going to do, Socrates? I don't want them to hurt you."

"I don't know." I said. "I'm going to have to think about it."

But I did know.

CHAPTER 85

I WAS HAPPY MY MOTHER WAS home again — safe for now — but worried because she continued to refuse to tell me details of what had happened to her during her second abduction. Even Thigpen and his partner couldn't pry any information loose from her. The woman could be maddening.

I finished dinner and was cleaning up when my cellphone rang. I checked the CallerID. It was Clotille.

I wanted to talk to her, to see her, and take her in my arms, but I didn't think I wanted to go up against Harte while Toula's wrath still lurked out there. But I also didn't think I should hide from Clotille, especially since she was calling.

"Hi," I said, trying with my light tone to mask my discomfort with the fact I'd been ignoring her.

"What have Ah done, Socrates, to rile y'all up so?" she asked.

I felt awful. I wanted to hug her and assure her we were okay with each other.

"You haven't done anything, Clotille. It's not—"

"Then why won't you—"

"Clotille, someone threatened to harm you because of me, and your father and I thought it would be better if—"

"Ah knew it," she said. "Ah knew it wasn't me angered you. Ah knew it."

I could hear her smile.

"That's wonderful, Socrates," she said, "but that doesn't change anything for me. Ah want to see you."

"That's not a good idea," I said. "Your father's right, I have to stay away from you for a little while, probably not much longer, but for now I do, just to be safe."

"No, Socrates, Ah'm not a child, me. Ah want to see y'all tonight. Ah won't allow you to keep me away."

I was boxed in. Harte was correct in insisting that Clotille and I keep apart until Toula could be dealt with or had moved on to someone else. But Clotille wasn't a child. She was capable of assessing her risk and deciding to avert it by not seeing me or to accept the risk, as she apparently wanted to. But she couldn't reasonably make that decision until she had all the facts concerning Toula, and Toula's threat.

"Talk to Harte," I said. "Let him bring you up to date. Then if you still want to see me, we'll talk about it."

"Uh, uh," Clotille said. "Ah want you to tell me. Ah'll decide if I'll take my chances, me." She paused, then said, "Y'all owe me that much, you."

I couldn't argue with that. Besides, I missed Clotille more than I'd realized until I first heard her voice a few minutes ago.

"Take me to lunch, Socrates. We'll talk. And we'll both be happy because we're together, us."

I smiled. "I will live with that single hope," I said.

———————

As I walked into Georgetown, I thought how much Clotille

had enriched my life in the short time I'd known her. I loved it when she talked, was captivated by the easy Cajun diction and syntax that masked her high intelligence. I found solace in her mere physical presence, in observing the easy way she moved and did things.

We met at *Café Milano*, a restaurant on Prospect Street near the campus of Georgetown University. Clotille was sitting at the bar when I arrived. She didn't have a drink in front of her. We kissed lightly, then I walked over to the *maitre d'* to see if we could get a table even though we didn't have a reservation.

We settled in on the second floor. We were by ourselves except for one other occupied table across the room.

Once we'd ordered drinks and the waiter left, I reached across the table and took Clotille's hand, kissed her fingers, and said, "I missed you, but I have mixed feelings about us being here together."

Clotille had a serious, almost impatient, look on her face. She pulled back her hand.

"Ah missed you, too," she said. "That's why Ah called, me. What's going on?"

I raised my glass in a toast. "First," I said, "to better times. For each of us, and together."

Clotille raised her glass, touched it to mine, and said, "Stop stalling, you."

I told Clotille about Toula, starting at the back end and how I had broken off a relationship with her. I described how she'd left the threatening voicemail. I also told her what Harte had passed on to me about Thigpen's interview with her.

"Ah don't understand," Clotille said. "you didn't really say why you broke off with that woman. Did Ah miss something, me? Ah know it wasn't the threat because y'all said that came after you stopped seeing her."

Clotille definitely had Harte's genes. She was a born detective. She saw right through my attempt to omit key facts.

I now told her how Toula and I had met, and told her about our *Friends With Benefits* relationship. This time I left nothing out and didn't sugarcoat what I said.

Clotille listened without interrupting me. I couldn't read her response by looking at her.

"So, Clotille, that's it," I said, "the whole story. Now Toula feels I owe her the obligation to keep seeing her, and since I refuse, she's tried to coerce me by threatening you."

"Why don't you see her?" Clotille said, "Didn't you enjoy your special arrangement?"

"I don't want anything to do with her, not anymore," I said, "not since I met you."

"We're you with her after we went out?"

"That's about when I ended it," I said.

I looked hard at Clotille, trying to read something in her body language, but she remained inscrutable.

"Are you upset," I said, "angry with me?"

She shook her head.

"Then what're you thinking?"

"Ah'm thinking, me, Ah'd like to have a similar arrangement with you, except for one aspect."

"What's that?" I said. I tried to mask my surprise and pleasure.

"Ah would want to leave out the just *friends* part, but keep the *benefits*. If y'all are willing to try that with me."

I don't shock easily, nor am I a prude. I also wasn't too worried how Harte might respond if Clotille and I started seeing each other on a serious basis, but I didn't buy into it.

"No," I said. "I can't. There's something else."

Clotille seemed disappointed and surprised, almost shocked.

"It's not I don't want to," I said, "believe me I do, but I'm not ready to commit to anyone. Not yet. It has nothing to do with you, it's me."

"Ah don't understand, Socrates," Clotille said. "Ah thought you liked me. You know Ah like you."

"Clotille, I swear it's not you or anything you've done," I said. "It's me. It's because I like you so much and will probably come to like you even more as I get to know you better that I can't be with you that way right now. I'm just not ready after my experience a few years ago with the Chinese woman I was involved with."

I could read the confusion on Clotille's face.

I reminded Clotille about my experience with Jade Li, how we'd been in love since college, and how, in effect, she'd abandoned me in her own way four years ago. I said that although I'd come a long way since then, I still had a long way to go to getting over my fear of abandonment.

I said I was afraid that if she and I became seriously involved, as we both wanted, I might anticipate my fear of abandonment and act on it, breaking-off our relationship before she could do so or, even worse, might act in some way that would force Clotille to break it off — all in order to validate my fear of being abandoned again.

"That's mighty insightful of y'all," Clotille said, "but it sets up a no-win situation for us. If you give in to your fear like you seem to be doing, then we don't win because we won't be together to find out if we can work through it. But you say if we try, then y'all might create a self-fulfilling prophesy, and bring us down. That sucks."

Definitely Harte's daughter, I thought.

"On the other hand," she said, "if we try, we might be surprised. We might make it work out. Ah'd rather have us try and mess up, than not try and just give up."

"Is that what you really want?" I said. "I might screw up."

"Ah'll take the chance if y'all will," she said, "but on one condition. You have to promise me that when you begin to feel frightened or worried, you'll tell me so we can talk it out, us. Ah'll do the same for you."

I stood up and walked around the table to Clotille. She looked puzzled and started to stand up. I waved her back down.

When I reached her I put my hand on her shoulder and bent down and kissed her. Then I walked back to my seat.

"I'll take the chance," I said.

CHAPTER 86

THE NEXT MORNING I SAT in my kitchen eating breakfast and thinking about my recent conversation at *Stan's* with George Kostas. His refusal to tell me more about the support group bothered me. Something about that organization poked at me and would not let me dismiss it from my thoughts.

I wasn't deterred by George's statement that no one who knew about the group would talk to me about it. I knew two people who might. I started with one of them by going to see my mother.

———— ·•·• ————

"All I know, Socrates, is what I told you. The support group is neutral territory. We don't discuss politics there."

My mother wasn't helpful so I called the other person who might be able to help me.

"Hello, Toula, it's me, Socrates."

After a charged half-minute of silence, Toula said, "What do you want?" Her tone was bone chilling.

"I know I shouldn't bother you, but I'd like to talk to you about the support group. It's for the investigation."

Again, a long pause.

"Meet me at *Zorba's* in half an hour," she said.

I arrived at the cafe first. Toula kept me waiting almost an hour before she imperiously strode in.

I stood up as she approached the table. She planted herself by the chair across the table and waited until I walked around the table to pull the chair out for her before she sat down. I could see a hint of a smirk on her face. I decided to swallow my pride in order to milk her knowledge of the support group. I had to remember my purpose in being here.

"I appreciate you meeting me," I said, as I sat down again.

She didn't say anything, but laughed lightly. It wasn't the friendliest laugh in her inventory.

"Like I said, I need some help in my investigation and thought you might give it to me."

"I see," Toula said. "Just like before, you call me when you need something. Otherwise I'm not good enough for you."

I bit my tongue. *This probably was a mistake.*

"That's not it, but if you're not willing to help me, why're you here?" I said. "I told you on the phone I needed your help." I was determined not to let her bully a relationship out of me just because I needed information from her.

"You really should learn some patience, Socrates. I didn't call you, you called me. Gratitude, too, can go a long way."

I swallowed hard and let that pass.

"What do you want to know?" she said, after half a minute of shared silence had passed. Her voice was hard, her words clipped.

I told Toula I was interested in knowing more about the support group — its origin, purposes, and role in the overall Metropolitan Washington Greek community.

"It seems to me," I said, "that by its very composition

it's a likely place for grievances to be nourished and possibly acted on.

"You think those old people were involved in the murders and assaults?" she said. She laughed. "You're bottom feeding now, Socrates. You must be desperate."

"I'd like your help," I said. "If you don't want to give it, say so. I'm not here to spar with you."

She made a *tsk, tsk, tsk* sound, then said, "Aren't you the righteous one." She stared at me for a few seconds, shook her head once as if to say, *How should I deal with this child*, but said instead, "Okay, have it your way for now. Here's what little I know?"

I let Toula talk at her own pace, not interrupting her with questions. It was a technique I learned interviewing witnesses or gathering information in my PI practice. Give people a silence to fill and they usually will fill it up with talk.

"I'm taking a risk talking to you about this," Toula said, "The support group is a cover for a secret lodge. What I know about it, I learned over the years from my mother. She swore me to secrecy."

I nodded.

"I can only say what I learned about lodges as a girl. I don't know nothing about the organization today."

Toula called over the waiter and ordered a glass of wine. I ordered hot tea.

"The Mount Parnassus support group," she said, "originated in Greek lodges — secret societies — formed to remove the Ottoman Turks from Greece. The support group is descended from the secret lodge called *Philiki Etaira,* a name that means the Friendly Society."

Again, I nodded to indicate my interest.

"But *Philiki Etaira,* itself, was not friendly," Toula said. "*Philiki Etaira* was active in the revolution of 1821 and played a major role in later struggles."

"Does *Philiki Etaira* play a role with the support group today?"

"I don't know," Toula said. "If I did know, I wouldn't tell you. But I will tell you this much: The rumor is that *Philiki Etaira* has teamed with *Oikoyennia,* the Greek mafia."

"All right," I said, nodding again. "Tell me what role the support group plays today in Washington's Greek community?"

"I'll tell you what you already know, that it acts as a support group for community members. That's all I'll tell you," she said.

This didn't add much to what I already knew from my mother and George.

"Is there anything you can tell me I haven't thought to ask," I said, "anything I should know for my investigation?"

Toula stared at me for a few seconds, not saying anything. I waited. Then she smiled — not a well-disposed smile — and said, "Watch yourself if you know what's good for you. These people don't play by your rules."

I was about to ask what she meant by that when she abruptly stood up, said, "Bye," and turned and walked out of *Zorba's.*

CHAPTER 87

WENT FOR A WALK IN Rock Creek Park to clear my head. After thirty minutes, I walked over to the Mount Parnassus to see my mother.

As I headed there, I thought about the ordeal my mother had recently been through. I knew I didn't have close to the whole story of what had happened to her during her second abduction because it wasn't in my mother's nature to disclose things about herself. She always held something back. But this morning when we spoke on the phone, she said she felt much better and would like to tell me all that had happened to her. Although I trusted her intent, I doubted she would follow through.

When I arrived, she was wearing a dressy nightgown and sitting up in bed. She broke into a big smile when she saw me. As she smiled, the color in her cheeks returned. It receded just as quickly when she stopped smiling.

The room was redolent with the fragrances of flowers and fruit that well-wishers from the condo and Saint Sophia had sent her. The window shades, which had been pulled closed on the other occasions I visited, now were rolled up so that sunlight poured into the bedroom, suffusing the room with the feeling of Spring.

I pulled up a chair from across the room and set it alongside the bed, leaned over and kissed her cheek, then sat down.

"You look pretty, Ma. I hadn't expected this so soon." I smiled.

"*Ach*! It's nothing," she said, brushing away my compliment with a slight shrug of her shoulders.

"Still feel up to talking?" I asked. I hoped she would say, Yes. Enough time had passed since her release in Lafayette Park that I worried she would lose memory of small, helpful details or would unintentionally create others from a false, recovered memory of the events.

"I'll try," she said. "If it becomes too much, we'll stop."

I reached over and squeezed her hand. "Fair enough."

"I already told you about the first time, so we can skip that."

"Okay."

"The second time was when I was walking back from Trader Joe's, pulling my cart of groceries behind me. I just passed the fire station. You know, the one on 23rd Street, across M from the CVS, when a van pulled up near where I was walking. I hardly paid any attention until I realized men were running from it toward me.

"I stopped and looked just as a man grabbed me by my shoulder and someone else put a cloth over my head. Then they pulled me into the van. I heard the door slide shut and felt us start to drive. I tried to sit up, but someone put a hand on my shoulder and pushed me back down on the floor. I was so scared. I felt my sleeve being pulled up by somebody, and then felt a needle jabbed in my arm. After that, I don't remember much."

"You were doped up so they could move you easily," I said.

"Next thing I remember, I was in a chair with my head still covered and my arms tied behind me. I thought I was alone so I started to call for help when someone slapped my face and told me, 'Shut up, Bitch.' After that, I don't remember nothing until I woke up in the hospital."

"Thanks, Ma," I said. "That helps. You don't have to say any more. We can pick it up with some questions I have another time, after you're rested."

"No, Socrates, I don't want to stop yet. I have some questions for you, too. I want you to answer them truthfully. Promise?"

I blindly agreed.

"Did anything happen to me while I was with them, you know, man/woman type things."

"No, Ma, it didn't. The doctors assured me. But they did keep you drugged while you were with them. That's why everything's a blur for you."

"*Dhóxa to theó* — Glory be to God for that," she said. She made the sign of the cross on her chest.

"The docs also said you weren't hit or otherwise physically harmed, except for the one slap you just told me about. It looks like it all was done to send a message to me that I'm not able to protect you, and that they will harm you if I continue the investigations."

"You're not going to stop now, Socrates, are you? Not after what these people did to me and my friends."

"No, Ma, I'm not quitting."

I filled her in on the information I'd gotten from the police and the hospital. I told her she'd been missing for three days before she was found wandering in the middle of the night. I also told her that her toxicity screen showed high amounts of morphine in her system, probably to keep her compliant during her confinement, and that she would have to go through detox rehab and counseling to make sure there were no addictive affects from her involuntary ingestion of the drug.

"I'm worried about you, Ma. I know we've been over this before, but I'd feel better if you would move—"

"Stop," she said, holding up her palm. She didn't say anything else. Her look said it all.

CHAPTER 88

ANOS SAT IN HIS CHAIR in the Treasure Room and thought about the events leading up to the recent theft of *The Mourning Woman*. He made two decisions: Milos and Aristides now would have to die, and he would recover possession of *The Mourning Woman* because he admired her so. He would do this, he decided, although she would be — and she would remain — the only artifact in his abandoned antiquities collection. He would decide later whether to keep her or destroy her.

The first thing he did to implement his decisions was to contact the *Patera* and arrange to have Milos and Theodoras murdered. The contract also required that the hitter recover *The Mourning Woman* and return her intact to him.

The second thing he did was resume his research into the authenticity of *The Mourning Woman* so he would know how to deal with her when he again possessed her.

The Tuesday following the day he made his decisions, Panos delivered the payment required by Kalakos in fulfillment of Panos' part of the contract.

On that same day, Panos also concluded his research. He still did not have a definitive answer. He still did not know if *The Mourning Woman* was genuine, but stolen, or if she was another fraud fostered on him by the Theodoros brothers.

CHAPTER 89

A S THE DAYS PASSED, MY mother seemed to be recovering nicely from her abduction, and in many ways seemed like her old self. She was in the kitchen baking when I stopped by to see her.

"Sit, sit, Socrates. Have some coffee. You're always in such a hurry," she said, as she pointed me to the table.

We drank coffee and ate pastries. When my mother stood up to get the coffee pot to pour herself another cup, she said, "So, to what do I owe the honor of your Saturday morning visit?"

"I'm always glad to see you, Ma, you know that, but I do have a few questions about your neighbors, if you don't mind."

"Why should I mind? You're not asking about me," she said, "so ask."

I pulled out the list of occupants and employees at the Mount Parnassus, and asked about those people who hadn't been home either time when I canvassed the building.

"Sorry," she said, when I arrived at the last name on the list, and she gave me the same answer she'd given me for all the others: 'I don't know them.'

"I wasn't very much help, was I? I guess I don't know many people here."

"No problem, Ma. I'll find out about them from somebody else."

I left my mother and walked toward Dupont Circle to go to my office. As I walked, I called George Kostas and asked him to meet me at *Zorba's*. He agreed, even though he clearly was annoyed I wouldn't tell him why I wanted to meet when he asked.

George and I had an early lunch, and a fairly pleasant talk until I told him the purpose of our get together.

"I don't feel comfortable talking about my mother's neighbors," he said.

His hypocrisy didn't sit well with me.

"That's bullshit, George," I said. I looked hard at him. "Either you want me to get to the bottom of your mother's murder or you don't. If you want me to, you'll cooperate. You can't have it both ways."

"I don't really know the people you mentioned."

"George," I said. "I don't believe you, but have it your way." I stood up, placed a twenty on the table, and walked away.

CHAPTER 90

TWO DAYS LATER, I MET with Harte at the Starbucks on M Street near 22nd.

"I told you to stay away from my daughter," Harte said. "What part of that didn't you understand?" He was furious.

"Clotille and I talked, and—"

"I didn't say it was up for debate and a vote. I told you to keep clear of Clotille until the problem with your wacko-stalker broad was done."

I couldn't argue with him. He was correct on all counts. I decided to risk setting him off by trying to put this in its proper perspective.

"Were you able to convince Clotille to stay away when you talked to her about it?" I said. I didn't give him time to answer. "Of course you weren't."

I knew how lame this must have sounded to him. It sounded lame to me. "You need to convince Clotille, not me," I said.

His face turned deep scarlet. "She has nothing to do with what I'm saying. I told you to stay away from—"

"That's my point, Harte," I said, now deliberately rubbing it in. "I couldn't convince her either."

That seemed to calm him. His face returned to its normal sallow color and his body relaxed, although his overall body language screamed frustration.

He shook his head. "That woman is more like Rosie than she should be considering they don't share any genes."

I smiled, but let that one go.

"Okay, Hotshot," Harte said. "How do you suggest we keep my daughter safe until this is wrapped up?"

It was ironic. We'd been verbally dueling with one another as if we were alone, but we weren't alone. Clotille was at the table with us. We had ignored her, and she had been quiet throughout my exchange with Harte, but now she loudly cleared her throat to grab our attention.

"Excuse me, y'all, but Ah have something to say."

Harte and I looked at Clotille as if we were surprised to discover her there with us. We glanced at one another and smiled.

"First off," she said, looking first at me and then at Harte, "Ah don't like being talked about as if Ah'm not here." She looked at each of us again. She did not looked happy.

"Second," she said, "Y'all don't get to make decisions for me, either of you. Ah'm not a child, me. Ah'll decide if Ah'm going to date you, Socrates, Harte won't," she said, speaking of her father as if he wasn't there. "You and I settled that," she said, "unless you changed your mind and didn't tell me."

"I haven't changed my mind," I said. I didn't dare look over at Harte.

"Then it's settled, you," she said, still looking in my eyes.

I nodded. Harte did not.

"Y'all okay with that now, Daddy?" she said.

Harte grumbled something I took to be, Yes.

"I'm just worried about you, Honey," he added.

"Me, too," I said. Once again, I didn't dare look at Harte. I could feel his scowl boring into me.

"Okay, then," Clotille said, her upbeat tone belying the conversation that had just occurred. "How do we protect poor little ol' me while Ah date Mr. Cheng here?"

"I have a thought," I said. I turned to face Harte. "Let's team up and solve the crimes together. Our combined abilities and resources should expedite the investigations. In the meantime, I'll try to get a restraining order from the court against Toula Xandereas to keep her away from Clotille."

"That sounds like a good idea, both ideas," Clotille said, smiling first at me and then at her father.

"I told you, Cheng, I don't work with civilians," Harte said. "Forget it."

He looked over at Clotille, who seemed about to say something. He gave her a severe look I interpreted to mean, *Stay out of this one if you know what's good for you.*

We left the restaurant together. Clotille gave me a peck on the cheek, while Harte looked on stoically. I caught his eye and surreptitiously nodded in the direction of a doorway across the street.

Harte looked over. I saw the color drain from his face.

Toula was standing in the doorway watching us. She was smiling and made no move not to be seen.

CHAPTER 91

MILOS STEPPED INTO HIS HOUSE, closed the front door, and reached for the light switch on the foyer wall. Before his finger made contact, a baseball bat, traveling at a head-speed sufficient to smack a hardball deep into the bleachers, smashed into his right knee.

Milos screamed and dropped to the floor, clutching his shattered knee with both hands. He lay on his side and turned his head to look up at his assailant.

The intruder flipped the light switch to its on position.

Notwithstanding the fog of pain, Milos was aware that the intruder was not wearing a mask to hide his identity, a factor that Milos, even in his shocked and anguished condition, understood did not bode well for him. The intruder didn't care if Milos could see his face because he did not intend to leave Milos alive to identify him.

Milos rolled over on his side and tried to use his left hand as a fulcrum to leverage himself into a kneeling position, but he didn't get far. This time the bat smacked him across his back, about ten inches below his neckline, sending excruciating pain throughout his torso, causing him to drop back down to the floor. Milos laid on his stomach, whimpering, unable to move or offer any resistance.

From the corner of his eye, Milos saw the intruder's shoes move next to his face. He watched as one shoe left his field of vision and then swiftly returned in a blur to kick him in the side of his head. Milos shrieked in pain, then moaned, and waited for the next blow to arrive, unable to move at all now.

He did not have long to wait.

The intruder raised the baseball bat over his head, then grunted from his effort as he brought the bat down against the back of Milos' knees.

Milos screamed.

After what seemed an eternity to Milos, the intruder rolled Milos over onto his back, and then, with two lightning fast swings, whacked Milos in the front of both knees, splintering the bones in both legs.

As Milos slipped into a welcomed coma, the intruder left the foyer. He soon returned with a small cooking pot full of cold tap-water which he threw into Milos' face, dragging Milos back into an unwelcomed state of semi-consciousness. Milos opened his eyes and groaned. Through the fog of pain, Milos could see his assailant standing alongside him, looking down at him.

As Milos watched through a gauze-like haze, the man gripped the bat with both hands and raised it above his head. The last thing Milos saw was the blur of the bat rushing toward his face.

It did not take Milos long to die after that.

———————————

When Milos' assailant went after Aristides later that same night, he changed his weapon of choice from the ball bat to two other favorites of his: a stainless steel ball tethered to the end of a telescoping steel rod; and a garrote consisting of a two foot length of piano wire, knotted in the center of its length, and secured by a wooden handle at each end.

The killer knocked twice on Aristides' front door. When Aristides looked through the security peep hole, he saw a well-dressed middle aged man, wearing a conservative suit and tie, standing on the front porch, his hands hanging by his sides.

Aristides frowned at the late hour, but opened the door. He'd barely said *Can I help you?* when the punch to his Adam's apple cut off his question and fully extinguished his ability to utter any sound other than a harrowing groan.

Aristides grasped his throat with both hands as he was pushed backward by the intruder, who bulled his way past the open door and into the foyer.

The intruder kicked Aristides in his left knee, crushing the bone and dropping Aristides to the foyer floor.

As Aristides held his knee with both hands and struggled to find his voice, the intruder removed the steel rod from inside his suit jacket, flicked his hand to extend the thin chain, and whipped the steel ball around in a circle, producing a steady hum as it whirled above Aristides.

Without warning, the intruder smashed the ball into the side of Aristides' head, and for the next fifteen minutes performed this same ritual on various other parts of Aristides' body. When the humming finally stopped, Aristides had sustained multiple broken bones and eighty-four lacerations. But, as his assailant intended, he still was alive.

The intruder collapsed the steel rod back into its storage size and slipped it inside his jacket pocket. He then removed the garrote from inside his suit jacket.

The garrote was the intruder's weapon of choice for close contact assassinations because it was quick, silent, and untraceable. All its parts could be purchased at any hardware store.

The intruder quickly slipped the wire loop over Aristides' head and around his neck, and slowly tightened the wires by twisting the wooden handles at each end until the knot at the center of the wire crushed Aristides' larynx.

Aristides was grateful when death finally visited him.

⸻

Two days later, FedEx delivered the brothers' package to Panos — seven identical *terra cotta* statuettes, each one *The Mourning Woman*, each one indistinguishable from the others, one or all of them fakes.

CHAPTER 92

CLOTILLE CALLED AND ASKED ME to meet her for dinner. She suggested we go to the *Prime Rib*, a restaurant located near her office on K Street between 20th and 21st. We met on the sidewalk outside the CFTC, and walked over to the *Rib*. As we walked, I furtively looked around to see if Toula was lurking, but I didn't see her.

We sat at the bar, sipped wine, and talked with Jimmie — the tender I'd known for about seventeen years — while we waited for a table to open up. We were remarkably relaxed with one another.

Clotille told me some stories from her childhood in New Iberia; I told her about growing up on Long Island in Levittown under the disparate influences of a strong Greek mother and an equally strong, but quiet, Chinese father.

After dinner, and another round of drinks at the bar, we said goodnight to Jimmie, and caught a taxi to Clotille's apartment in Arlington. She invited me to come in for a nightcap. I gladly accepted.

After a brief tour of Clotille's one bedroom home, we sat down on the sofa and sipped wine. The cumulative effect of the drinks we'd had at the restaurant, the wine we now were drinking, and our proximity to one another alone in Clotille's apartment, eventually led us into her bedroom. I spent the night.

When I got ready to leave in the morning to go home to shower and change my clothes, Clotille told me she felt wonderful. I, too, felt wonderful, but my feelings were tempered by my concern how Harte would react when he sensed, as I knew he would, that we'd slept together. Beyond that, I continued to feel guilty because Clotille and I hadn't fully come to terms with my fear of commitment, even though we'd discussed it briefly in general terms. Clearly, we needed to talk more about that issue.

The next night, disaster struck.

CHAPTER 93

THE FOLLOWING EVENING CLOTILLE LEFT her apartment a little after 8:00 p.m. and walked to the Clarendon Metro Station four blocks away. She was on her way to her parents' home to have late dinner with them as she did every Tuesday evening following her workout at her health club.

She was in a good mood. Her father, it seemed, had finally, if reluctantly, accepted her decision to date Socrates. Her mother, who had never expressed any problem with it, merely counseled her to be careful, not to position herself so she might be hurt.

When two hours had passed beyond the time Clotille was due to arrive at Harte's home, and she hadn't answered her home landline, her office phone, or her cellphone, Harte called in favors at the 2D.

The 2D's duty officer contacted the Arlington Police Department and the Virginia State Police even though not enough time had passed to officially treat Clotille as a missing person. The Arlington and state cops issued formal BOLO

[Be On the Lookout] alert notices, sometimes called All Alert Bulletins. The 2D did the same in the District.

Clotille was found later that evening in an alley one block from the Metro station. She was unconscious. She'd been beaten and, based on the condition of her clothing when she was found, appeared to have been raped. But she was alive. The Arlington EMS unit had taken her to the Virginia Hospital Center, a 334-bed hospital located on George Mason Drive in Arlington.

CHAPTER 94

I WAS AT HOME WHEN ROSIE Hart called. I immediately headed for the hospital.

Harte and a woman, who appeared sufficiently upset so that I assumed she was Rosie, were standing in the hallway outside a hospital room. A uniformed officer stood sentry by the door. I'd later learn that this was another ex-cop's favor called in by Harte.

When he saw me approaching, his face became dark. He started walking toward me.

"This is your fault, you sonofabitch," he said, as he came within normal speaking distance. "This never would've happened if you listened to me."

I held up both palms as if to ward off Harte and block his statements.

"You should have known better, not listened to her. She's too naïve to understand the danger—"

"Tell me what happened," I said. There was no point arguing culpability right then. My concern was for Clotille.

Harte told me the little he knew. I was devastated. I wanted to see Clotille and take her hand and assure her I would stand by her, but I'd have to wait. A medical tech was with her right then creating a Vitullo kit — a sexual assault evidence collection kit commonly known as a Rape Kit.

———————————

"Let's get some coffee," Harte said to me. "We aren't doing any good here." He looked over at his wife, and raised his eyebrows. "You wanna come?"

"You go," she said, shaking her head. "I'll call your cell when we can go in."

We took a small table in the cafeteria away from everyone else.

"This is your fault," Harte said to me.

"Do you have any reason to think this was connected to the Mount Parnassus or the Xandereas woman?"

Harte grunted, but didn't answer. His face and neck color were severe.

"Do the cops have any leads?" I asked.

Harte shook his head. "Not yet I know of. Thigpen's going to pick up that Toula woman, see what he can learn from her."

I nodded. I could see Toula arranging to have Clotille beaten, that wasn't beyond my imagination, but arranging for her to be raped? I just didn't know.

"Listen," I said, "I'm sorry about this, but I doubt it had anything to do with me."

Harte glared at me, but didn't say anything. He seemed to be waiting for me to say something else, maybe that I would stop seeing Clotille even if the assault could not be connected to my investigation or to Toula. I didn't take the bait.

"Look, Harte," I said. "I want you to reconsider working with me. It makes sense if we want to get to the bottom of the crimes and maybe even the attack on Clotille. I can do the investigation, and you can mine your sources at MPD, and call on your years of experience to advise me. Don't be so damned stubborn."

"I told you," he said, "I don't work with civilians."

"That's nonsense," I said. "If you don't want to work with me, because I'm me, say so, but don't give me that bullshit excuse anymore. There's too much at stake for both of us."

CHAPTER 95

H ARTE EVENTUALLY CAME AROUND AND agreed we'd work together, although I could tell from his comments when he called to tell me that he would be a reluctant collaborator. His resistance was overcome by the logic of combining our concerns for Clotille and heading off any other threats to her if there was a connection between the crimes at the Mount Parnassus and the attack on Clotille.

As a practical matter, however, all Harte could agree to was that we would collaborate on the crimes at the Mount Parnassus. We couldn't do anything with the crime against Clotille since that occurred in Arlington, another jurisdiction. All Harte could do with respect to Clotille's rape was call in his chits at the 2D to find out about the investigation by the Arlington cops, then share that information with me.

Harte and I got together the next morning at the *M Street Bar & Grill* to start brainstorming how we'd conduct the investigation. We divided up the roles and assignments, and generally started the slow process of becoming comfortable working together. I was nervous.

"What's the current deal with the stalker broad?" Harte said.

"I told you. She and I—"

"I know what you told me, Cheng, but there's got to be more to it than that. No woman could be that crazy over you?"

I chuckled. "She might be," I said. "After all, she's certifiable as far as I'm concerned. Thinks everyone's out to screw her over. Her ex-husband, her divorce lawyer, her co-workers, now me."

Harte didn't say anything for almost half a minute. I could tell he was running things through his mind.

"Okay, let's leave her out of this for now. What else we got?" he said.

I handed Harte a copy of the chronology I'd made. It was complete except for the assault against Clotille, since I didn't see any tie-in among it and the crimes at the Mount Parnassus. Time, and some burned-up shoe leather, would tell me if I was right.

Harte looked at the time-line. "This is good," he said.

"How should we go forward?" I asked.

"I'll talk to Thigpen, get his read on things, then I'll read through the files again," Harte said.

"Okay," I said.

"In the meantime, you concentrate on the people who live at the condo. Get me a list of everyone who lives and works there. I'll have Thigpen run the names for us, see who has a record that might be relevant."

I nodded again. I was feeling more positive already. "I have the list already," I said. "I'll e-mail it to you."

"Afterward, we'll get together and compare notes," he

said. He paused again, then stood up. "Don't forget, we're interlopers here. Don't get in the way of the cops. If you do, it'll be messy for both of us.

We split up after that. Harte said he was going back upstairs to meet his wife and say goodbye to Clotille. I planned on visiting my mother — she still was housebound — before going to my office to begin my part of the investigation. I would stop back at the hospital after Harte and his wife had left so I could spend time alone with Clotille.

After I visited my mother, I hurried to my office, booted up my computer, and opened my database software. I wanted to create a new database that would contain all I knew about the crimes at the Mount Parnassus. As I learned more facts, I'd add them. It was my plan to run various database queries from time-to-time against the records to see if any common themes emerge from among the crimes. I hadn't seen any so far, when I'd eyeballed the individual files or prepared the chronology, but I hoped the computer would disclose patterns not readily apparent to me.

CHAPTER 96

T HE HOSPITAL DISCHARGED CLOTILLE TWO days after her admission. She moved in with her parents while she continued to recuperate. I went over to Harte's home to visit her within an hour of her arrival there.

Rosie Harte answered my knock and opened the front door for me. It was clear she wasn't thrilled to see me.

"Oh," she said. "It's you. Well, come in." She stepped aside so I could enter.

"Ralph," Rosie shouted toward the back of the house, "Clotille's friend Socrates is here."

Harte came out to meet me.

"Cheng," he said, as he acknowledged my presence with a nod. He moved over and stood next to his wife, watching me.

"Harte, Mrs. Harte," I said, nodding my greeting, "I'm here to visit Clotille if she's up to it."

Rosie led me through the apartment to a bedroom in the back. She knocked on the door jamb when we arrived at the entrance.

"Your friend Socrates is here," Rosie Harte said, as she knocked again.

"Oh, come in, come in, Socrates," Clotille said. "Ah'm so glad you're here, you."

She was sitting up in bed with pillows propped behind her. She wore a nightgown and robe. I walked quickly across the room until I was close enough to reach her, then bent over and kissed her cheek.

"I'll leave you two alone," Rosie said. There was no warmth in her voice. "Call me if you need anything."

"How're you doing?" I said, as I straightened up.

Clotille shrugged, then patted the mattress alongside her. "Sit here, please. Stay close by me."

I sat on the edge of the bed and took her hand.

"Ah'm so glad you're here. Ah didn't know if y'all would come to see me after what happened."

"I'm here for you, whatever you need," I said.

She squeezed my hand and offered me a wan smile.

"Ah've never been so frightened in all mah life," she said. "It was even more horrible than Ah ever imagined, me, from reading about such things."

I patted her hand again. "You don't have to talk about this right now," I said. "We can talk later if you want."

I watched Clotille's eyes tear-up.

"Ah'll understand, Socrates, if you don't want anything to do with me after what that monster did, him. It'll be all right." She started to cry softly.

I took her hand in both mine, and held on.

"Listen to me, Clotille. I'll say this as often as you need to hear this. . . . I want to be with you. Nothing's changed between us. I promise. I want to be with you. Period."

Clotille cried harder. As I took my handkerchief from my pocket so I could wipe away her tears, I realized she was shaking. I dabbed her eyes, put my arm around her shoulders, and pulled her in closer to me. She put her head on my shoulder, and quietly wept.

CHAPTER 97

I LEFT CLOTILLE AFTER FORTY MINUTES because she seemed tired. I promised to come back the next morning.

As I walked toward the front of the house to say goodbye to Harte and his wife, I saw Harte standing in the doorway watching me. He motioned for me to follow him. We walked into the small 1950s-style living room.

"I'm going to look for some connection between the assault on Clotille and the crimes at the condo," Harte said. "I think the connection's you, but we'll see."

"That'll work for me," I said. I paused so he could continue, but he said no more.

"Have you considered the possibility that what happened to Clotille isn't related to the Mount Parnassus or to my investigations, that it was a coincidence?"

"I don't believe in coincidences," he said.

"Come on, Harte, give me a break," I said, "That's Hollywood leading-man, pulp magazine, private-eye bullshit, and you know it. We're not talking tough-guy Dashiell Hammett and Raymond Chandler here." I shook my head.

"Think so?" Harte said. "'I've been at this longer than you, Cheng. Dig deep enough, you'll find every time there are no coincidences."

"Sometimes, things just happen," I said.

Harte languidly shook his head. "You'll never get far as a PI with that attitude," he said.

"What if we forget about coincidences then," I said, "and think of it as unrelated?"

"Are you trying to talk me out of helping you?" Harte said. "That's where this is heading, you keep talking like that."

"I'm just trying to keep an open mind," I said.

Harte studied me for a few seconds, then said, "Let's see what we have and what we need to do. We're wasting time arguing."

CHAPTER 98

O VER THE NEXT TWO WEEKS, Clotille and I spent all or some part of most days together. It was nice, very nice. No pressure. Just, for me, the great pleasure of being in her company. Harte and Rosie now seemed reconciled to our relationship, at least that's how they behaved.

Clotille and I decided to take a weekend together away from Washington so we could relax and recharge. We booked dinner and a room for Saturday night at the five star internationally acclaimed, *Inn at Little Washington*, located in rural Washington, Virginia, seventy miles from Washington, DC.

We had a thoroughly enjoyable and relaxing weekend, but one without sex, as we had agreed in advance. Clotille was not yet ready to be intimate again. I had no problem with that. By agreement, we also didn't talk about the crimes at the Mount Parnassus or about what had happened to Clotille.

When I dropped Clotille off Sunday night at her parents' place, Harte came out to the car to talk to me. I rolled down my window as he approached.

"Harte," I said, as I nodded my greeting. I was a little uncomfortable. I braced for the coming verbal storm.

"Welcome back, Cheng," he said. "I take it no one

stalked you or committed other crimes against you in Little Washington."

"No," I said, "it was fine."

"I got that list of employees and occupants you sent," Harte said. I'll do a deep background search on everyone using the 2D's computers and its access to the national crime register. I already cleared it with Thigpen."

CHAPTER 99

GEORGE KOSTAS CALLED ME EARLY Monday morning. He asked to meet again to discuss the state of my investigation into his mother's murder. Since I had no more information than before, I offered to discuss it over the telephone, but he said, No. He insisted we do it face-to-face, saying I shouldn't be afraid to look him in the eye. He was becoming tiresome.

"Like I told you, George, unfortunately nothing new's happened in your mother's case," I said. "I'm still working on it."

"I find that hard to believe. There must be something."

I let his implication that I'd lied to him pass. I decided to make some small talk so my time coming to meet him wouldn't be a total waste.

"Somebody told me you're an artist, that you paint," I said.

George nodded, but still looked seriously sullen.

I didn't want to have to drag conversation out of him, so I decided to give it one more, low-key, try.

"What do you paint?"

"Religious themes."

"How'd you get interested in that?" I said.

"My Church and my father inspired me," he said.

Asking him friendly questions was becoming too much work. I decided I'd wrap it up to be polite and get out of there. I'd done my duty with George.

"So," I asked, "was your father a painter of religious topics?"

George shook his head. "He was a failed painter, but a great conservator. He was responsible for instigating the movement to recover the Elgin Marbles from the British Museum, to return them to Greece. It became his life's work. When he became the Minister of Arts for the king, he also devoted his life to preserving the masterpieces of religious art owned by our Church and country."

"That must have been nice for you growing up," I said, "having a father who accomplished so much for his Church and king." I waited while George smiled and nodded.

"Everything I paint," George said, "is in memory of my father. My mother and I honor — I mean, honored — his memory as best we could."

We made some other small talk for the next few minutes, then parted.

CHAPTER 100

T HE NEXT AFTERNOON, HARTE CALLED me to get
together. He said he had some questions about a few of
the people on the list I had e-mailed to him. He added
that although he could do this with me over the telephone,
he'd rather do it in person so we could begin to get used to
working together. That pleased me.

We met for dinner at *Otello*, an Italian bistro located near
Dupont Circle, north of N Street on Connecticut Avenue.

We greeted one another, ordered a bottle of Montepulciano
d'Abruzzo, and made small talk for a few minutes. After we'd
ordered our meals and while we waited for the food to arrive,
Harte pulled a small notebook from his jacket pocket, and
said, "Let's go over the names of the principal players. Tell me
what you know about each of them."

I nodded.

"Start with the Stamos DOA," he said.

"What I know, I know from my mother," I said. I paused
to collect my thoughts. "Let's see . . . . She originally came
from near Sparta. Her husband worked for the Colonels.
After the regime fell, Eugenia and her husband immigrated

to the U.S. He died shortly after that, from natural causes I think."

"What about before, the years she lived in Greece?" Harte said.

"This part of her history is interesting," I said. "Eugenia was one of several young girls taken from their villages to be trained to become the next Oracle at Delphi. Apparently, she ultimately was the one selected; the other girls returned to their villages."

"Why are you telling me this? Is that important to anything?" Harte said.

I shrugged. "Not sure," I said, "except being selected was quite an achievement and didn't just happen. The competition among families and villages to have their village's candidate selected was savage."

"Just like real life," Harte said.

"There's more. After Eugenia was selected, the priests trained her in the art and politics of rendering prophecies, and collecting gold and other valued remuneration in return for her divinations.

Harte smiled. "As I said, just like real life."

"The gold and other wealth delivered to the Cult of Apollo was shared among the priests and with the Oracle's family and village.

"Because the position of Oracle offered great wealth and prestige for the Pythia's family and village, the methods used to have the candidates selected involved bribes, threats, sex, politics, extortion, and, apparently, resultant anger and deep hatreds among those who lost out."

"Interesting," Harte said. "Anything else I should know? What about Arête Xandereas?"

"It's a similar story, up to a point. Arête, too, was from near Sparta. Her husband originally had been affiliated with the king as some kind of middle-level bureaucrat. When King Alexander fell, her husband went to work for the Colonels. Then, when the Colonels fell, he was arrested and eventually tried as a war criminal. He died in prison."

I waited while Harte finished making notes. When he looked up, I said, "She had two children, a girl and a boy. The girl you know. Toula, the stalker." I smiled without mirth.

"Oh, yeah," Harte said, "I know her all right."

"I don't know anything about the boy," I said. "except that he was left in Greece with a relative because he had a communicable lung disease. That wasn't so unusual with emigrants from the Balkans," I said.

Harte scratched out some other notes, then looked up and said, "And Serena Kostas?"

"My mother didn't know much about her when we talked. Selena immigrated to the U.S. without her husband when the Colonels came to power. Her husband had been King Alexander's Minister of Arts. They had one son, George. He's an artist, and a pain in the ass. I don't know anything else about them."

"There's that guy, Panos," Harte said. "What's his story?"

"He's the man Toula Xandereas called Uncle Panos when she introduced me to him at a support group meeting," I said. "He's an accountant or financial planner for people at the condominium and at Saint Sophia. That's all I know. Seemed decent enough when we talked."

"And last but not least," Harte said, "there's your mother. How does she fit in?" Harte looked at me hard. I wasn't sure what that was about, but I wasn't comfortable with it."

"My mother, as you know, also is Greek, but she grew up in China after her eighth birthday. Her father — my grandfather — worked in Shanghai for Secony Vacuum Oil Company. I knew him because he lived next door to us when I was growing up on Long Island.

I waited while Harte finished writing.

"When my father was alive, my mother didn't practice her religion or openly acknowledge her Greek culture. She deferred to my father's culture and Taoism. After he died two years ago, she returned to the Greek Orthodox Church, moved into the Mount Parnassus, and became active in its Greek community."

"Anything else I should know?" he said.

"Nothing I can think of."

Harte finished writing, closed his notebook, then pocketed it.

"I'll head to the 2D now and run all the names on the list," he said.

We shook hands, both said we enjoyed our dinner and work session together, and parted.

CHAPTER 101

CALLED CLOTILLE AFTER I LEFT Harte, and asked if I could come over to visit. She had moved back to her apartment in Arlington that afternoon.

Fifteen minutes later I knocked on her front door.

Clotille hadn't known I'd had dinner with her father, and was delighted when I told her.

"Ah'm glad mah daddy and y'all are getting along now, you two," she said.

Although I was still skeptical how my working relationship with Harte might play out, I said nothing about that. I decided to keep an open mind and enjoy watching Clotille enjoy the possibility that Harte and I might become friends or, if not friends, compatible as colleagues.

Clotille poured drinks for us and set out a platter of cheese and crackers. We settled on the couch, but at opposite ends, facing one another. I needed some physical distance so I could talk to her about my frustration with the investigation, yet not be so close to her that my need and desire to take her in my arms and hold her would take control.

"Something seems to be on your mind, you," she said. "Did Ah do something to offend you?"

"God, no," I said. "Thank goodness you're in my life. No, Dear, it's not you."

Clotille smiled warily, and slowly nodded.

"It's the investigation. I'm frustrated by it, by my lack of progress, and the danger that might be lurking out there threatening my mother and you."

After I said that I realized how feeble I sounded, given what Clotille had been through.

Clotille shook her head. "Don't y'all worry about me. I'm taking care now when I go out. I'll be all right. You just worry about your mother, you."

"I can't help but worry about you, too," I said.

Clotille smiled. "If what happened to me," she said, "was a warning for you to stop your investigation, it didn't work. You're still at it. So what are they going to do next to warn you away, kill me?"

I didn't want to say out loud that this was exactly what worried me, so I said, "Guess not."

CHAPTER 102

HARTE CALLED THE NEXT EVENING as I was getting ready to shower and call it a night.

"We need to get together," he said. "I've finished vetting the list you gave me."

We agreed to meet for lunch the next day at the new *Pot Belly* sandwich restaurant located in the space formerly occupied by the Mayflower Wine Shoppe on M Street, near the corner of New Hampshire Avenue.

We spent the first fifteen minutes ordering and eating lunch, saying very little. Harte seemed more relaxed and friendly than usual.

After we finished our meals, we left the restaurant and walked across the street to the same Duke Ellington Memorial pocket-park we'd sat in before.

"I turned up information on most of the people we talked about," he said. "There's nothing Earth shaking, not to me at least, but you might react differently. There was one thing you should've told me about, but didn't. I'll want to know why."

"What are you talking about?" I said.

"You'll see."

I had no choice but to wait, so I said, "Right." I wondered

if this information was the reason Harte had been so friendly at lunch.

"The information you gave me was good as far as it went," he said, "but you left out some things. The problem is, I don't know how important the omitted information is."

"Such as what?" I said.

"Such as, you told me Arête Xandereas was originally from Sparta, but she wasn't. She was from Mani. That's not even close to Sparta."

"Minor mistake," I said. "I had bad information. So what?"

"I don't know *so what*, but every piece of information is important until we find out it's not," he said.

I nodded. I couldn't argue with that.

"Eugenia wasn't from Sparta either. She was from a nearby village in Laconia."

"Okay," I said. "What else?"

"You didn't tell me your mother was related to Arête. Why not?"

"What are you talking about?" I said.

Harte raised his eyebrows. "Turns out your mother and Arête are cousins on their fathers' side. Why didn't you tell me?"

"Because I didn't know," I said, "but I intend to find out." I didn't want to think about the implications of this in terms of Toula and me.

PART FOUR

CHAPTER 103

"I CAN'T BELIEVE YOU NEVER TOLD me you and Arête are cousins," I said.

I didn't know which I felt more, anger or disappointment that she'd held back this information. Even though I didn't know if it was relevant or not to my investigation, it seemed like something I should have been told.

I was in my mother's kitchen sitting at the table with her, drinking coffee.

"It never came up," she said. "It's not a close relationship, Socrates. We're distant cousins."

"You never heard from your grandparents or parents that they'd lived in the province of Maniot, near Sparta?"

My mother shook her head.

"Arête never mentioned you were from nearby villages, and the same clan? I said.

"I told you, No," my mother said. Her rising anger was palpable.

I decided to drop it for now, except for one image I couldn't purge from my mind: As I looked at my mother, all I could see was Toula's feral smile.

CHAPTER 104

I LEFT MY MOTHER AND HEADED for my office to go online and research Selena, Arête, and George. After the revelation about my mother and Arête, I wasn't confident I had the full picture concerning any of them.

Google turned up nothing on Selena. I had the same result for her from the data warehouses.

I looked up Arête next. Google gave basic information about her such as her age, current address, and her telephone number. I had a slightly better response from the data warehouses. All three disclosed the same information: the date Arête had immigrated to the United States; the name of her children (Toula and Ari); the name of her deceased husband (Petreus); the village she'd grown up in (Mani); and her family surname. I was curious about Ari. I hadn't actually heard that name before although I knew he must be the brother Toula mentioned. I made a note to look into him later.

My search for George wasn't very fruitful except for one surprise. He had been arrested (but not brought to trial) for art forgery eleven years ago when he was living in Toledo, Ohio. Nothing more was said about this. I made a note to check on it with him. Other than that, George was described as a second- rate painter, with a minor talent for mimicry. He had not had any exhibits that were noted in the databases. He currently worked as a salesman for a local automobile seat cover manufacturer.

I left the computer satisfied I had exhausted one good avenue of research, even if nothing important had turned up. I had two matters (learn more about Ari and learn about George's arrest) to follow-up.

I swallowed my good sense, and called Toula. Much as I hated to reinvigorate the cycle of hostile dependency, I needed some information only she could give me.

CHAPTER 105

ARTE AND THIGPEN SHOOK HANDS and smiled. In spite of their disparate personalities, they had been good partners and friends. They had agreed to meet for lunch with the dual purpose of stoking their waning friendship and sharing information concerning the crimes at the Mount Parnassus.

Although Thigpen would have preferred that neither Harte nor Socrates had involved himself in the investigation, he'd resigned himself to the fact that as long as Harte and Cheng did not interfere with the official investigations, he couldn't stop them, and might even benefit from information they developed.

The former partners sat on a bench just across the sidewalk from a street vendor who sold hot dogs and other sausage-type sandwiches from an umbrella-covered cart. It was an eating spot they'd frequently ate at when Harte still was on the Job. He and Thigpen would get away from the noise and chaos of the detectives' bullpen and sit on the bench, savor the relative quiet of Idaho Avenue, eat hot dogs, and share information and ideas concerning cases they were working.

Today they were meeting because Harte had called Thigpen and asked if he could buy his friend lunch, bring him up to date on his side of investigation, and pick Thigpen's brain.

"So, what's up, Partner," Thigpen said, once he and Harte had settled onto a bench.

"Couple of things," Harte said. "First off, have you heard anything from Arlington? They blow me off when I call."

"I checked before I came here," Thigpen said. "Still nothing yet. How's Clotille doing?"

"Coping. . . . No, that's not right. Actually, pretty well, better than I thought she would. Better than me and Rosie are doing with it."

"Glad to hear that about the kid," Thigpen said.

"Here's what I know from my investigation with Cheng at the Mount Parnassus," Harte said. "Maybe you can fill in some holes."

Thigpen nodded. He clasped his hands behind his head, straightened out his legs, crossed them at his ankles. He stared across the sidewalk at the hot dog stand. He was all ears.

Harte spent the next twenty minutes telling Thigpen everything he and Socrates had learned about the two murders, the assaults, and the two kidnappings of Sophia Cheng. When Harte finished, Thigpen sat up straight and turned toward him.

"We're pretty much in the same place," he said. "We're close to declaring the cases cold again if something new doesn't turn up soon. The captain's getting itchy, and wants me to move on to something else."

"That's what I was afraid of," Harte said. "Before that happens, would you see if you can turn up anything on Selena and George Kostas, and on Ari Xandereas. He was the son Arête left behind in Greece."

"Will do," Thigpen said, "but don't get your hopes up."

CHAPTER 106

TOULA AGREED TO MEET ME, and insisted it be at *Stan's*. I was surprised after the little show she'd put on there. I made it clear I only wanted to discuss aspects of the investigation, not hook-up with her. She said, "Okay, your loss," then added, "We'll see."

When I arrived at *Stan's*, Toula was sitting at the bar talking to Danika. As we moved to a table, Danika raised her eyebrows, slowly shook her head, and winked at me.

After we engaged in small talk, I said, "I wouldn't have bothered you except I'd like your help."

"You mean you *need* my help, not just want it," she said.

I nodded. "Will you help me?"

"Sure," she said.

"Did you know your mother and mine are related?"

Toula laughed. "What's the matter," she said, "feeling guilty you were poking your cousin?"

I felt myself blush as my face grew warm.

"No," I said, "and we're distant relatives, at best, very distant." I waited a beat, then said, "Did you know?"

"Doesn't matter. We're both part of the clan."

"What clan?"

"Maniot. Once a Maniot," she said, "always a Maniot. Time and distance don't change that."

"What's a Maniot?" I asked.

Toula smirked. "Ask your mother, you really want to know."

I wasn't happy with her response, but I had an agenda to pursue today and I didn't want it lost among the flotsam and jetsam of Toula's quirky personality. I made a mental note to ask my mother about the Maniot.

"Who is Ari?" I said.

I guess I caught Toula off-guard because I could see her stiffen and her eyes narrow.

"Who is he?" I repeated.

Toula's eyes bore into mine. I didn't know whether she was going to answer me or stand up and walk out of the restaurant.

After a few seconds, her face and eyes softened. "Where did you hear about him?"

"Doesn't matter. Just answer me," I said. "I'm not here to waste time."

"Okay," she said. She paused a beat, then added, "He's my brother. I mean, he was my brother — when we lived in Greece. I don't even know if he's still alive or not."

"Why's that?"

"After my father died in prison, when my mother tried to bring me and my brother to America, my brother couldn't get an entry visa because he couldn't pass the physical at the American consulate office in Athens. They said he had tubercular growths in his lungs so would not be allowed to enter the United States."

I said nothing, just nodded. I didn't want to risk sending Toula off in some other direction.

"My mother left Ari behind with our grandparents at our village. They said they would care for him and send him to America when he was well. I never saw him again or heard anything about him, so I've always assumed he never became well enough to emigrate."

"All right," I said, "what do you know about Selena and her son, George?"

"Nothing much about Selena," Toula said. "I think her husband worked for the king, and died sometime during the reign of the Colonels. She then came to America with her son, George."

"That's what I've heard," I said.

"She was very creepy," Toula said, "always sneaking around."

If she creeped you out, I thought, *then she must've been something else.* "And George," I said, "what do you know about him?"

"He's a lecher, always hitting on me or other women around here," Toula said. "I don't know much else."

"What about his art? George as a painter?"

"He likes to say he was a serious artist. Once, he talked me into going with him to his apartment so he could paint my portrait."

"And?"

"He painted me, but the portrait sucked." She chuckled. "What was good, though, were the paintings he had sitting around, leaning against the walls. Beautiful old paintings like you only see on art postcards or in art books."

That caught my attention. "Were they paintings or printed reproductions?"

"They looked real to me, but I don't know. I asked him how come he had so many famous paintings."

"What'd he say?"

"That they weren't real, they were copies he made when he visited museums."

I didn't know where else to go with this or have anything else to ask, so I said, "Since we're here, can I buy you lunch?"

Toula smiled and slowly — very slowly — shook her head.

"Let's skip lunch and go back to your place where you can properly thank me for helping you," she said. She sported a mocking grin.

"Not a good idea," I said. "I told you on the phone, no hook-up. That's done for us."

I watched her face darken.

Toula stood up, and said, "Okay, then, Cousin, we're finished here. Go back to your redhead." She quickly strode out of the restaurant.

CHAPTER 107

FTER TOULA LEFT *STAN'S*, I used my cellphone to call my mother. I wanted to ask her about Toula's reference to the clan and the Maniots. She didn't answer my call so I left a message on her answering machine.

I checked my watch. I had a dental appointment in forty-five minutes so I walked over to I Street near 18th where my dentist had her office, and stopped at a nearby Starbucks to kill time. Somehow, I could never bring myself to arrive at a dental appointment early, not even for a routine, periodic checkup and cleaning.

It was almost 5:00 p.m. when my mother called back. In the time since I'd left my message for her, and I finished with my dental appointment, the questions I wanted to ask her had changed. I had gone home and Googled the term Maniot so I now knew who these people were. I also knew that they referred to themselves as the *family* or the *clan*, and that they were preternaturally insular.

Now I wanted to know what my mother knew about them and why she hadn't said anything to me. We agreed to get together the next day.

Clotille and I met for drinks at 7:00 p.m. Afterward we went back to my condo and cooked dinner. We ate steak *au poivre*, fresh green beans, and mashed potatoes. We opened a bottle of Ravens Wood Zinfandel.

After dinner I jacked my iPod to stationary speakers and turned on a Cedar Walton solo piano album. I poured a snifter of Courvoisier for each of us.

When we were eating dinner, I told Clotille about my meeting with Toula and my computer research into the Maniot. Clotille didn't seem to mind that I had tapped Toula as a source of information, probably because I was honest with her and told her I had refused Toula's offer to have me tap her.

"Ah'm amazed your mother and that old Greek woman, them, are related, but no one told you," Clotille said. "Do you think it was just an oversight?"

"I don't know. I've wondered about that. That's one of the questions I plan to ask my mother."

"It doesn't seem to have anything to do with what was going on at the condominium, or does it?" Clotille said.

I shrugged. "I don't know that either. I'm still thinking it through."

We finished our drinks, then caught a cab back to Clotille's apartment. I saw her to her door while the cab idled at the curb. We hugged and kissed, said goodnight, and I returned home.

CHAPTER 108

ARRIVED AT MY MOTHER'S THE next day in time for lunch. She was ready for me. She had set out a large serving platter of chicken, seasoned with herbs and basted with a sauce made from spiced tomatoes and caramelized onions, then baked golden brown; a large dish of Manestra pasta; and a bowl of green beans cooked in the same tomato and onion sauce as the chicken.

We hugged briefly, sat, ate, and talked while we ate.

"Why didn't you ever tell me about the Maniots?" I said.

"It never came up. I never think about it because it hasn't been part of my life since I was a little girl, since even before I moved to Shanghai."

I sipped my coffee.

"Why do you want to know?" my mother asked.

I repeated Toula's remark to me about once being a part of the clan, always a part.

"She's right about that," my mother said. "The Maniots are a clan and there's no getting away from it. But if you don't do anything to oppose the clan or harm someone who's part of it, there's no problem."

"What if you do go against the clan," I said, "then what?"

"You just don't, Socrates," she answered. "That's all there is to it."

It was clear she didn't want to discuss this any more so I switched to more pleasant topics.

I left my mother at 2:30 p.m., and headed home. I wasn't satisfied I had the full story yet on the Maniots, so I resolved to do my own, deeper investigation online.

CHAPTER 109

HARTE AND I MET AT my condo apartment so he could update me on the results of his research using the 2D's computers and access to restricted law enforcement databases.

"It's pretty much as you told me about the Selena woman and her son," he said.

"As for the son, I checked with a friend at the Department of State. You were right. He stayed behind in Greece because of a medical problem. Lived with the grandparents. He was clean as far as I could check, but he dropped off the map about fifteen years ago. No record at all that he ever tried to enter the United States or where he went."

Harte waited while I made some notes.

"As for George Kostas, it's pretty much as you said. He's a wannabe artist who couldn't make it, now works as a sales rep. He has one arrest that was pleaded out, no time served. His credit's good."

I scratched some notes into my notebook.

"The mother was in the U.S. since 1975, and kept a low profile. She showed up only once in the national crime database. She was rounded up with a bunch of other women in 1981 when they demonstrated in front of the British

Embassy protesting the refusal of the British Museum to return some marbles to Athens. By the way, why the hell do they care about marbles?"

I made a note in my notebook. I'd tell Harte another time about the Elgin Marbles.

"Why are you so interested in these people?" Harte asked. "Do you have something you haven't told me about?"

I shook my head. "No, I don't," I said, "but these are three people whose actions I can't explain."

"Such as?"

"Such as what was Selena doing in Eugenia's apartment when she was murdered? And why would someone kill her there? And why was her son so aggressive with me about finding his mother's killer, if he was involved?"

"Do you think the Selena woman was the one entering the apartment when the DOA went out for walks?"

I shrugged. "I don't know," I said, "but it seems likely, considering where she was found dead."

"Pretty convenient, don't you think?" Harte said.

"I don't know what to think," I said. "Not yet. I hoped you might turn up something. I guess that's not to be."

"Not yet," he said. "But stay tuned."

CHAPTER 110

CHECKED MY WATCH. IT WAS 8:15 p.m. I called Clotille, but she didn't answer. I decided to work for a while, then try her again. If I didn't reach her soon, I'd go out alone in the neighborhood for a bite to eat.

I cleared off my desk and took out a yellow legal pad, filled my fountain pen with ink, and prepared to review what I knew about the people and crimes at the Mount Parnassus. I would create a list of all the persons who were involved, directly or indirectly, and below each name would write notes for a narrative describing how they seemed to fit in. I also would make a list of unanswered questions that seemed to be associated with each person. This would differ from the chronology I'd already made because it would not be determined by sequence. When I finished, I would enter it all into my computer.

I started with Eugenia Stamos, and thought about the circumstances under which I met her.

I'd met Eugenia as a favor to my mother who wanted me to help her elderly friend, who believed someone had been entering her home. I was skeptical, but I was wrong.

In the course of this, Eugenia made or hinted at some prophecies. She had alluded to her own death and to the death of people around her, and perhaps she'd been right. Both Selena and Eugenia now were dead.

The only other matter I'd learned about Eugenia that might be relevant was her early history. She had been one of several young girls in Greece competing to be the next Pythia, and had been selected as the chosen one. She eventually gave it up to move to Athens with her husband.

I couldn't think of anything else to add to my notes about Eugenia so I turned the page of my yellow pad and wrote 'Arête Xandereas' at the top.

Arête, I decided, was one strange woman. Old World in every apparent respect — her way of dressing, her mannerisms, her belief in the power of the Evil Eye, her secretiveness.

From what I'd learned, Arête grew up in a Maniot village in the southern Peloponnese, just south of Sparta, in the Greek prefecture of Laconia. I also learned that throughout their history, the Maniots were known as fierce warriors who were proudly independent and who practiced blood feuds.

Arête's husband had worked for King Alexander, but after the King was deposed had worked for the Colonels. When the democratic forces brought down the Colonels, Arête's husband had been arrested and tried for war crimes. He died in prison. Arête soon thereafter left Greece and came to the United States with her daughter, Toula.

The final thing I knew about Arête was that she was related to my mother through their fathers, who were distant cousins. Although I didn't know if Arête knew this, I believed Toula had known it, at least it seemed so when Toula and I talked about it. I wasn't sure what the relevance of this might be to my investigation, if at all. It did mean, however, that my mother, too, was a Maniot, although she'd never said so to me. She always referred to herself as a Dorian.

I put down my pen and pad and went out to the kitchen to get a beer. I returned with a long-neck Yuengling and settled back in my chair. I thought about Selena.

She was a puzzle. She had yielded no information to me the few times we met, and left two significant questions: What was she doing in Eugenia's apartment when she was murdered and why was she murdered?

What did I know about Selena? Not much, it seemed. Her husband had been the Cultural Minister under the king, and had unsuccessfully devoted his life to recovering the Elgin Marbles from the British Museum. Other than that, he apparently died a natural death from old age, after which Selena and her son moved to Washington.

Then there was George. Selena's pain-in-the-ass son.

I had to give George this much: He'd been right about his mother when he insisted she hadn't committed suicide. But where did George fit into all this, if he did?

I took a long pull on my beer, licked my lips clean, and thought about Toula and her missing brother. *Now there's a pair*, I thought.

Toula was too weird and calculating for me to consider apart from Arête. I saw Toula as a younger extension of her mother, a paranoid in training.

I put down my pen and yellow pad, closed my eyes, and leaned my head back on the chair's cushion. I tried to think what all this might mean, or if I'd forgotten anyone. Then I remembered. I had forgotten Panos.

I got up from my chair and went to my list of condominium

unit owners so I could see his full name. I wrote it down at the top of a new page: Panos Makeresos.

I didn't know much about him. I knew he was a financial planner or accountant, but I didn't know much more than that. He seemed friendly enough, but had cold, flat eyes, so I didn't trust his smile or his kind words. I made a mental note to find out more about Uncle Panos.

CHAPTER 111

THE NEXT MORNING AT 11:00 I showed up at Toula's door without first calling. Arête answered my knock. She stared at me, said nothing, then turned away, leaving the door wide open. I followed her into the foyer and through the hallway to the parlor. Toula wasn't there.

I waited while Arête shuffled out of the room. Toula walked in a few minutes later. She wore a grin that gave voice to her expectation of my carnal capitulation.

"I didn't know you were coming here," she said. "Change your mind, cousin?"

I ignored her question. "Sorry I didn't call first. This'll only take a few minutes. I have a few more questions you can help with, then I'll go,"

Toula didn't say anything. She walked by me to an overstuffed chair and sat down. I followed to a nearby seat.

"Did your brother ever leave Greece? There's no record of him after about fifteen years ago."

"I have no idea," she said. "I told you, I never had any contact with him. . . .Why do you care?"

"I'm still gathering pieces to fill in the puzzle, and trying to eliminate loose ends so I can deal with whatever remains."

"As I said, I don't know. I haven't seen him or heard anything about him since I was three."

"Is it possible he came to the U.S. later, but you don't know it?"

"It's possible, but since I wouldn't know about it, I don't know. Why do you care?"

"He's dropped off the face of the Earth," I said. "It's possible he left Greece and took advantage of the European Union's borderless states to travel to another country, and settled under another name."

Toula shrugged. "You still haven't told me why you care."

"Just touching all bases," I said.

"I don't believe you," Toula said.

CHAPTER 112

WANTED TO CONTINUE TO BUILD a good relationship
with Detective Thigpen, so when I left Toula I called him
and said I would bring him up to date on my investigation
and thoughts whenever he wanted to meet. Although he didn't
offer up the flip side of my tender, I hoped he'd reciprocate
and share his information and thoughts with me when we got
together.

I arrived at the 2D and was shown into an interview room
by Thigpen's partner. She said my timing was good, that
Thigpen and Harte were meeting elsewhere in the building,
and would be along in a few minutes. "Thigpen," she said,
"envisioned this meet as an all-hands-on brainstorming
session to light a fire under the cases, that the cases were
almost to the point where they were going to be classified
again as cold."

Five minutes later, Thigpen and Harte walked in and sat
down.

Thigpen opened the session by describing MPD's progress
on the cases to date. When he finished, he asked if I had
anything to add to what I'd said.

I ran through the various players at the Mount Parnassus
who'd had any contact with the crimes, stating the facts I

knew about them, the questions that were raised by each person, and my resolution of those questions I could answer. When I finished, Thigpen, his partner, and Harte said they had nothing to add.

"That's good work, Cheng," Thigpen said. "Now you can step back. We'll take it from here."

"What do you mean, take it from here?" I said. "You're not suggesting I stop my investigation are you?"

"That's exactly what I'm saying. My partner and I are going full out before the cases go cold." He looked hard at me, obviously awaiting my acquiescence.

I looked at Harte who stared back at me, but did not signal his position on this.

I looked back at Thigpen.

"No, Detective," I said, "I'm not backing off. Not unless you can assure me my mother's not in any danger and that the assault on Clotille was unrelated to the crimes at the Mount Parnassus. Can you do that?"

Thigpen glanced over at his partner, then at Harte, then looked back at me. "No," he said, "I can't do that. Not yet."

"Then I'm still in," I said. I turned to Harte.

"What about you?" I said. "You still with me?"

Harte looked away from me and over at Thigpen. Then he turned back to face me.

"I'm in as long as Clotille's rape might be related," Harte said. "Until we find out otherwise."

Thigpen closed his notebook and stood up. He looked at me. "The usual warnings about interfering with an investigation apply, but stay in touch. You did good work on this, Cheng."

Harte and I left the 2D together. I walked him over to the Red Line Metro at Tenley Circle and watched him ride the escalator down into the station. Then I walked along Wisconsin Avenue toward Georgetown. When I reached R Street, I turned east and walked over to Connecticut Avenue, heading for my office.

As I walked, I thought about the meeting we'd just had. A solid sense of unease shrouded me. It wasn't because Thigpen had basically warned me away from the investigation. I was confident he was just going through the prescribed motions, which is why he told me to stay in touch. Nor was it my realization that after all these weeks investigating, I still didn't know whether my mother was in any danger or not.

What bothered me was I felt as if I was in a race against Thigpen to be the first to solve the crimes, because if he finished before me, some questions I'd rather have remain under wraps might come out and then come back to bite my mother and me.

CHAPTER 113

I CALLED GEORGE KOSTAS, AND TOLD him I wanted to meet, that I had some information concerning his mother's death.

"Do you know who killed her?" George said.

"We need to meet," I answered.

"But you said—"

"George, cut the crap, and let's just get together. It'll save us both time and questions."

We met at the *M Street Bar & Grill.*

It was clear when I looked at George, the way he was fidgeting, and the way his eyes wouldn't meet mine, he was anxious to get this over with.

"George," I said, "I know your mother, and sometimes you, were entering Eugenia's apartment when she was out. I want you to tell me why."

"That's not true," he said. "You have no evidence—"

"Then tell me how and why your mother wound up in Eugenia's apartment when she was murdered." I paused to give him the opportunity to see the absurdity of his position.

"I dunno," he said. He didn't look at me as he said this.

"George," I said. "I don't have time to waste. The cops found a camera near the body with your mother's and your fingerprints on it. The film had eleven exposures of the ikons on Eugenia's walls." I paused again to give him an opportunity to come clean.

"Oh, damn," George said. "I suppose it won't hurt then to tell you."

This was too much for him. I watched his shoulders slump. He wiped one eye with the back of his hand.

"Go ahead," I said. "Get it off your chest."

He took a deep breath, and let it out with a sigh. "All right," he said. "My mother did enter the apartment when Eugenia was out. She'd gotten hold of Eugenia's key early in their friendship, and had a copy made."

"Why?"

"Eugenia's husband, when he worked for the Colonels, stole art and religious ikons from churches all over Greece. The ikons on Eugenia's walls, the figurines on her shelves and piano, were probably all plundered." He sighed again.

"Did Eugenia know that?" I said.

"I dunno. Doesn't matter. The art and ikons have to be repatriated and returned to the churches."

I nodded. "Go on," I said, although I thought I knew where this was headed.

"Eugenia's husband, whatever his lofty title, was nothing more than a common art thief. My mother was only doing what my father would have done through the courts if he was still alive."

"Okay," I said, "tell me how it worked. Where did you fit in? And what did your mother do once she was in Eugenia's condo?"

George sank back in his chair.

"Once inside, my mother inspected the objects scattered throughout Eugenia's apartment. She wanted to see if she recognized any as stolen. She rarely succeeded because we didn't have much information on that aspect of the thefts. But we did have good references on the looted ikons, so we were able to recapture them and ship them back to our sources in Athens."

"How'd that work?" I said.

"My mother or I would make several photographs of the ikons on Eugenia's walls. We then would compare the images to our reference books. If we determined an ikon had been stolen, I would use the photo to paint a copy."

George paused to sip his coffee.

"When the copy was ready, we would re-enter Eugenia's apartment and substitute the copy for the stolen original on the wall. No one was the wiser. Certainly not Eugenia."

"Seems like a lot of trouble. Why not just confront Eugenia and have the ikons returned?"

"We didn't have proof they were plundered, if she resisted. Nor did we think she had been culpable in the thefts. We didn't want to hurt her. This way, no one was the wiser."

"Okay," I said. "Then what?"

"Then nothing. That's what we were doing when someone murdered my mother. I wasn't with her that day, but if I had been—"

"I have another question," I said. "Did you follow Eugenia when she took walks?"

"Sometimes," George said. "My mother was always nervous about being caught in the apartment, so sometimes

I would follow Eugenia, and call my mother when we neared the condo building on her return."

That made sense. "How many ikons did you swap out before your mother was killed?"

"About a third of them."

"Do you have any idea who killed your mother?"

He shook his head. "I wish I did. I'd fix the sonofabitch."

"Any thoughts as to why she was murdered?"

"It must have had something to do with stopping us from repatriating the ikons, I guess. I can't think of any other reason someone would want to kill my mother."

I wondered about that. His explanation didn't ring true.

CHAPTER 114

WHEN GEORGE AND I FINISHED, I walked over to the Mount Parnassus to talk to my mother. As usual, we settled ourselves at the kitchen table.

I recounted my conversation with George.

"I believe you," my mother said, "but I find it hard to believe that Selena was the person frightening Eugenia. She didn't seem cruel to me. George, I could see, but not his mother."

"I haven't yet worked out why anyone would kill Selena just because she was switching fake religious art for stolen art?" I said.

"Maybe that wasn't the reason," she said.

"What then?"

My mother shrugged. "Maybe she just was in the wrong place at the wrong time."

"Meaning what?" I said.

My mother didn't answer. Instead she stood up, walked over to the counter, and said, "I made some fresh coffee. Have some."

CHAPTER 115

I LEFT MY MOTHER AFTER TWENTY minutes. There wasn't much to say about Selena, her actions, and her fate. My mother remained adamant she wouldn't tell me her theory why Selena had been murdered.

I called Toula from my cellphone as I left the building. She picked up on the third ring.

In spite of the obstacles she presented so far, she'd proved to be a reliable source of information.

I could tell from the way she played coy with me that she was eating up the conversation and her self-perceived power over me. I told her I had a few more questions and would appreciate it if we could meet and talk. I offered to buy her lunch. She agreed to meet me.

We met at *The Mad Hatter*. Once we were seated, not too far from the mahogany bar, I looked at Toula and smiled. She seemed unnaturally relaxed. Even friendly. So far she'd made no snide references to Clotille, and hadn't yet said that the only reason I'd had sex with her was so I could later pump her for information. I wondered how long this unnatural state of tranquility would last.

"I'll make it easy for you, Socrates, so you don't have to

work your way up to it. What do you want to know?" she said.

I told her about my conversation with George, and said, "So I know why Selena was in Eugenia's apartment, but I don't know why she was murdered. Any thoughts?"

"Maybe you're making it too complicated," she said.

"Meaning?"

"Meaning, maybe she wasn't supposed to be killed, but was in the wrong place at the wrong time."

That was the second time someone had recently said that to me.

"As in, the real target was Eugenia?"

Toula shrugged, and fanned out her palms.

"Then why kill Selena?"

"I'll leave that one to you to work out." She smiled the menacing smile I'd seen too often and had come to dread.

I asked if she had any thoughts why someone might assault and kidnap my mother.

"No," she said.

I switched subjects.

"That cop, Detective Thigpen," I said, "he did some research into your brother."

Toula's eyebrows knitted together. Her eyes narrowed. "Why would he do that?" she said.

"Seems Ari dropped off the face of the Earth. Any thoughts on why and where he might be?"

She shook her head.

"So you still say you haven't seen him or heard from him or anything about him in the past fifteen years?"

"Longer," she said. "Since I was three. I told you that. Don't you believe me?"

I wasn't going to touch that one. Not with Toula's demonstrated record of paranoia.

"Could he be in the U.S.," I asked, "but you not know it?"

Again, Toula shook her head. "I suppose it's possible, but how would I know?"

"Do you think your mother's been in touch with him?"

"She would have told me," Toula said.

I wondered about that.

CHAPTER 116

SHIFTED SUBJECTS.

"Tell me about your mother," I said, "about her life in Greece before you were born? There must have been stories the family told about her, if your family was anything like mine."

"I know my mother had a very special childhood in her village even though everyone was very poor."

"How so?"

"She was groomed to be the next Pythia. Her family and village expected her to be selected to become the Oracle when the one then living retired or died. Everyone counted on it."

"What did that involve?" I said.

"It meant her family, the village occupants, even her school mates — everyone — treated her as special in every way."

"That sounds like a nice childhood," I said.

"While it lasted," Toula said.

I watched her face darken as she made this last comment.

"What happened to change it?" I asked.

"Some other girl from another village was selected by the priests."

"Then what happened?"

"Apparently, cultural shock followed. Suddenly, my mother not only wasn't special, she'd become a pariah. It was as if it had been her fault she wasn't the chosen one."

"I guess a lot of people were counting on her," I said. "There must have been disappointment, anger, loss of face for her family, and a sense of betrayal. All understandable, if unfortunate, responses from those people around your mother."

Toula shrugged.

"What'd your mother do about it?"

"What could she do? She was eleven years old. She had gone overnight from being a rock star to being an outcast. It was very hard on her. It still is. My mother won't talk about it."

We ate lunch and talked about other things. In general, it was more enjoyable than I ever would have predicted, even though we talked briefly about why we wouldn't go back to my apartment, and how I would pay her back for her information since I wouldn't hook-up with her. We left that part unresolved.

"It'll be worth your while if we go back to your place," Toula said, "believe me, it will. I'm ready."

When I remained silent and didn't bite, she said, "Besides, I have other information you'll want to hear, but I'll only tell you in bed."

Toula's proffer wasn't even tempting. I had no trouble declining Toula's offer of sex. That was Clotille's influence, and the fact I now knew we were relatives. It was hard, however, to pass up the chance to learn what other information Toula could offer that might be useful to me.

Toula laughed, seemingly without malice, but would not tell me what information she was withholding from me.

I never did find out what it was.

CHAPTER 117

For once Toula had acted civilly. Well, moderately so for her.

Notwithstanding Toula's improved attitude at lunch, I could not shake the unease I felt after I left her. Her friendliness was so out of character that instead of welcoming it, as I should have, I distrusted it.

I soon shelved these feelings and thought about our conversation. If nothing else — because I hadn't really learned any new information from her — Toula had whet my appetite to learn more about her family.

I decided to begin with Arête.

I spent the afternoon online using Google and several new databases, not the ones I regularly subscribed to, which I'd already exhausted as far as this case was concerned. I didn't turn up anything Toula or Harte hadn't already told me.

I also looked into the culture and history of the Maniots. Then I read about the Cult of Apollo and its practice of selecting girls to become the Pythia.

When I finished, I repeated all my research, but substituted Eugenia's name for Arête's.

My research, reading, and note-making took almost two hours. When I finished, I shut down my computer and called

Harte and Thigpen. I set up a meeting with them for the next morning. I had some answers for them.

CHAPTER 118

W E MET AT *STAN'S*.
Although I had no smoking gun to offer, no confession to hand over, I did have facts I posited as true, based on my meetings with George, Toula, and my mother. I also had much circumstantial evidence, my power of analysis, and common sense. I would offer all this to Thigpen. I was confident my conclusions were correct, and that I had solved the crimes.

"Okay, Cheng," Thigpen said, "tell us something you have that we can actually use in court."

The first thing I did was walk them through my interviews. I started with Selena.

I recounted what George had told me about why she entered Eugenia's apartment, and why I believed she was found dead there with a camera.

"So, if we ask him," Harte said, "this George will back you up, show us the ikons he and his mother took, and the copies they substituted for them?

I nodded.

"And he'll testify to this in court?"

I shrugged. "You'll probably have to offer him immunity."

Thigpen opened a small notebook and made a note in it.

"Should we like him for killing his mother?" Thigpen asked.

"No," I said. "Else why would he have insisted his mother's death wasn't suicide. It wouldn't have been in his self-interest to open up the cause of death again."

"Obviously," Harte said.

"Do you know who killed her and why?" Harte asked.

"I think I do," I said. "Selena was killed because she was in the wrong place at the wrong time. As for who? I'll get to that soon," I said.

"What about the Stamos dame?" Thigpen said. "What do you know about her homicide?"

"If you recall, several things happened to Eugenia. Someone repeatedly entered her home when she was out; someone assaulted her and my mother; and, someone eventually murdered her."

"How did your mother fit-in?" Harte asked.

"Okay, I said, "I'll do that first." I gathered my thoughts. "I first assumed Eugenia was the target of the beatdown, that my mother just happened to be with her, and got caught up in it. I don't think that anymore." I paused. "I believe it was the other way around. My mother was the target. Eugenia was a victim of circumstances."

Thigpen and Harte looked at each other, jointly frowned, then looked back at me.

"Eugenia was beaten because she was with my mother, who was the target. The beating was to convince my mother to have me stop my investigations, and to punish her for her friendship with Eugenia."

"Do you know this or are you guessing," Thigpen said.

"Educated, informed guess," I said.

Thigpen shook his head and made a note in his notebook.

"And now," I said, "that takes us to the question: Who murdered Eugenia, and why?"

Harte and Thigpen glanced at one another, then looked attentively at me.

CHAPTER 119

"L ET'S START WITH WHAT EUGENIA and Arête had in common that might play into this, and then why the murders were committed," I said. "Then we'll get to the *who*."

"You'll recall that both women claimed to be from Sparta. In fact, neither was. Each woman was from a different village near Sparta, in the Maniot region, but not from Sparta itself.

"Is this really relevant?" Thigpen asked.

I noticed he was tapping his foot. "Yes," I said.

"As children, both women were groomed by their families and villages to be the next Oracle at Delphi. But it was a zero-sum game. There could be only one winner. For the family and village whose candidate was selected, the rewards were immeasurable. There would be fame, notoriety, and unbounded riches. For the families and villages whose young girls weren't selected, there was disappointment, shame, loss of face, and vast loss of treasure in the form of bribes and other expenditures that had been made by them."

"Hold on," Thigpen said, "while I write something." When he finished, he looked up and said, "Go on."

"When the priests selected Eugenia, Arête's family and village took the historically and culturally predictable step for Maniots. They declared a vendetta against Eugenia and all her family. Had the selection gone the other way, had Arête been the one chosen, Eugenia's family and village would have declared a blood feud against Arête and her family. It's what they did in Mani."

Thigpen frowned again, looked briefly at Harte, then said, "Walk us through this."

I took a deep breath and considered what I wanted to say.

"Certain communities in Greece," I said, "have a tradition of long-running feuds among families and villages. These *honor conflicts* frequently began because one family or village believed it had been wronged by some other family or village.

"We know that," Thigpen said. "Tell us about this feud."

"In this instance," I said, "when Eugenia was selected to train to be the next Pythia, Arête's rejection triggered intense feelings of resentment which, in turn, initiated a cultural desire for revenge."

"Are you serious?" Thigpen said. "You really mean a pissed-off family in Greece, after all these years, would carry out a vendetta in the States?"

"That's exactly what I mean," I said. "It fits with the Greek cultural notion of personal vengeance against offenders who have harmed them. The family or village vendetta is a natural outgrowth of this cultural imperative."

Harte shook his head. "So, you're telling us this is what they believe, what they do, where that woman Arête came from?"

"The blood feud has defined the history of Maniot for centuries. The region was notorious for its vendettas. It sometimes led to entire family lines and villages being wiped out. Under the canon of the vendetta, Eugenia had to die."

"Okay," Harte asked, "who killed her then? Was it Arête? Or Toula?"

CHAPTER 120

I CONTINUED MY EXPLANATION.

"The vendetta required that the revenge be carried out by the eldest son, if there was one. That would be Arête's lost son, Ari."

"The missing kid in Greece?" Thigpen said.

"The same," I said, "but not missing. Just under the radar."

Thigpen turned to look at Harte, then looked back at me, and glowered. "Meaning?"

"Meaning sometime around fifteen years ago he changed his identity, dropped out of sight, and came to the United States with his new ID."

I looked at Harte, then at Thigpen, and said, "Nikos, the elevator operator, is Arête's long-lost son, Toula's older brother, the son left behind in Greece all those years ago."

Harte and Thigpen looked at one another, then back at me. "You're serious?" Thigpen said.

"Think about it," I said. "It fits the profile of a blood feud. He probably had help from members of the secret lodge — the one called *Philiki Eteria* — but Nikos ran the vendetta as he was obligated to do as the oldest male."

I paused to let them takes this in. Then I said, "I researched him. Ari Xandereas dropped off the map in Greece about the same time Nikos made his appearance in this country. Everything I have been able to learn about Nikos is consistent with an ID switch by Ari."

Thigpen held up his finger for me to wait while he jotted down a note.

"Did he kill Selena?" Harte said.

"I believe so," I said, "but I don't think that was his original intent. Most likely he went to Eugenia's home to murder her, and once inside encountered Selena. She probably recognized him as Nikos the elevator operator, so he killed her to protect his secret."

"Assuming this is true, did he beat Eugenia and your mother?" Thigpen said.

"Not him personally, but someone who worked with him did because the intent wasn't to kill my mother, but to warn and punish her. He couldn't do that and not be recognized, so he had someone do it for him."

"What about the two kidnappings of your mother?" Harte asked.

"That was intended to warn me away, just as my mother told us."

"And Clotille?" Harte said. "Was she raped and beaten because of you?" Harte's face was dark.

That threw me.

"Not as far as I know," I said. "I don't think what happened to Clotille had anything to do with the events at the Mount Parnassus."

"That jives with what the Arlington cops tell me," Thigpen said. He turned to faced Harte, and nodded. He turned back to me.

"I have a problem with your theory that the elevator operator's the doer," Thigpen said. "When we checked DNA for elimination against the sample from the Stamos crime scene, he didn't come up a match. What do you say to that?"

"You took Nikos' sample from the wrong part of his body," I said.

Thigpen frowned. "What the hell are you talking about, Cheng? That's nonsense."

I shook my head. "Actually, Detective, it's not nonsense. Nikos has two different DNAs. He is one person on the outside, but two people on the inside. At least genetically he is. Nikos is what is known to science as a human blood chimera.

CHAPTER 121

Harte and Thigpen said in unison, "A human *what?*"

I almost smiled at the look on their faces.

I couldn't blame them. It had taken me a while and some heavy-duty reading before I was able to wrap my mind around this genetic condition that affects at least eight percent of non-identical twins in the U.S. population.

"He's a chimera," I said. "Nikos is a person with two genetically different cell types in his body. In Greek mythology, the Chimera was an awesome, fire-breathing monster with the head of a lion, the body of a goat, and the tail of a serpent.

"In genetics, a chimera is most easily recognized as those people who have two different blood types. They also have certain physical abnormalities they share in common.

"In some cases the chimerical person is one of two non-identical twins who shared a blood supply in the uterus. In other cases, the chimerical person was the surviving twin of another twin who died early in gestation, and whose DNA the surviving twin absorbed."

"You gotta be kidding," Thigpen said.

I shook my head.

"This has to be bullshit," he said. "I don't know much

about DNA, but I do know each perp has one type, and no one else has it."

"Not so, Detective," I said. "First of all, we know that statistically there can be more than one person with the same DNA. That's why the numbers are given as a probability, for example, as one in X billion, not stated as a certainty.

"We know, too," I continued, "that one person can have two types of DNA in his cells, one type in one group of cells and another type in another group of cells. That's what being a chimera is all about," I said.

""Are you saying," Harte asked, "that when the lab boys checked the elevator operator's DNA, they checked the wrong DNA?"

"To put it simply, Yes. I assume the sample was the usual swab from inside his cheek. If the sample had been a blood sample instead, it's likely his other DNA would have been a match for the crime scene DNA. It was just fortuitous that the wrong elimination sample was taken."

Thigpen pulled out a handkerchief and blew his nose. "Are you ready to say this to our lab people?"

"Sure," I said. "We're not talking screw-up here, just a curious fact of nature."

"Tell us more," Harte said. "How come this is the first we're hearing about this thing? It must've come up before."

"It did. In a case reported in 1983 in the British Medical Journal, a Cleveland woman was told she wasn't the mother of her two children because their DNA differed from hers. Yet the woman insisted she had have given birth to the children.

At first the authorities thought the babies had been switched in the nursery, but that was ruled out when the woman gave birth to a third child under highly-controlled conditions where the baby could not be switched. This baby, too, had DNA that differed from her mother's. Yet the doctors had watched the childbirth.

"It turns out," I said, "the woman was a chimera.

"This condition resulted from cells the woman received from her twin brother — who had died in utero — entering her system when she was a fetus. The other twin's DNA continued to live within the woman's cells.

"Originally, the lab had tested the woman's DNA using her skin cells. Then, when they tested the baby immediately after birth under controlled conditions, and the baby did not match his mother's DNA, they immediately tested the mother again, this time using the mother's blood cells. This time, the baby's DNA matched the mother's DNA.

"You're saying we can't rely on genetics and DNA anymore?" Harte said.

"No," I said, "I'm not saying that. Chimerism doesn't mean genetics, as we know it, is wrong. It's just an aspect of genetics that has to be considered when there isn't a match."

"I have a different question," Thigpen said.

"If we assume you're right and this isn't just *la la land*, how'd you tie it to the elevator operator? You can't see his two DNAs."

"His appearance," I said. "Remember earlier I mentioned there are two physical traits common to chimeras?"

Harte and Thigpen nodded *in tandem*.

"The most common traits are having eyes with different colors and having the so-called hitch-hiker's thumb. Nikos shows both traits. His left eye is dark brown; his right eye is blue. If you check his thumbs, his right is normal; his left thumb looks like he's trying to hitch a ride."

Harte and Thigpen looked at one another.

"So you're saying if we retake his DNA from some other body place, we'll get a different result?" Thigpen said.

I nodded. "But take it from several places to exclude coincidence," I said, looking at Harte. "You'll get a match to the crime scene from at least one test."

Harte and Thigpen again looked at each other. Harte shrugged.

CHAPTER 122

"I GUESS THE BALL'S IN MY court," Thigpen said. "I'll check out what you've told us, pick up the elevator operator, and anybody else involved, if you're right."

"I'm right," I said.

What I didn't say, however, was that even though I was right about Nikos, I hadn't told them everything that was important to know. I still had something to sort through for myself.

I'd done all I could for Thigpen. I'd given him the ammunition to pursue the resolution of the crimes. No smoking gun, to be sure, but enough for Thigpen and the MPD to build cases against the culpable individuals. Prosecutions and consequent convictions have been built on less.

Thigpen was true to his word. As I learned later from Harte, Thigpen took the information I passed on to him and initiated a thorough investigation of all the crimes. He also stayed in touch with the Arlington cops investigating the assault on and rape of Clotille.

After three weeks, the United States Attorney for the District of Columbia presented evidence to the grand jury. Indictments were handed down: Arête for soliciting murder and conspiracy to commit murder; Nikos (a/k/a Ari), the same as his mother, plus first degree murder; George for unlawful entry — grand theft was waived as part of an immunity deal. in return for George's expected testimony at trial; and, against several John Does for the assault and unlawful detention and kidnapping of my mother — two counts. Ironically, only Toula escaped indictment. There wasn't sufficient evidence to tie her to any of the crimes.

"Don't worry, Cheng," Thigpen said, when I indicated I was surprised Toula had skated. "That dame will indict herself before too much time goes by. She'll stalk the wrong person and wind-up on the wrong side of the fence, one way or another. Trust me on that."

That was some comfort.

CHAPTER 123

BY TACIT AGREEMENT, MY MOTHER and I did not talk about the events leading up to the trials, which were scheduled to begin three months after the indictments. Although we spent much time together, I sensed my mother was feeling guilty for having involved me in Eugenia's problems. For my part, I was happy to avoid discussions of the events until the trials were over in case I was called as a witness. I had already been formally deposed and subpoenaed by both sides.

One week after the last trial, I went to see my mother. I was taking her out to lunch. I also intended to bring up and, hopefully, resolve some questions I still had.

We settled at a table for two at *Paolo's*. My mother had a glass of Chianti before our meal; I drank something stronger because I had to face an awkward agenda.

"Ma," I said, "we need to talk about some of the things we've been avoiding."

"So, talk," she said. "I haven't been avoiding nothing. Why would you say that?"

I sucked in a deep, deep breath. This was going to be even more awkward than I'd anticipated.

"Why didn't you tell me you and Arête were distant cousins?"

"Like I said before, I didn't think it was important. If I thought it was important, I would have told you."

"The police might think it's important if they learn about it," I said.

"I don't see why."

"Ma, this is a subject you don't know as much about as me. From the cops' point of view, if you knew you were related to Arête, and that you both were Maniots, then you probably knew about the vendetta. That also means you probably knew Arête was tied into the crimes."

"Well, it is what it is," she said. "Let it go."

"If the cops want to pursue this, they probably can make out a good case you were a co-conspirator or an accessory."

"It's all over now, Socrates, unless you turn me in. Is that what this is about?"

I shook my head. "That's not the point, Ma." I paused, then said, "I have another question."

She nodded, but clearly was annoyed.

"Why'd you involve me in all this if you knew about the vendetta?"

I watched her frown and consider her answer.

"For the reason I said: to help my friend, to ease the fears of an old woman. That had nothing to do with the vendetta, as you now know."

"Is that why you were kidnapped?" I said.

"You were getting too close and might have discovered the vendetta. Probably, too, because Arête decided I had become a traitor to the clan by getting you involved and by being friends with Eugenia. Arête had warned me months before not to keep up my friendship with Eugenia." She cleared her throat and held up her empty glass for the waitress to refill.

"Arête was wrong," she said. "I wasn't a traitor. I didn't see any reason why you giving Eugenia peace of mind would interfere with the conduct of the feud, especially since all but the last break-ins had nothing to do with the vendetta."

That last statement removed any lingering doubt I might have had. My mother had known about the vendetta and, therefore, probably knew all along who was responsible for the killings.

"I was right, wasn't I?" she said. "The break-ins by Selena had nothing to do with the vendetta."

I nodded and kept quiet. I didn't know how to deal with that sort of self-serving rhetoric.

"So now what, Socrates?" she said. "Are you going to turn me in?"

I thought I'd make light of her question. "You *are* an accessory, you know, if not worse." I watched her eyes narrow. "As a member of the DC Bar, I'm an officer of the court, and probably have a duty to give you up."

"You'll do nothing of the sort," she said. Her anger was clear. "You, too, are a Maniot, whether or not your father was one of us. We stand by one another. You never, ever, go against the clan. Not ever. Understand?"

That shocked me. I had been treating this lightly to avoid a tense situation, but my mother came back with both guns blazing.

You never want to think your mother has been deceiving you, but sometimes you have no choice but to accept that. There was no reason to carry on this discussion. Her statement, *Understand*, was not an idle question; it was a command.

After lunch I walked my mother back to the Mount Parnassus. We no longer spoke of the crimes. We hugged, made plans to have dinner together in a week, then I walked back to my office, a chastened, but changed son.

THE END

ACKNOWLEDGEMENTS

Thanks to Dominica — my wife. Also my thanks to my mother-in-law, Josephine Thomas, who read the manuscript and offered many useful suggestions. Thanks, too, to Margaret Sarris (Birmingham, AL) for her help with Greek Orthodox rituals and other Greek cultural matters.

Please Review *THE MOURNING WOMAN*

If you enjoyed *THE MOURNING WOMAN*, please leave a review on Amazon at www.Amazon.com [Type into the search box: Roth THE MOURNING WOMAN] and/ or leave a review at your other favorite online retailer.

Reviews not only help me, but help other readers decide if they want to read my book.

FREE BOOK

Get a free copy of *MANDARIN YELLOW*, the first Socrates Cheng mystery, by going to: http://eepurl.com/chLh1D

For more information on my other books,
Visit my web site: www.stevenmroth.com

Coming soon. The second Trace Austin suspense novel:
NO PLACE TO HIDE
and
The third Socrates Cheng mystery novel:
THE COUNTERFEIT TWIN

Sign-up for my book updates sending you information about these and my other upcoming books:
http://eepurl.com/chLiUD